P. BAZHOV

MALACHITE CASKET

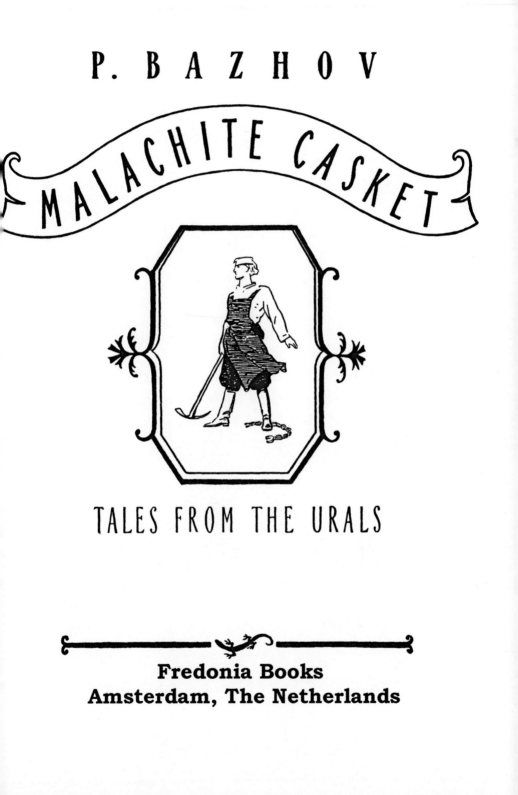

TALES FROM THE URALS

Fredonia Books
Amsterdam, The Netherlands

Malachite Casket:
Tales from the Urals

by
Pavel Bazhov

ISBN: 1-58963-731-3

Copyright © 2002 by Fredonia Books

Reprinted from the original edition

Fredonia Books
Amsterdam, the Netherlands
http://www.fredoniabooks.com

CONTENTS

MALACHITE CASKET

THE MISTRESS OF THE COPPER MOUNTAIN

One day two of the men from our village went to take a look at the hay. Their meadows were quite a bit of a way off. Somewhere the other side of Severushka.

It was a Sunday and real hot. That sort of fine weather you get after rain. Both of them worked in the mines, on Gumeshky. They got malachite, and the kind of stone called lapiz lazuli, and sometimes nuggets of copper, and anything else they could find.

One was quite a young fellow, not married yet, but all the same he was pale and tired, with that green look about him. The other was older, and he was quite worn out, his eyes were sunk into his head and his cheeks too. And he never stopped coughing.

It was sweet there in the woods. The birds were singing as happy as you like, the earth smelled good, and the air seemed sort of light. Now, they were both tired, our two. They got as far as Krasnogorsk mine, folks used to get iron ore from it then, and there they lay down on the grass under a rowan, and fell asleep.

But all of a sudden the young one—it was as if someone had nudged him—he woke up. And there in front of him he saw a woman sitting on a pile of ore by a big rock. She'd got her back to him, but you could see from her plait she was a maid. It was a sort of deep black, that plait of hers, and didn't dangle as our maids' do, but lay close and straight down her back. And the ribbons at the end weren't quite red and weren't quite green, they'd something of both. You could see the light shining through them and they seemed to clink a little, like thin leaves of copper. The lad stared at that plait and then went on looking at her. She was not very tall, with a pretty figure, and she was a real fidget—couldn't sit still a minute. She'd bend forward as if she was looking for something under her feet, then she'd sit up again and twist to one side and the other, she'd jump up and wave her hands about, then sit down again. Like a bit of quicksilver, she was. And all the time she kept on talking and talking, but what language it was you couldn't say and who she was talking to you couldn't see. But all the time she had a laugh in her talk. Seemed as if she was feeling real merry.

The lad wanted to say something, then all of a sudden it hit him like a blow over the head. Mercy on us, why, that's the Mistress herself! That's her robe. Why didn't I see at once? It was that plait of hers I kept looking at. . . .

Her robe, now, it was something you'd never see anywhere else. It was all made of silk malachite, that's a kind you get sometimes. It's stone but it looks like silk, you want to take and stroke it.

Here's bad luck, thought the lad. Can I get off before she sees me?. . . He'd heard, you see, from the old folks that the Mistress, the Malachite Maid, liked to beguile folks and fool them.

But he'd barely thought of it when she turned round. She gave him a merry look and then she laughed and said jestingly: "How's this, Stepan Petrovich, will ye stare at a maid's beauty and give naught for the looking? For a peep ye must pay! Come here, closer. Let's talk a bit."

The lad was frightened all right, but he didn't show it. He took hold of his courage. She might be a demon, but all the same she was a maid. Well, and he was a lad, and a lad must think shame to let a maid see him faint-hearted.

"I've no time for chat," said he, "we've slept too long anyway. We're going to take a look at our grass, how it's coming along."

She laughed, then she said: "Have done wi' your make believe. Come here, I tell ye, there's a thing we must talk of."

Well, the lad saw there was no way out. He went up, and she beckoned him to come round the pile of ore to the other side. He went, and there he saw a lot of lizards, more than you could count. And all of them different. Some were green, and some light blue, and some dark blue, every shade and colour, and some were like clay or sand with golden specks. And some shone like glass or mica, and some were like withered grass and some had all sorts of patterns on them.

The maid just sat and laughed. "Don't tread on my soldiers, Stepan Petrovich," she said. "Look how big and heavy you are, and they're but tiny." Then she clapped her hands and all the lizards ran this way and that and left him a clear path.

He came right up to her and stopped, and she clapped her hands again. "Now there's nowhere ye can tread," she said, and she was still laughing at him. "If ye crush my servants—it will be bad."

He looked down and he could not see the earth at all. All the lizards had crowded together, like a patterned floor round his feet. He looked again and—why, it was copper ore! Every sort and finely polished. And there was mica, and blende, and colours like malachite.

"Well, d'ye know who I am now, Stepanushko?" asked the Malachite Maid, and burst right out in peals of laughter. Then she stopped and said: "Don't be afraid. I'll do ye no harm."

13

The lad was shamed and angered too to have a maid laugh at him and speak words like that. He got so hot he even shouted at her.

"Who would I be afraid of, when I work in the mine!"

"That is well," said the Malachite Maid. "That's the one I need, one who fears naught. When ye go down the mine tomorrow the bailiff will be there. Tell him this, and see ye forget no word of it. The Mistress of the Copper Mountain, you must say, has ordered you, ye stinking goat, to get out of the Krasnogorsk mine. If you break up my cap of iron there, I shall sink all the copper in Gumeshky so deep ye'll never find it again."

That's what she said, and then she looked at him hard.

"D'ye understand, Stepanushko? You work in the mine, you say, and there's naught you fear? Then tell the bailiff what I bid ye. And now go, but say naught to your companion there. He's all tired, worn out he is, no need to worry him and get him into trouble. I've told one of my lizards to help him a bit."

She clapped her hands again and all the lizards scattered. And she herself, she jumped up and took hold of the rock with her hands, then she skipped on to it and started running about on all fours like a lizard. And instead of hands and feet she had little green paws and a tail came out and there was a black stripe that went half way down the back, but the head was still a maid's. She ran up on top of the pile of rock and then she looked back.

"Don't forget, Stepanushko, what you're to say. The Mistress orders you, ye stinking goat, to get out of Krasnogorka.... Tell him that and I'll marry you!"

The lad actually spat in his disgust. "Ugh—a reptile! Me—marry a lizard!"

She saw it and she laughed.

"Be it so," she cried. "We'll talk about it afterwards. Maybe ye'll think better of it?"

Then she was gone round the rock with a flick of her green tail.

The lad was left alone. It was very quiet. All he could hear was his companion snoring behind the pile of ore. He wakened the man and they went to their meadows to see how the grass looked, and returned in the evening. And all the time Stepan kept thinking and thinking—what should he do? To say that to the bailiff wasn't a small thing, and it was true, as well, he did stink, folks said there was something rotting inside him. But not to say it—that was fearsome too. After all, she was the Mistress. She could turn any ore you found into worthless blende. And how would he get his task done then? But most of all, he was ashamed to show himself an empty braggart before a maid.

He thought and he thought, and he took courage.

"Let come what may, but I'll do what she ordered."

Next morning when the men were waiting by the cage, the bailiff came along. Of course they all took off their caps and stood silent, but Stepanushko marched right up to him.

"I saw the Mistress of the Copper Mountain yesterday," he said. "And she orders you, ye stinking goat, to get out of Krasnogorka. And if ye spoil this iron cap, she says, she'll sink all the copper in Gumeshky so deep nobody'll ever get at it."

The bailiff's very whiskers shook with rage.

"What's that? What's that? Are ye drunk or daft? What Mistress? Who d'ye think you're talking to? You—I'll make ye rot in the pit!"

"Have it your own way," said Stepan. "It's what she told me to say."

"Flog him!" yelled the bailiff. "And send him down the pit and fetter him in the working. Feed him the dogs' oats to keep life in him and give him the full task, no easement. And if he tries any tricks—flog him again."

Well, of course, the lad was flogged and sent down. The overseer, as big a cur as the bailiff, put Stepan in the worst working he could find. It was wet and there was no good ore, it ought to have been abandoned long ago. And there they fastened him with a long chain, so he'd be able to work. You know what it was in those days—serfdom, they abused folks all they wanted. And the overseer jeered at him. "Cool down a bit here," he said, "and your task'll be pure malachite—so-and-so much," and the amount he said was out of all sense or reason.

15

Naught to be done. As soon as the overseer had gone Stepan started to swing his pick, and he was a brisk, able young fellow. When he looked, he was real pleased at what he saw. For malachite came tumbling down as if someone was throwing it. And all the water had drained away somewhere, so it was quite dry.

Well, he thought, that's not so bad. Seems like the Mistress hasn't forgotten me. And while he was thinking it, there came a flash of light and there was the Mistress herself standing in front of him.

"You're a lad of mettle, Stepan Petrovich," she said. "Ye can be proud of yourself. Ye weren't feared of the stinking goat. Ye spoke well. Come and see my dowry. I too stand by my word."

But she was frowning as if she didn't like it much. She clapped her hands and all the lizards came running up and took the chain off Stepan, and then the Mistress gave them her orders. "Get ready double the task, and see it's all the best silk malachite." Then she turned to Stepan again. "Come, my betrothed, and see my dowry."

They went into the mountain, she in front, Stepan following behind. Wherever she turned, it opened before her. It was like great chambers underneath the ground, and all the walls different. Some were green, and some were yellow with golden specks, and others again had copper flowers on them. There were blue walls too, of lapiz lazuli. The way it was, no words can tell. And her robe, too, it kept changing. Sometimes it shone like glass, and then it would shimmer with colours, or sparkle like it had diamonds all over it, or go coppery red and then shine a silky green again. So they went on and on, until at last she stopped.

"After this," she said, "there's but yellow and grey rock for many versts. Naught to see. But here, we're right under Krasnogorka. After Gumeshky, this is the place I love best."

Stepan saw they were in a huge chamber, with a couch, and tables and stools all pure copper. The walls were of malachite studded with diamonds and the roof dark crimson with a tinge of black, and flowers of copper on it.

"Let's sit down here," she said, "and talk a bit."

They sat down on stools and the Malachite Maid said: "Now you have seen my dowry."

"Aye, I've seen it," said Stepan.

"Well, and now what d'ye say to marrying me?"

Stepan didn't know what to say. You see, he had a betrothed maid already. A good maid, an orphan. Of course if you put her beside the Mistress, she was nowhere for looks. Just an ordinary maid like you see every day. Stepan stuttered and stumbled, and "Your dowry's enough for a Tsar," he said, "but I'm just an ordinary plain fellow, a worker."

"My friend," said she, "stop hedging and speak out. Will ye marry me or not?" And she frowned till her brows met.

So then Stepan just said plain and straight: "I can't. I'm promised."

He waited. Now she'll be really angry, he thought. But she seemed sort of pleased, even.

"True heart, Stepanushko," she said. "I praised ye for the bailiff, but I have double praise for this. You didn't snatch at my wealth, you didn't give up your Nastasya for a maid of stone." It was quite right, Nastasya was his sweetheart's name. "And now," she said, "here is a gift for your maid." She gave him a casket of malachite. And inside, jewels and ornaments of every sort. Rings and earrings and such, even the richest maid didn't have the like.

"But how," asked Stepan, "am I to get such a thing out of here?"

"Don't ye fret about that. All will be done, and I'll get ye away from the bailiff too, and ye'll live in plenty with your young wife, only beware—see ye don't get thinking and remembering me after. That'll be my third test."

She clapped her hands and the lizards came running in again and laid the table with all sorts of things. She fed him good cabbage soup and buns stuffed with fish, and mutton and boiled grain and all sorts, the way the Russian custom is at feasts.

When he'd finished she said: "Now fare ye well, Stepan Petrovich, and see ye don't remember me." And there she was in tears. She held out her hand and the tears fell down—drop-drop-drop into her hand, and turned into hard grains, a whole handful. "Here," she said, "take these for a nest-egg. Much money is given for these stones. You will be rich." And she gave them to him.

The stones were cold, but her hand, now, it was hot, like it was live, and it trembled a bit too.

Stepan took the stones and he bowed low and then he asked: "Where shall I go?" And he was sort of downcast himself. She pointed, and a way opened in front of him, like a drift, and it was as light as day in it. Stepan followed the drift, and again he passed all the wealth of underground, till at last he found himself back in his own working. Then the drift closed behind him and all was as it had been. A lizard ran in and put the chain back on his leg, and the casket suddenly got quite tiny so he could hide it inside his shirt. Soon after that the overseer came along to jeer at him, but stopped and stared—for Stepan had done much more than the task set, all fine malachite, you couldn't find better anywhere. Now how's this, he thought, where's all this come from?... He climbed down and took a good look.

"Ye can get anything ye want in this working, seemingly," said he. So he had Stepan taken to another, and put his own nephew in that one.

When Stepan started working the next day, malachite came tumbling down again, and nuggets of pure copper; but that nephew—all he could get was rock and blende. So the overseer smelt something queer and went to the bailiff with it.

"Stepan," said he, "must ha' sold his soul to the devil."

"That's his own business, who he's sold it to," said the bailiff. "Ours is to make all we can out of it. Tell him he'll be a free man if he finds a hunk of malachite of a hundred poods."

What with all this, the bailiff had the chain taken off Stepan, and he had all work stopped on Krasnogorka, too. Who can tell, he thought, maybe that dolt spoke truly. And the ore's getting mixed with copper anyway, only spoils the iron.

The overseer told Stepan what the bailiff had said, and Stepan answered: "Who doesn't want his freedom? I'll do my best, but whether I find it, that's as luck goes."

18

Soon Stepan did find a hunk like the overseer told him. They lugged it up to the top, and the overseer and the bailiff were real proud of it. "See what we've got," they said. But they didn't give Stepan his freedom. They wrote a letter about it to their Master, and he came himself, all the way from that Petersburg to take a look at it. He heard all about it and he had Stepan come to him.

"I give ye my word as a gentleman," said he, "to set ye free if you find me a piece of malachite big enough to make columns thirty-five feet long."

But Stepan said: "I've been made game of once already. I'll not be caught twice in the same snare. First write me a paper that I'm free, then I'll try, and we'll see what comes of it."

Well, of course the Master shouted at him and stamped his foot, but Stepan just went on talking.

"Aye, and I near forgot—there's a maid I'm plighted to, write a paper making her free too, or what'll it be, I'm free but my wife's still a serf."

The Master saw Stepan was not to be turned, so he wrote out a paper.

"There," he said, "but now see you do your best."

Stepan only answered: "That's as luck goes."

Of course he found it. Easy enough for him, when he knew all the inside of the mountain and had the Mistress herself helping him. They carved columns out of it, the way they wanted them, and hauled them to the top, and the Master sent them as a gift to the very biggest church in all St. Petersburg. And that hunk Stepan found first, they say it's still in our town. It's kept as a curiosity.

Well, after that Stepan was free. And then it seemed like the riches of Gumeshky all vanished. There was a lot of lapiz lazuli, but mostly it was just blende they found. Never a sign of copper nuggets, and no malachite, and water started coming in. It got worse and worse, till at last all the mine was flooded. Folks said the Mistress was angry about the pillars, because they'd been put in a church. And churches were something she'd no use for at all.

Stepan was never really happy, though. He married and there were children, and he built himself a house, everything right and fine. You'd have said he'd all to make a man glad, but he went about moping and his health and strength went. He just pined right away.

But sick as he was, he took it into his head to go hunting. He'd pick up his shot-gun and away to Krasnogorsk mine, but he never brought a thing home. Then one day, it was in the autumn, he went and he didn't come back. He didn't come and didn't come. ... Where could he be? Well, of course, folks went out to seek him. And they found him, lying dead by a great rock, and he was smiling; his shot-gun lay there beside him, it hadn't even been fired. The ones that got there first, they said they saw a green lizard by him, such a big one as none had ever seen in our parts. It was sitting there by the dead man, its head up and tears dropping. But as soon as they came close it ran up on to the rock and disappeared. And when they brought Stepan home and started to lay him out they found one hand closed tight, but they could just see something green in it, little grains, a whole handful. And there was one there as knew something about it, and he looked and said: "Those are copper emeralds! They're rare stones, and cost a mint o' money. That's a fortune he's left ye, Nastasya. Where did he get them?"

Nastasya, that was Stepan's wife, she said he'd never told her a word about the stones. The malachite casket he'd given her before they married. It had many rare things in it, but no stones like those. She'd never seen them before.

They started getting the stones out of Stepan's dead hand—and what d'you think?—they all crumbled into dust. So no one ever knew where he'd got them. After that they tried digging in Krasnogorka. But all they found was ore, brown, with copper in it. But then someone found out those were the tears the Mistress of the Copper Mountain had dropped. He'd never sold them, he'd kept them and let none see them, and when he died he took them with him. Aye.

That's what she's like, the Mistress of the Copper Mountain.

It's a chancy thing to meet her, it brings woe for a bad man, and for a good one there's little joy comes of it.

1936

THE MALACHITE CASKET

Nastasya, Stepan's widow, was left the malachite casket with every kind of women's ornaments in it. There were rings and earrings and all sorts. The Mistress of the Copper Mountain herself had given it to Stepan before he married.

Nastasya had grown up an orphan, she wasn't used to such rich things, and she didn't like making a lot of show either. At first, when Stepan was alive, she used sometimes to put on this or that. But she never felt easy in them. She'd put on a ring, you'd say it fitted just right, neither too tight nor too loose, but when she'd go to church in it or to visit friends, her finger would start aching as if it was pinched and the end would even turn quite blue. If she put on the earrings it was worse still. They'd pull and pull on her ears till the lobes were all swollen. Yet if you picked them up they didn't seem any heavier than the ones she always wore. The necklace, six or seven strands of it, she only tried on. It felt like ice round her neck and never got any warmer. And anyway, she was ashamed to let folks see her in a thing like that. "Look at her, all decked out like a tsarina," they'd say.

Stepan didn't try to make her wear them, either. He even said once: "Better put them away, lest misfortune befall."

So Nastasya put the casket in her bottom chest, underneath the others— the one where she kept her store of homespun and things of that sort.

When Stepan died and they saw the stones in his hand, it happened that Nastasya showed the casket to some folks. But that man who knew about all those things, the one who told them what Stepan's stones were, they say he warned Nastasya: "Mind out, see ye don't sell that casket for naught. It's worth many a thousand."

He'd got learning, that man, and he was free, too. Once he'd been foreman at the mine, but they took him off it. He was too easy on the men. Well, and he liked his glass too. Always in the tavern, he was, though I should speak no ill of the dead. But in all else—a real good man. He could write a petition or mark off sections, and he made a proper job of it, not like some. Our folks would always treat him to a glass on holidays, whoever else might be left out. He lived like that in our village till he died. The people kept him going.

Nastasya had heard from her husband that the foreman was an honest man with a good head on him, the only trouble was the drink. And she heeded what he said.

"So be it," she said, "I'll keep it for a rainy day." And she put the casket back in its old place.

They buried Stepan and mourned forty days, all right and proper. Nastasya was a fine, comely woman, and well off, so suitors soon started sending matchmakers. But she'd got plenty of sense.

"A second, though he's good as gold, still he's but a stepfather to the children."

So after a time they let her alone.

Stepan had left his family well off, as I say. They had a good solid house, a horse, a cow, everything they needed. Nastasya was a hard worker, the children were good and obedient, so they'd little to fret them.

They went on like that for a year, and another, and a third, and then they found they were getting a bit poorer. After all, you couldn't expect a woman with small children to farm real well. And they needed a bit of money now and then, too. To buy salt and such like.

Then Stepan's family started pestering Nastasya: "Sell the casket. What d'ye want with it? There's all those jewels just lying there doing no good. After all, Tanyushka'll never wear them. Things like that! It's only gentry and merchants buy such like. You can't put them on with our poor clothes. And you could get money for them. It'd give ye a bit of a lift up."

They kept nagging and nagging at her like that. And buyers flocked like crows to a bone, merchants all of them. One offered a hundred rubles, another two hundred.

"We're sorry for your children," they said, "we're being kind to ye because you're a poor widow."

They thought they'd got hold of a simple village woman they could fool, but they'd caught the wrong bird.

Nastasya minded what that old foreman had told her, not to let the casket go for naught. And she was loth to part with it, too. After all, it was a gift from Stepan, her dead husband. And then again, there was her little girl, the youngest child. She kept begging and crying: "Mummie, don't sell it! Don't sell it, Mummie! I'll go out and work, I'll be a servant, but keep it for Father's sake!"

Now, Stepan had left three children. Two were boys, just lads like any others. But the girl, she wasn't like her mother or her father either. Even when Stepan was alive and she was just a babe, folks wondered at her. And not just the maids and wives, but the men too. "Where've ye got her from, Stepan?" they'd say. "Who does she take after? All jimp and pretty, with her dark hair, and then those green eyes! Not like the other maids round our way."

Stepan would turn it off with a joke. "Naught to wonder at if she's black-haired, with her father working underground since he was a little lad. And green eyes—naught strange there either, with all the malachite I've brought up for our Master Turchaninov. I've got her for a remembrance."

So he started calling her Remembrance; when he wanted her he'd say: "Come here, my little Remembrance!" And when he bought something for her, it was always green or blue.

Well, the child grew, and all took note of her. She was like a bright bead dropped from a gay necklace—she stood out, like. And though she wasn't a child to make friends with folks, they all smiled at her. Even cross-grained shrews had a good word to say. A real beauty, she was, everyone liked to look at her. Only her mother sighed.

"Beauty, aye, but not our kind of beauty. Like a changeling."

She took it real hard when Stepan died. She got thin, seemed to waste away till she was nothing but eyes. So one day her mother got the idea of giving her the malachite casket to let her amuse herself with the things in it. She might be little but still she was a maid, even when they're children they like to adorn themselves. So Tanyushka tried on this and that, and it was a wonder, whatever she put on, you'd have thought it was made for her. Some of the things, her mother didn't even know what they were for, but she seemed to know everything. And that wasn't all. She kept on saying: "Oh, Mummie, I feel so nice in Father's presents, they're all warm, it's like sitting in the sun and somebody stroking you very, very softly."

Now, Nastasya had worn them, and she hadn't forgotten how her fingers had got swollen and her ears had hurt and the necklace had been icy cold. And she thought to herself: There's something queer here. Uncanny, it is. So she put the casket away in the chest again. But after that Tanyushka was always at her with "Mummie, let me play with Father's presents."

Nastasya wanted to deny her, but she hadn't the heart, so she'd get out the casket, and only warned the child: "See ye don't break aught."

When Tanyushka was a bit older she'd get out the casket for herself. Nastasya would take the lads to mow or some other work and leave Tanyushka to mind the house. First, of course, she'd get through the jobs her mother had left her—wash the dishes, shake out the tablecloth, sweep up, feed the hens and see the fire was all right. She'd hurry up and finish, and then get out the casket. There was only one chest left now on top of the bottom one, and it had got real light at that. So Tanyushka could easily move it on to a stool and get the casket out of the bottom chest. Then she'd take out the trinkets, and start trying them on.

One day a robber came when she was busy with them. Maybe he'd hidden in the garden early, or maybe he'd slipped in some way, for none of the neighbours saw him in the street. He was a stranger, but it looked as if someone had told him everything, when to come and how.

After Nastasya left, Tanyushka did a few bits of work outside, and went into the house to get the casket. She put on the jewelled head-dress and the earrings. And that was when the robber slipped in. Tanyushka looked round and there stood a man she'd never seen before, with an axe in his hand. It was their own axe, it had been standing in the entry. She had put it in the corner herself after sweeping up. Tanyushka was frightened all right, she just sat there, but that man, he cried out and dropped the axe and clapped both hands over his eyes as if they burned him. "Oh, I'm blinded, oh Heavens, I'm blinded," he groaned and kept rubbing his eyes.

Tanyushka saw something had happened to him, so she plucked up courage.

"What have ye come for," she asked, "and why have ye got our axe?"

But that man, he just groaned and kept rubbing his eyes. Tanyushka began to feel sorry for him, she got a mug of water and wanted to give it him, but he stumbled to the door and yelled: "Keep off!"

He backed into the entry and stopped there, and held the door so Tanyushka couldn't get out. But she climbed through the window and ran to the neighbours. Well, they came with her and started asking the man who he was and what he wanted. He blinked a bit, he was beginning to see again, and then said he'd been passing and come to ask alms, and then something had happened to his eyes.

"It was like the sun in them, I thought I was blinded. Maybe the heat made me sick."

Now, Tanyushka hadn't told the neighbours about the axe or the casket either. So they said to each other: "It's naught, she maybe forgot to fasten the gate and he came in, and then something happened to him. All sorts of things happen."

Still, they kept him there and waited for Nastasya. When she came with the boys the man told her the same as he'd told the neighbours. Nastasya saw everything was in its place, nothing gone, so she didn't bother about him. The man went away and the neighbours too.

Then Tanyushka told her mother all about how it really had been. Nastasya guessed he'd come for the casket, but it seemed it wasn't such an easy thing to steal it. All the same, she thought, I'd better be careful.

She said nothing to Tanyushka and the other children, but she took the casket into the cellar and shovelled earth over it.

Again they all went out and left Tanyushka alone. She wanted to get the casket, but it wasn't there. Tanyushka was real upset, but suddenly she felt something warm about her. What could it be? Where did it come from? She looked round and saw a light coming up through the cracks of the floor. That frightened her—was something on fire down there? She opened the trapdoor and looked down—yes, there was a light coming from one corner. She got a bucket of water to put out the fire, but she couldn't see anything burning and there wasn't any smell of smoke either. So she felt about in the loose soil where the light was coming from and there she found the casket. She opened it and the stones seemed even more beautiful than they had been before. They were all sparkling in different colours and a light came from them like from the sun. Tanyushka did not take the casket up into the room, she stopped where she was and played with the trinkets till she was tired.

So it went on from that day. The mother thought: I've hidden it well, no one knows where it is.... And the daughter, as soon as she was all alone, would spend an hour or so playing with her father's presents. As for selling them Nastasya wouldn't listen to a word about it.

"If it looks like we'll have to go and beg our bread, then I'll do it, but not before."

She had a hard time, but she stuck to it. She struggled through a few years and then things got better. The older children started to earn a bit, and Tanyushka wasn't idle, either. She learned to embroider with beads and silk, and she did it so well that the cleverest embroiderers in the gentry's sewing-rooms threw up their hands in amaze—where did she get the designs, and where did she find the silks?

It had been a strange chance, how that had all come about. A woman knocked at the door one day. About Nastasya's age, she was, not very tall, dark, with sharp, keen eyes, and quick enough to take your breath away. She had a homespun bag slung on her back and a cherry-wood staff in her hand like a pilgrim. She came to the door and asked Nastasya: "May I stop and rest a day or two, Mistress? I've a long road ahead and I'm dropping on my feet."

At first Nastasya wondered if it was someone after the casket again, but she let her stay all the same.

"I don't grudge ye a rest," she said. "Ye won't wear a hole in the floor or take it with ye. But it's poor fare here. In the morn it's onions and kvass, in the evening kvass and onions, that's all the change there is. If that'll do for ye, stop as long as ye like, and welcome."

But the traveller had already put down her staff and laid her bag on the seat by the stove without waiting for leave, and was taking off her boots. Nastasya wasn't too pleased at that. Pretty free and easy she is, thought Nastasya, starts taking off her boots and opening her sack without waiting for yea or nay. . . . But she said no word of it.

Sure enough, the woman was unfastening her sack; then she beckoned Tanyushka.

"Come here, child, and look at my handiwork. If it pleases ye, I'll teach you to do it too, I can see ye've an eye for it."

Tanyushka went up close, and the woman gave her a strip of cloth with both ends embroidered in silk. And it was such a brilliant pattern, the very room seemed the brighter and warmer for it.

27

Tanyushka couldn't stop looking at it, and the woman laughed. "So it takes your eye, my work, does it?" she said. "Would you like me to teach it ye?"

"I would!"

But Nastasya snapped: "Don't ye even think of it. We've no money to buy salt with, and ye want to do silk embroidering! Silk costs money."

"Don't fret yourself about that, Mistress," said the traveller. "If your daughter has skill she'll have the silk too. For your kindness I'll leave her enough to last a while. And after that ye'll see how it'll be. Folks pay money for our craft. We don't give our work away. We earn our bread."

So Nastasya had to agree.

"If ye'll give her the silk, she can learn well enough. Why not, if she can do it? And thank ye kindly."

So the woman started to teach Tanyushka and the maid learned it all as quick as if she'd known it before. And there was another thing. Tanyushka wasn't friendly with strangers, or loving with her family either, but this woman—she was clinging to her all the time. Nastasya looked askance, she wasn't too pleased. Found herself a new mother, she thought. Doesn't want to come to her own mother, but hugs a tramp!

And that woman, just as though she wanted to rub it in, kept calling Tanyushka "child" and "daughter," and never once used her christened name. Tanyushka saw her mother was put out, but it seemed like she couldn't help herself. She was so taken up with the woman, she even told her about the casket.

"We've got a costly remembrance of Father," she said, "a malachite casket. And the stones in it! I could look and look at them and never tire."

"Will you show it me, Daughter?" asked the woman.

It never even came into Tanyushka's head that she mustn't.

"Aye, I'll show ye," she said, "when there's none of ours at home."

As soon as the chance came, Tanyushka took the woman down in the cellar. She got out the casket and opened it; the woman looked a bit, then she said: "Put them on, I can see them better that way."

Tanyushka didn't need telling twice, she put them on, and the woman, she started praising them.

"Aye, they look fine, but they just need a touch or two."

She came up close and started touching a stone here and a stone there with her finger. And whatever stone she touched, it sparkled quite differently. Tanyushka could see some of them, and some she couldn't. Then the woman said: "Stand up straight, Daughter."

Tanyushka stood straight, and the woman started stroking her hair and her back, very gently. She stroked her all over, then she said: "When I tell you to turn round, mind you don't look back at me. Look straight in front, watch all you see and say naught. Now turn round."

Tanyushka turned, and there was a great hall in front of her, she'd never seen the like in all her life. It looked like a church, and yet it wasn't quite the same. The ceiling was very high up, supported on columns of pure malachite. The walls were covered with malachite to the height of a man, and there was a pattern of malachite all along the top. And right in front of Tanyushka, like in a mirror, stood a beautiful maiden, the kind you hear of in fairy-tales. Her hair was dark as night and her eyes shone green. She was decked with precious stones, and her robe was of green velvet that gleamed all shades. It was a robe made like the ones worn by tsarinas in pictures, you wonder what keeps them up. Our maids would take shame to let folks see them like that, but the green-eyed maid stood there quite quiet, as if that was the proper way. And that hall was full of people, dressed city way, all gold and medals. Some had medals hanging in front, others had them sewn on the back, and some had them all over. It was clear they were very great lords. And there were women, too, just the same with naked arms and naked bosoms and jewels hung all over them. But none could hold a candle to the green-eyed maid. Not one of them worth a look, even.

Beside the maid stood a tow-headed man; he'd a squint and big ears that stood out, so he looked for all the world like a hare. And the clothes he wore—a fair wonder, it was. Gold wasn't enough for him, he'd got precious stones on his shoes, even. And the kind you'd find once in ten years. He must have had a lot of mines of his own. He kept babbling something to the maid, that hare did, but she didn't so much as move an eyebrow, just as if he wasn't there.

Tanyushka looked at the maid, wondered at her, and then she suddenly noticed something. "Why, those are Father's stones she's wearing!" she cried, and in that moment it all vanished.

The woman just laughed.

"You didn't look long enough, Daughter! Now don't ye fret, you'll see it again, all in good time."

Of course Tanyushka was full of questions—where was that place she'd seen?

"It's in the Tsar's palace," said the woman, "it's the hall that's decorated with the malachite your father got."

"And who was that maid wi' Father's gems and who was the man as looked like a hare?"

"That, my child, I'll not tell ye, you'll soon learn it for yourself."

When Nastasya came home that day, the stranger woman was getting ready to go. She bowed low to the mistress and gave Tanyushka a bundle of silks and beads. Then she took out a little button, it might have been glass or it might have been crystal cut smooth.

"Take this, Daughter, for a remembrance," she said, and gave it to Tanyushka. "If you forget something in your work, or if you're in a difficulty, look at the button. You'll find your answer there."

With that she turned and went away. Vanished all of a sudden.

From then on Tanyushka was skilled at her craft. She was coming to the age for marriage, too—she looked a grown maid already; the lads would eye Nastasya's window, but they didn't dare to make free with Tanyushka. She wasn't the friendly sort, you see, she was grave and aloof. And besides, what would a free maid want with a serf? It would be just putting her head in the yoke.

In the Big House they heard of Tanyushka's skill at her craft, and started sending lads to her. They'd pick one of the lackeys, one that was young and handsome, give him a fine suit, hang a watch and chain on him and send him to Tanyushka with some message or other. Maybe, they thought, a dashing young fellow like that would catch her fancy. Then they'd have her a serf. But it was no good. When the lackey gave his message she would answer him, but for all other talk she had no ear. And when she got tired of it she'd make a mock of him too.

"Go along, go along, they're waiting for ye. They must be feared you'll spoil that fine watch and rub the gold off the chain. Can't keep your fingers off it, it's that new to ye."

She'd got words that scalded like hot water thrown on a dog. He'd slink off snarling: "Call that a maid? A stone statue with green eyes! There's plenty better!"

He could snarl all he liked, but still he'd seem bewitched, like. Whoever they sent was mazed with Tanyushka's beauty. Something seemed to pull them back, even though it was only to walk past and eye the window. On feast days all the young fellows in the village found something to do in that street. They beat a track past the window, but Tanyushka never so much as looked at them.

The neighbours began to reproach Nastasya.

"Who does she think she is, your Tanyushka? She keeps away from the girls and she won't look at the lads. Is she waiting for the Tsarevich, or does she think to be the Bride of Christ?"

Nastasya could only sigh.

"Eh, Neighbour, I can't make aught of it myself. She always was a strange maid, but since that sorceress was here, she's beyond me. I start talking to her, and she just stares at that witching button of hers and says no word. I'd throw it away, that button, but it helps her in her work. When she needs to change her silks and that, she looks at the button. She showed it me once, but my eyes must be getting bad for I saw naught there. I could give her a whipping, but she's a right good worker. It's really her craft as keeps us. So I think and think till I start crying. And then she says: 'But Mother, I know this won't always be my place. I don't beguile the lads, I don't even join the games. Why should I want to plague folks for naught? If I sit by the window it's because I have to, for my work. Why d'ye scold me? What have I done bad?' Now how can I answer that?"

But with it all, life was better for them. Tanyushka's work got to be the fashion with the gentry. It wasn't only the ones near the village and in our town that bought it, people sent from other places too, and paid well for the work. Many a good man doesn't earn as much. But then there came a great mishap—a fire. It broke out in the night. The sheds and shelters for the livestock, the horse and cow, the farm tools and other gear—all were lost. They just managed to get out with what they stood up in. Except that Nastasya did snatch up the casket.

The next day she said: "Seems like we've come to the end. We'll have to sell the casket of gems." And the sons all said: "Aye, sell it, Mother. But don't let them go cheap."

Tanyushka looked secretly at the button, and there was the green-eyed maid nodding—aye, sell them. It was a bitter thing for Tanyushka, but there was naught else to be done. Besides, soon or late they would go to that green-eyed maid anyway. So she sighed and said: "Aye, sell them if ye must." She didn't even take a last look at the gems. Besides, they had taken shelter with a neighbour, so there was no place to lay them out.

No sooner had they made up their minds to sell, than the merchants were there. Maybe one of them had started the fire himself so as to get hold of the casket. They're that sort—got claws that'll pierce aught to grab what they want. They saw the lads were grown now, so they started offering more. Some five hundred, and one even went up to a thousand. There was plenty of money about, Nastasya could set herself up quite comfortable with those gems. Well, so she asked two thousand. They kept coming to her, bargaining; they'd raise their prices a bit and keep it from each other, for they never could agree among themselves. It was a tempting bit, you see, that casket, none of them wanted to lose it. And while they were still at it, a new bailiff came to Polevaya.

There were times when bailiffs stopped a long while, but in those years they kept changing and changing. The Stinking Goat who was there in Stepan's days maybe got to stink too much even for the old Master's stomach, anyway, he was sent to Krylatovskoye. Then came Roasted Bottom—the workers sat him down on a hot ingot one day. After him there was Severyan the Butcher, the Mistress settled him, turned him into rock. Then there were two more, and at last the one I'm going to tell you about.

Folks said he was from foreign parts and knew all sorts of languages, all but our Russian, he spoke that badly. But there was one thing he could say well enough: "Flog him!" He'd draw it out, like, as though he was singing: "Flo-o-o-og him!" Like that. And whatever a man had done, it was always the same: "Flo-o-og him!" So folks called him Flogger.

That Flogger wasn't really so bad, though. He made a lot of noise, but he didn't use the whipping post very much. The tormentors got fat and lazy, they'd naught to do. Folks had a chance to breathe a bit when Flogger was there.

You see, it was this way. The Old Master had grown feeble, he could hardly get about. And he wanted to marry his son to a countess or someone like that. But the young gentleman had a kept woman and he was real foolish over her. There it was, a puzzle for the Old Master. It was kind of awkward. What would the bride's parents say to it? So the Old Master began persuading that woman—his son's light o' love—to marry the music teacher. The Old Master had one there to learn the children music and foreign tongues, the way the gentry did.

"Why go on living wi' a bad name?" he said. "Marry the music teacher. I'll give ye a good portion and send your husband to be bailiff in Polevaya. It's all plain and easy there, so long as he's strict wi' the folks. He ought to have sense enough for that, even if he is a musician. And you'll live real well, you'll be the lady of the place. You'll be respected and honoured and all the rest of it. Naught wrong wi' that, is there?"

The woman was ready to listen. Maybe she'd quarrelled with the Young Master, or maybe she was just clever.

"It's what I've been wanting a long time," she said, "but I didn't like to ask."

As for the music teacher, well, of course he jibbed at first. "I don't want her," he said. "She's got a bad name, she's a trollop."

But the Old Master was sly. That's how he'd got rich. And he turned that music teacher right round. Whether he scared him or flattered him or got him drunk I don't know, but he soon had the wedding day fixed and then the young couple went off to Polevaya. That was how Flogger came to our village. He didn't stop long but—give him his due—he wasn't so bad. Afterwards, when they got Double Jowl instead, folks wished him back.

Flogger and his dame came just at the time when the merchants were round Nastasya like flies round a pot of honey. Now, that woman of Flogger's was a handsome piece, all pink and white—a real light o' love. Trust the Young Master to pick a tasty bit! Well, this fine lady heard about the casket. "Let's have a look at it," she said, "maybe it's really worth buying." So she dressed herself up and drove to Nastasya. They had all the estate horses to use.

"Here, my good woman," she said, "show me those stones you're selling."

Nastasya got out the casket and opened it. And Flogger's dame—her eyes nearly popped out of her head. She'd lived in Petersburg, and been in other lands with the Young Master too, and she knew something about gems. And she was real amazed. What's this, she thought, the Tsarina hasn't gems like these, and here they are in Polevaya, with folks as have been burnt out! I must see they don't slip through my fingers.

"What d'ye want for them?" she asked, and Nastasya told her: "I'm asking two thousand."

The dame bargained a bit, just for decency's sake, then she said: "Well, I'll give ye your price, my good woman. Bring the casket to my house, and you'll get your money there."

But Nastasya told her: "Bread doesn't run after a stomach in our parts. Bring the money and the casket's yours."

Well, Flogger's dame saw she'd have to do it the way Nastasya wanted. So she hurried home for the money. But first she told Nastasya: "See you don't sell to anyone else."

"Don't ye fret," said Nastasya. "I keep my word. I'll wait till evening, but after that I do as I like."

Off went the dame, and all the merchants came hurrying in, they'd been watching, you see. And they wanted to know what had happened.

"I've sold them," said Nastasya.

"How much?"

"Two thousand, the price I asked."

Then they all shouted at her: "Are you crazy or what? Give them to a stranger and refuse your own folk!" And they started bidding again, putting up their prices. But Nastasya wasn't to be caught.

"Those may be your ways, say this and promise that and turn it all round, but they're not mine. I've given my word, and that's the end of it."

Flogger's dame was soon back. She brought the money, put it into Nastasya's hand, picked up the casket and turned round to go back home. And there on the threshold she met Tanyushka, the maid had been away somewhere when the casket was sold. Tanyushka saw the dame holding the casket and looked well at her, but it wasn't the one she'd seen that time. And Flogger's wife stared back.

"What's this sprite? Whose is she?"

"Folks call her my daughter," said Nastasya. "It ought to have gone down to her, that casket you've bought. I'd never ha' sold it if we hadn't got to the end. Ever since she was a bit of a thing she's always played wi' those gems. She'd try them on and say they made her feel warm and happy. But what's the good, talking o' that now? What falls off the cart's lost and gone!"

"You're wrong there, my good woman," said Flogger's dame. "I'll find a place for those gems, they won't be lost." But what she thought to herself was: A good thing that green-eyed maid doesn't know her own power. If she got to St. Petersburg she'd turn the heads of tsars. Better see my fool Turchaninov doesn't set eyes on her.

On that they parted.

Flogger's wife came home and started to brag to her husband.

"Now, my friend, I don't need to be beholden any more to you or to Turchaninov either. The first thing that doesn't suit me—off I go! I'll go to St. Petersburg, or maybe I'll go abroad, I'll sell the casket and then I'll buy husbands like you by the dozen if I want."

That's how she bragged, but all the same she badly wanted to show herself in those gems she'd bought. A woman, after all! So she ran to the mirror and first of all she put on the head-dress. But—oh, oh, what's this? It nipped her and pulled her hair so she just couldn't bear it. And she had a job to get it off. But still she itched to see herself in the things. She put on the earrings and they nearly tore her lobes. She put on a ring and it nipped so she could hardly pull it from her finger, even when she soaped it. And her husband just sat and jeered at her—not meant for you to wear, those things!

It's queer, she thought. I'll have to go to town and let a good craftsman take a look at them. Shape them and make them fit—but I must see he doesn't change the stones.

No sooner said than done. The next morning off she went. It didn't take long to get to town with three good horses pulling. She asked folks where she could find a good craftsman and an honest one, and sought him out. He was an old man, real ancient, and very skilled. He took a look at the casket and asked her where she'd bought it. The dame told him all she knew. The old man looked at the casket again, but he never even glanced at the gems.

"I won't touch them," he said, "no matter what ye offer me. The craftsmen that made all this are none of ours. And I'm not the one to vie with them."

Of course the dame didn't understand what it was all about, she sniffed and went off to find another craftsman. But it was as if they were all in a plot. One after another they looked at the casket, admired it, never so much as glanced at the gems and refused to have anything to do with it. Then the dame tried cunning, she said she'd bought the casket in St. Petersburg. There were plenty like it there. But the man she served with that tale only laughed at her.

"I know where the casket was made," he said, "and I've heard tell of the craftsman that made it. There's none of us can try to vie with him. If he's made things to fit one, no other'll be able to wear them, try as ye will."

The dame still didn't understand the whole of it, but one thing she could see—the man was scared of something. And then she called to mind how Nastasya had said her daughter liked to put on those trinkets.

Could they be made for that green-eyed creature? Bad fortune, indeed!

But then came second thoughts. What does it matter to me? I'll sell them to some rich fool. Let her bother herself about them, the money'll be safe in my pocket!... So back she went to Polevaya.

When she arrived she found news. The Old Master had gone to his eternal rest. He'd been cunning enough, the way he'd fixed it all with Flogger, but Death had been one too many for him. Knocked him over the head. He hadn't had time to get his son married, so now the young man was his own master. And it wasn't long before Flogger's wife got a letter. It told her this and that, and when the spring floods go down, my sweeting, I'll come and have a look at the village and take you back with me, and as for your music master, we'll get rid of him somehow.... Flogger found out about it and made an uproar. It shamed him before the folks. After all, he was the bailiff, and now here was the Master coming to take away his wife. He started drinking hard. With the clerks and such like, of course. And they were glad enough so long as he stood treat.

One day when he was carousing with his flatterers and boon companions, one of them started to brag.

"We've got a real beauty in our village, you'd have to go a long journey to find another like her."

Flogger was quick enough to catch that. "Whose maid is she? Where does she live?"

They told him all about it, and reminded him of the casket—that's where your goodwife bought it, from that family.

"I'd like to take a look at her," said Flogger, and the carousing band thought of a way to do it.

"We can go now, see if they've built the new cottage right. They're free, but they live on the village land. There's always ways to compel them."

Off they went, two or three of them, and Flogger too. They took a chain for measuring, to see if maybe Nastasya had filched a bit of land from the neighbours, and if the boundary posts were the right distance apart. Tried to catch her out. Then they went into the cottage, and Tanyushka happened to be alone there. Flogger took one look at her and lost his tongue. For he'd never seen such beauty in any land he'd been in. He just stood there like a fool, and as for her—she sat quite quiet as though it was all naught to her. Then Flogger got his wits back a bit and asked her: "What's that you're doing?"

"It's embroidery folks have ordered," she said, and showed him.

"And would ye take an order from me?" asked Flogger.

"Why not, if we come to terms."

"Then," said Flogger, "can ye make me a portrait of yourself in fine silk?"

Tanyushka looked quietly at her button, and the green-eyed maid signed to her—take the order, and then pointed at herself.

"I won't make my own portrait," said Tanyushka, "but I know a woman wearing precious gems, in the robe of a tsarina, I can do that. But it won't be cheap, such work."

"Ye needn't fret about that," said Flogger, "it can be a hundred rubles or two hundred, if only the woman's like you."

"The face'll be like," she said, "but the clothes will be different."

They agreed on a hundred rubles. Tanyushka said it would be ready in a month. But all the same Flogger kept coming and coming, making as though he wanted to see how it was getting on, but it was something quite different really. His wits seemed turned, but Tanyushka, she took no notice. She'd say two or three words, and that was all. Flogger's boon companions started to mock him.

"You'll get naught there. Wasting boot leather!"

Well, Tanyushka finished that portrait. Flogger took a look and—God above!—it was her very self, only in rich robes and gems. He gave her three hundred rubles instead of one, but Tanyushka handed two of them back.

"We don't take gifts," she said, "we work for our bread."

Flogger hurried home; he kept looking at that portrait but he hid it away from his wife. He didn't drink so much, and started to take a bit of interest in the village and the mine.

With springtime, the Young Master arrived. Came driving into Polevaya one fine day. The people were all called together, there were prayers in the church, and then all kinds of dancing and prancing in the Big House. A couple of barrels of wine were rolled out for the common folk too, so they could drink to the memory of the Old Master and the health of the new one. It was like priming a pump—the Turchaninovs were good at that. Add ten bottles of your own to the Master's goblet and then it would look like something, but at the end of it all you'd find your last kopek gone and naught to show for it.

The next day the people were back at work again, but there was still feasting and drinking in the Big House. And so it went on. They'd sleep a mite and then back to their carousing again. They'd go rowing about in boats, or riding horses in the woods, and then the music would start—there was everything you could think of. And all this time Flogger was drunk. The Master gave the wink to his hardest drinkers—fill him up and keep him that way. Well, of course, they were glad enough to curry favour with the new Master.

Flogger was drunk, but he'd a good idea what was coming, all the same. He felt awkward, ashamed like, in front of the guests. So when they were all at table, he burst out: "What do I care if Master Turchaninov takes my wife! He can have her for all of me! I don't want her. Take a look at the maid I've got!" And what does he do but pull that portrait from his pocket. They all gasped, and Flogger's dame, her mouth dropped open and she couldn't seem to get it shut again. As for the Master, he just stared and stared. And he wanted to know more.

"Who is she?" he asked.

Flogger just laughed. "If you heap the whole table wi' gold I shan't tell ye!"

But what was the good of that, when everyone knew Tanyushka! They all fought to be the first to tell him. But Flogger's dame, she kept arguing and trying to stop them.

"Stuff and nonsense! You don't know what you're talking of! Where'd a village maid get a dress like that, and gems, too? That portrait, my husband brought it from abroad. He showed it me before we were married. He's drunk, he doesn't know what he's saying. When he's sober he won't remember a word of it."

Flogger could see his wife was all in a taking and started snarling at her.

"You're a shameless hussy, that's what ye are! Trumping up a cock-and-bull tale to fool the Master! When did I ever show ye that portrait? I got it here. From that maid they're talking of. About the dress, I won't tell a lie, I don't know anything about it. You can put any dress on her. But the gems, she did have those. And now they're here, locked in your cupboard. You bought them yourself for two thousand, but you couldn't wear them. A Circassian saddle won't go on a cow. The whole village knows how ye bought them!"

The Master no sooner heard of the gems than he said: "Get them out, show me them."

Now that Young Master, hark 'ee, was a spendthrift, played ducks and drakes with his money. Like heirs often are. And he was real mad about gems. He couldn't boast much of looks, so at least he'd boast of jewels. As soon as he heard of fine gems, he'd be itching to buy them. And he understood about them right enough, though in general he hadn't much wits.

Flogger's dame saw there was no way out, so she brought the casket. And the moment the Master saw the gems he asked: "How much?"

She named a figure beyond all sight or reason. The Master started bargaining. They came to terms on the half, and the Master signed a paper for the money—he hadn't that much with him, you see. Then he put the casket on the table in front of him and said: "Send for that maid ye've been telling of."

Some of them went off running to fetch Tanyushka. She came at once, thinking naught of it—she expected some big order for work. She came into the room, and there it was full of people, and in the middle a man with a face like a hare, the same one she'd seen that time. And in front of the hare stood the casket, her father's gift. Tanyushka guessed at once it was the Young Master.

"What d'ye want of me?" she asked.

But it seemed like he couldn't speak. He just stared and stared at her. Then at last he found his tongue again.

"Are those your gems?" he asked.

"They used to be, but now they're hers," and she pointed to Flogger's dame.

"No, they're mine," said Turchaninov.

"That's your affair."

"Would you like me to give them back to ye?"

"I've naught to give for them."

"Well, you won't refuse to try them on—I want to see how they look when they're worn."

"I don't mind doing that," said Tanyushka.

She took the casket, sorted out the trinkets the way she was used to doing, and quickly put them on. The Master looked and he just gasped. Gasped and gasped and naught else. And Tanyushka, she stood there in the ornaments and said: "There they are. Have ye looked your fill? I've no time to be standing here. I've work waiting."

But right there, in front of them all, the Master said: "Marry me. Will ye?"

Tanyushka only laughed.

"It's not fitting to talk that way, Master, to one as isn't your equal." Then she took off the trinkets and went.

But the Young Master couldn't let her alone. The next day he came to her cottage to make his proposal in all form. He begged and urged Nastasya—give me your daughter.

"I won't force her one way or the other," said Nastasya. "Let it be as she says. But to my mind it's not suitable."

Tanyushka listened and listened, and then she said: "Here's my word. I've heard tell there's a chamber in the Tsar's palace decorated with the malachite my father got. If you show me the Tsarina in that chamber, then I'll be your wife."

The Master was ready to agree to anything, of course. He started off at once getting ready to go to St. Petersburg, and wanted to take Tanyushka with him—I'll get you horses, he said. But Tanyushka told him: "It's not our custom for a maid to use a man's horses before she's wed, and we're still naught to one another. We'll talk of that later on, when ye've kept your word."

"When will you come to St. Petersburg, then?" he said.

"I'll be there by Intercession Day," she said. "Ye can rest easy about that. And now go."

The Master left; of course he didn't take Flogger's dame with him, didn't even give her a look. As soon as he got back to St. Petersburg he told the whole town about the gems and the maid. He showed the casked to many. And of course folks were real curious to see the maid. By the autumn he'd got a house for her, and bought all kinds of robes and shoes and put them ready. And then she sent word she had come, and was living with some widow right on the edge of the town.

Of course Turchaninov went straight off there.

"Why are you here? How can you live in a place like this? I've got a house all ready, you couldn't want a better."

But all Tanyushka said was: "I'm quite comfortable where I am."

The talk about the gems and Turchaninov's maid got to the Tsarina too. "Let Turchaninov show me that bride of his," she said, "for what's told of her is beyond belief."

Off he went to Tanyushka—she must get herself ready; she must have a robe to wear at court, and put on the gems from the malachite casket.

"About my dress ye needn't concern yourself," she said, "but the gems I'll take as a loan. Only mind ye don't think of sending horses for me. I'll come my own way. Wait for me by the entrance to the palace."

Turchaninov wondered a good bit—where would she get horses? And a court robe? But he didn't dare ask.

All the grand folks gathered at the court, they came rolling up in carriages, in their silks and velvets. Turchaninov was early by the door, fidgeting about, waiting for Tanyushka. And there were others curious to see her, they stood about waiting too. But Tanyushka, she put on the gems, fastened a kerchief round her head the village way, put on her sheepskin and came along quietly on foot. And the folks who saw her, they wondered where she'd come from and followed her in a crowd. She came to the palace but the lackeys wouldn't let her in. "Villagers can't come in here," they said. Turchaninov saw her when she was a good way off, but he was ashamed to have his bride come on foot and in a country sheepskin, so he went and hid himself. Tanyushka opened her sheepskin and the lackeys stared. That robe—why, the Tsarina herself hadn't one like it! They let her in at once. And as soon as Tanyushka took off her kerchief and sheepskin all the people gasped in wonder and started asking: "Who is she? What land's this Tsarina come from?"

Turchaninov was there in a moment.

"This is my bride," he said.

But Tanyushka looked at him very sternly.

"That's still to be seen," she said. "Why didn't ye keep your word, why weren't ye at the entrance?"

Turchaninov mumbled and stumbled, there'd been a mistake, please forgive him, and so on.

They went into a chamber of the palace, the one where they were told to go. Tanyushka looked round and saw it wasn't the right one.

"What's this, are ye trying to deceive me?" she asked, more sternly still. "I told ye it must be the chamber that's decorated with the malachite my father got." And she started walking through the palace just as if she were at home there. And all the senators and generals and the rest followed after her. "What's this?" they said. "That must be where we're all to go."

The people crowded in till it was as full as could be, and all of them staring at Tanyushka. And as for her, she stood close up to the malachite wall and waited. Of course Turchaninov was there right by her. He kept babbling that it wasn't fitting, the Tsarina had said they were to wait for her in another chamber. But Tanyushka stood there quietly, didn't even move an eyebrow, just as though he wasn't there at all.

The Tsarina went into the chamber she'd said and found it empty. But her informers quickly told her that Turchaninov's maid had led them all away to the Malachite Hall. The Tsarina scolded, of course—such high-handed goings-on!—and she stamped her foot, too. She was a bit angry, you see. Then she went to the Malachite Hall. Everybody bowed low, but Tanyushka stood there and never moved.

"Now then," said the Tsarina, "show me this high-handed maid, this bride of Turchaninov's!"

When Tanyushka heard that she frowned and said to Turchaninov: "What does this mean? I told ye to show me the Tsarina, and you've done it so as to show me to her. You've lied again! I don't want to see any more of ye. Take your gems!"

With those words she leaned against the malachite wall—and melted away. All that was left was the gems sparkling on the wall, stuck there in the places where her head, neck and arms had been.

Of course all the courtiers were real scared and the Tsarina swooned right away. There was a great to-do till they'd raised her. Then when everything had quietened down a bit, Turchaninov's friends said to him: "Take your gems, at least, before they're stolen. It's the palace you're in! Folks here know their value."

So Turchaninov started trying to pick them off the wall, but each one he touched turned into a drop—some clear like tears, others yellow, and others thick and red like blood. So he got none of them. He looked down and there on the floor was a button. Just a glass button, bottle glass, it looked like. A worthless bit of a thing. But in his trouble he even picked that up. And as soon as he had it in his hand, it was like a mirror and the green-eyed maid looking out of it, wearing the precious gems, and laughing and laughing.

"Eh, ye stupid cross-eyed hare!" she said. "For you to think of getting me! What match for me are you?"

After that Turchaninov lost the last of his wits, but he didn't throw away the button. He'd keep looking in it, and it was always the same thing he saw—there stood the green-eyed maid and laughed and laughed and mocked him. He was so cast down he started drinking, and got into debt right and left, our village and mines almost went under the hammer in his time.

As for Flogger, after he was put out of his job he spent his time in the tavern. He drank all he had, but he still kept that portrait in silk. What happened to it after, nobody knows.

Flogger's dame was left empty-handed too. Try to get your money on a note of hand when all the iron and copper's mortgaged!

About Tanyushka nobody ever heard a word more from that day on. It was just as though she'd never been.

Nastasya grieved, of course, but not over much. Tanyushka, you see, had always been like a changeling, not like a daughter to her at all. And then, the lads had both grown up. They got married. There were grandchildren. Plenty of folks in the cottage. Plenty to do and think of—watch one, give a slap to another—no time to brood!

But the young fellows didn't forget Tanyushka for a long time. They still came round Nastasya's window. Maybe some day she'd be there. But she never was. Then in the end they got married one by one, but time and again they'd remember: "Eh, that was a rare maid used to live in our village! Ye'll never see another like her."

But there was one other thing; talk started going round that the Mistress of the Copper Mountain had a double: folks would see two maids in malachite robes, two of them together.

1938

THE FLOWER OF STONE

It wasn't only Mramor that was famous for stone carving, folks say there were craftsmen in our villages too. Only ours mostly worked with malachite, because there was plenty of it, and the very finest kind. The things they made, you'd just stare and wonder how they did it.

There was a master craftsman in those days called Prokopich. He was the best there was in carving, none other could come near him. But he was getting old, so the Master told the bailiff to give Prokopich an apprentice.

"Let some lad learn his craft, all of it, to the last secret."

But Prokopich—maybe he just didn't want to give away the secrets of his craft, or maybe it was something else, but he didn't teach any of them much. All they got from him was bumps and bangs. He'd buffet a lad till his whole head was bruised and pull his ears nearly off, and then tell the bailiff: "He's no good. His eye's not straight and his hand's like a foot. He'll never learn."

The bailiff must have been told to humour Prokopich.

"If he's no good, he's no good.... We'll find ye another." So the next lad would be sent.

The boys all heard about Prokopich's teaching. They'd roar and howl at the very thought of going to him. And fathers and mothers too, they were loth to send their boys to be knocked about, and tried to keep them out of the way if they could. Besides, it wasn't a healthy trade, carving malachite. The dust was real poison. Folks kept away from it.

But the bailiff had his orders from the Master so he went on sending lads to Prokopich to learn his craft. And Prokopich would torment them a while as his way was, and then send them back. "No good."

At last the bailiff lost his patience. "How long will ye keep this up? No good, no good—when'll ye say 'good'? Make something of this one."

But Prokopich was stubborn. "All the same to me... I can teach him ten years if ye like, but naught'll come of it."

"What lad do ye want, then?"

"You needn't send any, for me. I'm not pining for 'em."

So it went on. The bailiff and Prokopich tried plenty of lads, but it always ended the same—with bruises on their heads and only one idea inside, to get away. Some spoiled things on purpose so Prokopich would turn them off.

Then it came to Danilo Nedokormysh's* turn. An orphan, he was. Twelve, maybe, or a bit more. A tall, spindly lad with long legs, thin as a rail— you'd wonder how he kept body and soul together. But he'd a comely face, with blue eyes and curly hair. First he was made a page at the Big House, to pick up handkerchiefs and snuff-boxes and the like, and run errands. But he didn't seem made for it. Other lads are quick and smart, as soon as you look at them they're standing up straight—yessir, yes ma'am, what

* *Nedokormysh*—famished.—*Tr.*

47

can I do? But that Danilo, he'd be off in some corner staring at a picture or decoration, just standing there staring. They'd call him and he wouldn't even hear. He was flogged at first, of course, then they gave him up as a bad job.

"Head in the clouds. Moves like a snail. Never make a good lackey of him."

He wasn't sent to the mines, though. He'd never have lasted a week on that work. So he was put to help the herdsman. But he was no good at that either. He seemed to be trying his best, but everything went wrong with him. Half the time he was in a sort of daze. He'd stand staring at some bit of grass while the cows wandered off. The herdsman was a kindly old fellow and sorry for the orphan, but all the same he had to rate him.

"What's going to come o' ye, Danilo? Ye'll ruin all for yourself, and my old back'll get the whip too. What good are ye? What are ye thinking about?"

"I don't know myself, Grandad. . . . Just—naught special. I was watching, like. . . . There was a bug crawling on a leaf. It was not quite blue and not quite grey, and there was just a mite of yellow under the wings; and the leaf was a long wide one. . . . The edge was jagged, curling a bit, like a fringe, and darker, but in the middle it was real bright green, as if it had just been painted. And there was the bug crawling about on it."

"Well now, aren't ye a fool, Danilo! Are ye here to watch bugs on leaves? Let it crawl where it wants, ye're here to herd cows. Get all that nonsense out o' your head before I tell the bailiff!"

There was one thing Danilo could do, though. He learned to play the horn better than the old man himself. Real tunes, it was. When the cows came home in the evenings, the women and maids would ask him: "Play us a song, Danilushko."

He'd start playing, but it wasn't like any song they'd ever heard. It would be like the forest rustling and the brook babbling and birds singing all at once, real nice it sounded. Because of those tunes all the women started making much of Danilushko, some would mend his clothes, others would cut him new foot-rags of homespun, or make him a new shirt. And food, they all vied in treating him to the best and finest. The old herdsman, he was real pleased with Danilo's tunes too. But not always. For once Danilo began playing it was just as if he'd no cows to mind at all. And that was what brought misfortune on them.

Danilushko got lost in his tunes one day when the old man had dozed off a bit, and some of the cows strayed away. When it was time to get them together and drive them to the common, there was this one gone and that one gone. They sought and sought, but what chance was there to find them? It was right by Yelnichnaya, that's close to the woods, they're thick and dark, with plenty of wolves about. They found one cow and that was all. So they took the herd home, and told about the missing cows. Of course, men went out on horseback and on foot to search, but they never found a single one of them.

You know the way it was in those days. For every fault, bare your back. And to make it worse, one of the lost cows belonged to the bailiff. No hope of getting off lightly this time. First they had the old man to the whipping post. Then came Danilo's turn, and he was so thin and spindly, the flogger looked at him and said: "That one'll faint wi' the first stroke—if it doesn't let his soul out at once."

All the same he gave his whip a good swing, but Danilushko didn't make a sound. A second blow, and a third—and not a cry from the lad. Then the flogger got savage and started laying on as hard as he could.

"I'll make you yell, you stubborn cur! Yell you shall! You shall!"

Danilushko was shaking all over, tears rolled down his face but not a sound did he make. Bit his lips and kept it in. He was flogged till he fainted, but never a cry out of him. The bailiff—he was there, of course—was real amazed.

"There's one that can stand knocking about! I know now where I'll send him, if he's still alive."

Well, he did get better, Granny Vikhorikha put him on his feet again. That's an old woman they tell of. She was famous round about for her simples. She knew the powers of herbs, what to use for toothache, or sprains, or the rheumatics—all of it. She'd go out and seek the herbs herself, each one at the time when it had its full strength. And then she'd brew her leaves and roots, or make salves of them.

It was Heaven for Danilushko, living with that old woman. She was kind, you see, and liked to chat; and all her hut was hung with her dried grasses and flowers and roots. Danilushko would look at this one and that and ask her—what's it called? Where does it grow? What's the flower like? And the old woman told him about them.

One day Danilushko asked her: "D'ye know all the flowers round our way, Granny?"

"Well, I won't boast," she said, "but I can say I know those that flower for men to see."

"But are there any that flower in secret?"

"Aye, that there are," said old Vikhorikha. "Ye know the fern? They say it flowers on St. John's Day. It's a magic flower, that is. It'll show where there's hidden treasure. But it's evil for a man. Then there's a flower that breaks rock—it's like a will-o'-the-wisp. Catch it and it'll open all locks for ye. It's a robber's flower. And then there's the Flower of Stone. It grows in the malachite mountain, folks say. It has great power on the Snake Festival. But unhappy the man that sees it."

"Why's he unhappy, Granny?"

"That, my child, I can't tell ye because I don't know myself. It's the way it was told me."

Maybe Danilushko would have gone on living with Vikhorikha, but the bailiff's lickspittles saw the lad was getting on his feet and hurried off to tell of it. So the bailiff sent for Danilushko.

"Off you go to Prokopich," he said, "learn to carve malachite. Just the job for you."

Naught to be done, so Danilushko went, though it seemed like a puff of wind would blow him over.

Prokopich took one look at him. "Picked a fine 'un this time. There's strong, lusty lads can't learn my craft, what'll I do with a lad who can hardly stand on his feet?"

So Prokopich went to the bailiff. "He's no good. Might kill him by accident, like—and then have to answer for it."

But the bailiff—not a word would he listen to.

"He's given ye to teach—teach him and less talk about it. He's tough, that lad is, for all his sickly looks."

"Well, be it as ye will," said Prokopich. "I've said my say. I'll teach him, but I hope I won't be blamed."

"None to blame ye, the lad's alone in the world, do as ye like with him."

So Prokopich went back home again, and there was Danilushko at the work-bench, staring at a slab of malachite. There was a mark on the slab where the border was to be carved. Danilushko was looking at it, shaking his head. Prokopich wondered what the new lad could be about. So he asked in his usual gruff way: "What's that ye're doing? Who told ye to meddle wi' the work? What are ye staring at?"

"Seems to me, Grandad," said Danilushko, "ye oughtn't to carve the border that side. Look, here's how the pattern goes, ye'll cut right through it."

Well, of course, Prokopich started to shout at him.

"What's that? Who d'ye think you are? A master craftsman? Seen naught, know naught and start airing your ideas! What do you understand about it?"

"I know this is spoiled, that I do know," said Danilushko.

"Who's spoiled it? Eh? You say that to me—you, ye snot-nose, to me, the best craftsman? I'll give ye spoiled—ye'll be under the sod!"

He went on shouting and bawling, but he didn't even touch Danilushko. You see, he'd puzzled a good bit over that slab himself, over which side he'd carve the border. And Danilushko had hit the nail right on the head. So Prokopich shouted till he got tired and then he said kindly enough: "Well, Master Craftsman, show me how you think it ought to be done."

Danilushko started pointing out this and that.

"Look, the pattern could go this way. Or better, make the slab narrower, carve the border where there's no pattern and just leave the natural pattern on top."

Prokopich growled: "H'm—aye.... Ye're full o' knowledge. Mind ye don't spill it." But to himself he thought: the lad's right. Something ought to come of this one. But how can I teach him? One thump and he'll turn up his toes.

He thought this way and that, and then he asked Danilushko: "Whose son are ye, Clever?"

Danilushko told him all about himself. An orphan, couldn't remember his mother and as for his father, didn't even know who he was. Always been called Danilo Nedokormysh, but what his real surname was he'd never heard. He told Prokopich how he'd been at the Big House and why he'd been sent away, how he'd spent the summer herding and how he'd been flogged. The old man felt quite sorry for him.

"I can see ye've not had a good time of it, lad, and now on top of it all ye've been sent here to me. Our craft's no easy one." Then he made a show of anger again and growled. "That's enough, now, that'll do! Chatterbox, that's what ye are. If tongues were hands they'd all be grand workers. Chit and chat day and night! An apprentice—huh! We'll see tomorrow what you're made of. Get your supper, it's time to sleep."

Prokopich lived alone. His wife had died long before, and one of the neighbours, old Mitrofanovna, came in to look after things. In the morning she'd cook something and clean up, and in the evening Prokopich managed all he wanted for himself.

They had supper, then Prokopich said: "Lie down here on the bench."

Danilushko took off his shoes, put his knapsack under his head, covered himself with his homespun coat, shivered a bit—it was chilly in the hut in autumn—but soon fell asleep. Prokopich lay down too, but he couldn't get to sleep, all the talk about the malachite pattern kept going round and round in his head. He tossed and grunted a bit, then he got up, lighted the candle, went to the bench and started measuring the slab this way and that. Tried one band of carving, then another, made the border wider, made it narrower, then he turned it all round the other way. But no matter what he tried, it always came out that the lad's way was the best.

"So that's the sort he is, this Nedokormysh!" Prokopich marvelled.

52

"Green as grass, and teaches an old craftsman. What an eye! Oh, what an eye!"

He went softly into the lumber room, got a pillow and a big sheepskin coat, put the pillow under Danilushko's head and covered him with the skin. "Sleep well, Sharp Eyes," he said.

The lad didn't waken, he just turned over on the other side and stretched out under the sheepskin—nice and warm he felt—and breathed sort of heavy, like a cat purring. Now, Prokopich had never had any children of his own, and Danilushko just caught at his heart. He stood looking down at the lad, while Danilushko slept on, breathing heavily with just a bit of a whistle in it. And Prokopich kept wondering how he could make the lad stronger and sturdier, so he wouldn't look as if a puff of wind would knock him off his feet.

"A sickly boy like that to learn my trade! The dust—it's poison, it'll get on his chest before we know it. He ought to rest and put some flesh on him first, then I'll teach him the work. There's a craftsman in him."

The next morning he told Danilushko: "You start off by doing odd jobs round the house. That's the way I have it. Understand? First, go and gather hips, the frost's just touched them, they ought to be right for buns. But see ye don't wander off too far. Just get as many as ye find. Take a crust o' bread with ye—something to bite on in the woods. And go to Mitrofanovna, tell her to fry a couple of eggs and give ye a pitcher of milk. Understand all that?"

The next day he told the lad: "Go and catch me a goldfinch wi' a good loud voice, and a linnet, a lively one. See ye're back by nightfall. Understand?"

Danilushko caught both and brought them home.

"Aye, they're good ones," said the old man. "Go catch some more."

So it went on. Every day Prokopich gave Danilo some job, but it was all play. As soon as the snow came he sent the lad off with the neighbour to help bring wood. Well, what sort of work was that! Going, he just sat on the sledge and drove the horse, coming back he followed the load on foot. Stretched his legs a bit, ate his dinner and slept like a log. Prokopich got him a warm coat and cap, gloves and felt boots. The old man wasn't so badly off, you see. He was a serf, but he paid quit-rent and managed to earn a bit for himself. And soon he was real fond of Danilushko. The boy got to be like a son to him. So he didn't grudge him aught, and kept him out of the workshop for the time being.

Living so well, Danilushko began to pick up, and he got real fond of Prokopich too. Who wouldn't? He could see Prokopich was kind to him, and it was the first time in his life he'd ever been so well off. Winter passed, and Danilushko could run wild all he liked. One day he'd be on the pond, the next in the woods. And he'd keep looking and looking at Prokopich's work. As soon as he came home they'd be talking, Danilushko would tell Prokopich things and ask him—what's this, and why's that? So Prokopich would explain, and show him too. Danilushko took it all in. Sometimes he'd try for himself—"Here, let me do it." Then Prokopich would watch him work and help him when he needed it and show him how to do it all better.

In the end the bailiff noticed Danilushko by the pond. He asked one of his lickspittles: "What lad's that? He's always here. I've seen him plenty of times. Fishing on a weekday, a big lad like that! Ought to be at work. Someone's keeping him back."

Of course they soon found out, the bailiff's spies, and when they told him he couldn't believe it.

"Bring him to me," he said, "I'll look into this."

So Danilushko was brought to the bailiff.

"Whose lad are you?" he asked. And Danilushko said: "I'm an apprentice, I'm learning to carve malachite."

The bailiff took him by the ear. "So that's how ye do your learning, ye rascal!" And by the ear he led Danilushko to Prokopich.

The old man saw there was trouble brewing and thought how to shield the lad.

"I sent him myself to catch a perch. I felt a real hankering for fresh perch. I've a bad stomach, I can't eat other food. So I told the lad to catch me some."

The bailiff didn't believe the story. And he could see Danilushko looked quite different, he'd put on weight, he'd a good shirt and trousers and even top-boots. So the bailiff thought he'd find out how much Danilushko knew.

"Now then," he said, "show me what your master's taught ye."

Danilushko put on an apron, went to the bench and started telling this and showing that. And whatever the bailiff asked him, he knew it all. How to rough out the shape of the stone, and file it off, and polish it, the different mortars and when to use them, how to grind, how to inlay on copper and on wood—he had it all pat.

The bailiff tested him with one thing after another, and then he asked Prokopich: "Seems like you're suited wi' this one?"

"I don't complain," said Prokopich.

"You don't complain, but ye let him idle about. He's sent here to learn your craft, and spends his time fishing in the pond! Take heed! I'll give ye fresh perch, the kind ye'll mind to your dying day, and the lad'll get a taste of it too."

He stormed and threatened a bit, and then he went. But Prokopich turned to the lad in amaze.

"When did you learn it all, Danilushko? I've not taught ye anything at all yet."

"You showed me things and told me things," said Danilushko, "and I saw the way you do it."

Prokopich, he was so pleased the tears came to his eyes.

"Danilushko, son," he said, "whatever I know, I'll learn ye it all. I'll keep naught back."

But of course that was the end of Danilushko's easy, free life. The next day the bailiff sent him some work, and from then on he had his task to get done. Simple things at first, of course—brooches and boxes. Then it was candlesticks with decorations on them, till it came to the real fine work. Petals and leaves, flowers and patterns. It's a tedious craft, that with malachite. A thing may look naught, but the hours it takes to do! Well, Danilushko grew up on it.

When he made a snake bracelet from one piece of malachite, the bailiff said he was a real craftsman. He wrote of it to the Master. "We've a new craftsman in malachite carving, Danilo Nedokormysh. He works well, but he's young and he's slow. Shall I give him task-work or put him on quit-rent like Prokopich?"

Danilushko didn't really work slowly at all, it was amazing how quick and skilful he was. But Prokopich taught him to be clever. The bailiff would give Danilushko five days for some task, and Prokopich would say: "He can't do it. He needs a fortnight for work like that. The lad's only learning yet. If we hasten him he'll only spoil the stone."

Well, the bailiff would argue a bit, but he'd add on a few days. So Danilushko could take his time. He even learned to read and write a bit without the bailiff knowing. He didn't get much, of course, but still it was something. It was Prokopich put that idea in his head too. Sometimes the old man would do part of Danilushko's task himself, but the lad would never allow that if he saw it.

"Grandad—stop! For shame—am I to let ye sit at the bench and do my work for me? Why, your beard's green from malachite, your health's gone, and look at me!"

In those years, you see, Danilushko had grown into a real proper-looking lad. They still called him "Nedokormysh" out of old habit, but he was as big as *this*. Tall, rosy, curly-headed and gay—a lad to draw any girl's eye. Prokopich had even started talking about a wife for him, but Danilushko just shook his head.

"Time enough for that, they won't run away. First I'll be a real craftsman, then we'll think about it."

The bailiff got an answer back from the Master. "Have that apprentice of Prokopich's make a goblet for my house," he wrote. "Then we'll see whether to let him off on quit-rent or give him task-work. Only mind, see Prokopich doesn't help Danilo. If you let aught slip you'll answer for it."

The bailiff read that letter and sent for Danilushko.

"You'll work here, under my eye," he said. "You'll get a bench and tools, and stone'll be brought, all ye want."

When Prokopich heard it he was real cast down. What was this? What was the reason? He went to the bailiff, but of course the bailiff wasn't telling him anything, only shouted: "Mind your own business!"

So Danilushko had to go and work in a strange place. Before he left Prokopich warned him: "Mind, see ye don't work over quick, Danilushko! Don't let 'em see what ye can do."

At first Danilushko was careful, he'd keep trying this and that and measuring here and there, but it was dull and tedious. Whether he did much or little, he had to sit there from morning to night. He got so tired of it, he couldn't stand it any more and started working the way he really could work. The goblet seemed to grow like a live thing and soon it was made. The bailiff took it as a matter of course and told Danilushko: "Make another like it."

Danilushko made a second and then a third. And when that was finished, the bailiff said: "That's the end o' your tricks. I've caught you and Prokopich both. The Master gave you this much time for one goblet, the way I told him when I wrote, and ye've made three. Now I know what ye can do. You don't fool me any more, and as for that old fox, I'll teach him to cover ye up. So it'll be a lesson to others!"

He wrote all that to the Master and sent the three goblets. But the Master —maybe he was getting weak in the head, or maybe he was angered with the bailiff for something, anyway, he did it all just the opposite. He put Danilushko on quit-rent, but so small it was naught to speak of, and forbade the bailiff to take the lad away from Prokopich; maybe if they worked together they'd be more like to think up something new. He sent a drawing with the letter, it was another goblet with all kinds of designs and adornments. There was a carved edge, and more carving round the middle, and leaves all over the foot. Real fancy, it was. And the Master wrote: "Let him take five years, but make it exactly like this."

So the bailiff had to eat his words. He told Danilushko what the Master had said, sent him back to Prokopich, and gave him the drawing.

Danilushko and Prokopich were real glad, of course, and the work seemed to go of itself. Danilushko soon started on the new goblet. It was difficult work, one wrong stroke would mean the whole thing spoilt, he'd have to start right from the beginning again. But Danilushko had a true eye, a sure hand and plenty of strength, so the job went well. Only one thing bothered him, there was plenty of difficulty but there was no beauty. He said as much to Prokopich, but the old man just scratched his head.

"What's that to you? They've drawn it that way, so it's how they want it. Plenty of things I've carved and polished, but what was the good of 'em, I couldn't tell ye."

Danilushko tried to talk to the bailiff, as though that were any use! The man stamped and brandished his fists. "Have ye gone clean daft? That drawing cost a mint o' money. It was mebbe done by the best artist in the city, and you think you know better!"

But then seemingly he called to mind what the Master had written, that the two of them might find something new, so he said: "Here's what you can do. Make that goblet from the design the Master sent, and then if you want to make another your own way, do as ye like about it. I won't stop ye. We've plenty of stone."

Well, Danilushko fell into deep thought. We all know, it's easy enough to see what's wrong with others' work, but try thinking up something yourself! Many a sleepless night it costs. Danilushko would sit working on the goblet he'd been given the drawing for, but his mind was far away, turning over flowers and leaves, picturing which would be best for patterns in malachite. He went about thinking all the time, real moping he got. Prokopich noticed it.

"Are ye sick, Danilushko lad? Go easy wi' that goblet. What's your hurry? Go out for a bit of a walk, ye do naught but sit over that work all day."

"Aye, I will," said Danilushko. "I might go into the woods a bit. Maybe I'll see what I want there."

After that he started going into the woods nearly every day. It was just at haymaking time, with wild flowers and berries everywhere. Danilushko would stop a bit in the meadows, or go to a glade and stand there looking all round. Then back he'd go to the meadow and stare at the grass and flowers, sort of searching. There were a lot of folks about at that time, and they'd ask him if he'd lost something. He'd smile sort of sadly and say: "It's not what I've lost, it's what I can't find."

They began to say the lad wasn't all there.

Then he'd come home and go straight to the bench, and sit at it till morning; and when the sun rose he'd go back to the woods and meadows. He started bringing home flowers and leaves, mostly poisonous ones, wild garlic and hemlock, thornapple and marsh tea and all sorts of other marsh plants. His face got thin and his eyes were sort of wild, and his hand lost its sure cunning. Prokopich got real concerned, but Danilushko told him: "That goblet gives me no peace. I want to bring forth all the power of beauty in the stone."

Prokopich tried to talk him out of it.

"Why fret yourself over that? You're fed and warm, what more d'ye need? Let the gentry play wi' their whims and fancies. So long as they let us alone. If they get some idea of a design, we'll make it, but why should we rack our brains for them? Picking up an extra load, that's all it is."

But Danilushko stuck to it.

"It's not for the Master I'm racking my brains," he said. "I just can't get it out of my head. I can see the stone we've got here, look at it, and what do we do wi' it? Grind it and carve it and polish it, and all the wrong way. And now I'm taken wi' the wish to work it so I can see its full power of beauty, and let others see it, too."

Times Danilushko would sit down again with that goblet the Master ordered. He'd work on it and laugh at it all the time.

"A stone ribbon the moths ha' been at, and a border the rats ha' nibbled."

Then all of a sudden he pushed that work to one side and started on something else. He stood there by the bench without even stopping to rest. "I'll make my own goblet with a pattern of thornapple," he said to Prokopich.

The old man tried to stop him. Danilushko didn't want to hear a word at first, but after three days or maybe four, when he got a bit stuck, he gave way.

"All right, then," he told Prokopich, "I'll finish the Master's goblet first, and work on my own after. Only don't you try to put me off then.... For I can't get it out of my head."

"Well and good," said Prokopich, "I won't bother ye." But to himself he said: The lad'll get tired of it, he'll forget. He needs a wife, that's what's wrong with him. Nothing like a family to drive the vapours out of his head.

So Danilushko set to work on the goblet. There was plenty in it to keep him busy, enough for a year and more. He worked hard and never spoke of the thornapple; Prokopich began talking of a wife.

"There's Katya Letemina, what's wrong with her? A real good maid, she is. Not a thing ye can say against her."

Now, there was a bit of cunning in Prokopich's talk. He'd seen Danilushko looking Katya's way a long time, and she didn't seem averse. So Prokopich led the talk to her, as though by accident. But Danilushko was as stubborn as a mule.

"That can wait," he said. "First I'll get the goblet done. I'm sick of it. I'd as soon smash the hammer down on it, and you start telling me to wed. I've talked to Katya, she'll wait for me."

Well, Danilushko finished that goblet, the one made like the Master's drawing. He didn't tell the bailiff, of course, but he thought to have a bit of a merrymaking at home. Katya, his sweetheart, came with her parents, and a few more, mostly malachite carvers. Katya was amazed at the goblet.

"How could ye carve a pattern like that," she said, "and never break the stone! And all so smooth and polished!"

The craftsmen too had their word of praise.

"Line for line with the drawing. Not a fault anywhere. And clean work. Couldn't be done better, and ye did it quickly too. If ye go on this way, we'll have a job to keep up wi' ye."

Danilushko listened and listened, and then he burst out: "That's just what's wrong, naught to find fault with. Clean and smooth, the pattern plain, all just like the drawing, but where's the beauty in it? Here's a flower, just a common weed, but when ye look at it, it brings joy to your heart. But the goblet—who'll rejoice to look at that? What good is it? Folks'll look at it and they'll marvel like Katya here, they'll say—what an eye, what a hand

that man had that made it, and where did he get the patience to do all that finicking work and never break the stone?"

"And if he did chip it," laughed the craftsmen, "he stuck the bit back and polished it so ye'll never find the place."

"Aye, that's it. . . . But where's the beauty of the stone itself—tell me that? A vein runs down here, and you bore a hole in it and cut a flower. What's the good of it there? Just spoiling the stone. And look what stone it is! The very best—the best, d'ye understand me?"

He got all hot about it. He'd drunk a glass or two, you see.

The craftsmen started telling Danilushko the same thing Prokopich always said.

"Stone's stone. What'll you do with it? Our job's to grind and cut, that's all."

But there was an old man sitting there. He'd taught Prokopich and the others too. They all called him Grandad. He was ancient and shaky, but he understood what the talk was about, and he said to Danilushko: "Ye'd best keep off them kind o' thoughts, son. Put 'em from your head. Or mebbe the Mistress'll take ye for a mountain craftsman."

"What are those, Grandad?"

"They're skilful craftsmen who live in the mountain, and no man ever sees them. Whatever the Mistress wants, they make it for her. I saw a bit of their work once. Eh, that was real work, that was! You'll never see the like here."

They all pricked up their ears at that, and wanted to know what he'd seen.

"It was a serpent," he said, "like ye make for bracelets."

"Aye, well, what was it like?"

"Naught like the ones here, I tell ye. Any craftsman who saw it would know at once it wasn't our work. Our serpents, no matter how good they are, they're but stone, but this was like as if it was living. A black line down the back, and eyes—ye'd think it was just going to up and sting ye. They can make anything! They've seen the Flower o' Stone, they've got the understanding of beauty."

Now, when Danilushko heard that flower spoken of again, he started asking the old man what it was and all about it. And Grandad answered him honestly.

"I couldn't tell ye, my son. I've heard tell of such a flower. But it's not for our eyes. If a man sees it life loses all its sweetness for him."

Danilushko only said: "I'd like to look at it."

Then Katya, his sweetheart, she got all upset.

"What are you saying, Danilushko! Have you got tired already of life's sweetness?" And she burst into tears. Prokopich and the others tried to smooth it over, and laughed at the old man.

"You must be getting weak in the head, Grandad. It's all nonsense. Why d'ye muddle the lad's head with your fancies?"

Then the old man got angry and struck the table with his fist.

"That flower exists! It's truth what the lad says—we don't understand the stone. And that flower holds the heart of all beauty."

The other men laughed at him.

"Ye've taken a drop too much, Grandad!"

But the old man stuck to it. "There *is* a Flower of Stone!"

The guests went their ways, but that talk about the Flower of Stone stayed with Danilushko. Again he began wandering in the woods and stood staring at his thornapple, but not a word about the wedding. Prokopich began to urge him.

"Why d'ye put the maid to shame? How many more years is she to wait unwed? Soon she'll be the laughing-stock o' the village. Don't ye know the gossips' tongues?"

But it was the same old story with Danilushko. "Bide a bit, let me finish thinking and find the right kind of stone."

He started hanging about the copper mine, the Gumeshky one. Times he'd go down, and times he'd hunt among the stone when it was carried up.

One day he'd picked up a bit of stone and was turning it over and over in his hands, thinking—no, that's not it, when suddenly he heard someone say: "Seek in another place, on Serpent Hill."

Danilushko looked about him, but saw nobody. Who could have spoken?

Was someone playing a trick?. . . But there was nowhere to hide. He looked round again, then turned to go home. And from behind him the voice came again.

"You heard me, Danilushko the Craftsman? On Serpent Hill, I tell ye."

He looked round again, and there stood a woman, faint and shadowy as though made of blue mist. And then she was gone.

What could that be? he thought. Could it be *her?* Suppose I do go to Serpent Hill?

That was a place Danilushko knew well, for it wasn't far from Gumeshky. It's been gone a long time now, all dug away. But in the old times they used to get the stone from right on top of it.

The next day Danilushko went there. It was a low hill, but steep. And on one side it fell sheer as though it had been sliced off. You couldn't ask for a better scanning cut. The layers were opened up, look all you want.

Danilushko went up to that cut, and there lay a hunk of malachite that had tumbled down. A big piece, too heavy to carry, and shaped and patterned like a bush. Danilushko looked it over and over. It was just what he wanted—darker at the bottom, with veins running the right way—everything he could hope for. Well, of course, Danilushko was real happy, he ran off to get a horse and brought the stone home.

"Look at this," he said to Prokopich. "Just as if it was made for me. Now I'll soon get it done. And then I'll wed. It's right, Katya's been waiting a long time. Aye, and I haven't found it easy either. It's only this job that's keeping me. The sooner it's done, the better!"

Danilushko set to work on the stone and day and night were one to him. Prokopich said naught. Maybe, he thought, the lad'll quiet down when he's got it done. . . . The work went fast. Danilushko trimmed away the stone at the bottom and you could see at once it was a real thornapple bush. The broad leaves in bunches, the jagged edges, the veins—all real as life. Even Prokopich said it was so like you wanted to touch it. But when he got to the top part, the trouble began. He'd carved the stem and the thin leaves at the side—how it all held together was a marvel. And the cup was just like the thornapple, but somehow it wasn't right. It had gone dead and the beauty

63

was lost. Danilushko couldn't sleep, he sat there over his goblet thinking how he could make it right, make it better. Prokopich and the other craftsmen who came to look at it were amazed—what more did the lad want? He'd made a goblet like nobody'd ever made before, and still he wasn't pleased. He must be sick, he should see a leech. Katya heard all this talk and began to weep. That brought Danilushko to his senses.

"Very well," he said, "that's enough. It seems I can go no higher, I can't grasp the power of beauty in the stone." And he himself started to hurry on the wedding all he could. That's easy when the maid's had everything ready and waiting long ago. So they fixed the day. Danilushko got his good spirits back again. He told the bailiff about that goblet. The bailiff came and took a look—eh, what a piece of work! He wanted to send it away to the Master at once, but Danilushko wouldn't agree.

"Bide a while, there's a bit more to do."

It was autumn, for the wedding day was close to the Serpent Feast. Somebody spoke of it—soon all the serpents'll be gathering. Danilushko heard that, and it was like an omen. He remembered the talk about the Flower of Stone. And something seemed to be pulling at him. Maybe I'll go up Serpent Hill one last time, he thought, maybe I'll learn something there. And he remembered that piece of stone. Just as if it had been put there for him. And the voice by the mine—it had told him to go to Serpent Hill.

So Danilushko went. There was already a bit of frost and a sprinkling of snow on the ground. Danilushko went to that cut where he'd found the stone, and there he saw a big hollow, as though someone had been quarrying. He didn't stop to think who it could be, he went in. I'll bide here a bit, he thought, and shelter from the wind. It's warmer.... He looked round, and there by one wall was a grey boulder like a chair. Danilushko sat down on it and stared at the ground, and all the time he couldn't get that Flower of Stone out of his head. If only I could just glimpse it, he thought. All of a sudden he felt quite warm, as though it were summer again. He lifted up his head and there just opposite, sitting by the other wall, he saw the Mistress of the Copper Mountain. Danilushko knew who it was at once, because of her beauty and her robe of malachite. But he thought: Maybe I'm just fancying it, there's naught there really. So he sat quiet, staring at the place where the Mistress sat just as if he saw nothing at all. And she sat there quiet too, sort of thoughtful. At last she spoke.

"Well, Danilo the Craftsman, so naught came of your thornapple?"

"No, naught came of it," he said.

"Don't lose heart," she said, "try again. You shall have the stone ye want."

"Nay," he said, "I can do no more. I'm all worn out wi' it. Show me the Flower of Stone."

"That's easy enough," she said, "but afterwards you'll be sorry."

"Ye won't let me leave the mountain?"

"Why not? The way's open. But they always come back to me."

"Show me! Of your charity!"

But still she tried to dissuade him.

"Maybe ye'll try once more with your own powers." She reminded him about Prokopich too. "He's cared for you, now you must care for him." Then she spoke of his sweetheart. "The maid's given ye all her heart, but you've got yours set on other things."

"I know all that!" cried Danilushko. "But unless I see the Flower life's worth naught to me. Show me!"

"If that's the way, Danilo the Craftsman," she said, "then come to my garden."

As she said it she rose. There was a sort of rustle like a landslide, and when Danilushko looked round, he saw no walls at all. All round him were tall, tall trees, but not like the ones in our woods, they were made of stone. Some were marble, some were serpentine—every kind. But they were living trees, with little twigs and leaves. When the wind swayed them there was a sound like when you throw down a handful of pebbles. And underfoot the grass was of stone too, of lapiz lazuli and red stone—all sorts. There was no sun, but the light was like it is just before sunset. In between the trees were golden serpents swaying and twisting as though in some dance. It was from them the light came.

Then the Maid led Danilushko to a big glade. The earth there was like ordinary clay, with bushes velvety black. Great green bells of malachite swung from the bushes, and in each was a star of golden antimony. Glowing fiery bees hung over the flowers and the stars tinkled softly as though they were singing.

"Well, Danilo the Craftsman, have you looked your fill?" asked the Mistress.

"Stone to make these," said Danilushko, "is not to be found."

"Had you thought o' them yourself, I'd have given ye the stone, but now I cannot," she said and waved her hand. There was the same rustle again, and Danilushko found himself sitting on the boulder in the hollow. The wind was howling round him the way it does in autumn.

Danilushko went back home. Now that day the folks had come to his sweetheart's home to make merry. At first Danilushko pretended to be mighty gay, he sang songs and danced, but then he seemed to sink down under a cloud. Katya got quite frightened.

"What's the matter, Danilushko? You look like it was a funeral."

"My head's aching," he said, "and it's all red and green and black before my eyes. I can't even see the light."

Well, with that the party broke up. Now, it was the custom that the bride and her friends should see the bridegroom home. But how far would that be when he lived only two or three houses away? So Katya thought of something better.

"Let's go a long way round. We'll go to the end of our street, and then back by Elanskaya." And she thought to herself—maybe the fresh air and wind'll do Danilushko good.

The girls were glad enough to spin out the merrymaking a bit longer. "Of course," they cried, "we must see him home properly. And he lives so close we wouldn't have time for a farewell song, even."

It was a quiet night with a little snow falling. Just the time for walking. So off they went. The two sweethearts walked in front, and Katya's friends and the young fellows who'd been at the party a bit behind. The maids started singing a farewell song. It was sort of melancholy, more fit for a funeral. Katya saw this wasn't the thing at all. There's Danilushko feeling low as it is, she thought, and they start that wailing.

She tried to turn his mind to something cheerful. He'd talk a bit, and then get gloomy again. Katya's friends finished their farewell songs and started having fun again, running after each other and laughing, but Danilushko went along all glum, his head hanging. However hard she tried, Katya couldn't cheer him up. And so it went on till they got to his home. The maids and the young fellows parted, some here, some there, and Danilushko took his sweetheart to her door without any more rites or ceremonies, and then went back home himself.

Prokopich had been asleep a long time. Danilushko very quietly lighted the lamp, dragged his goblets out into the middle of the room and stood looking at them. Just then Prokopich's cough started to rack him. He coughed till he was nigh choked. He was getting an old man, you see, and he was frail and ill. That cough of his was like a knife right in Danilushko's heart. He minded all their years together. He felt real sorry for the old man. Well, and Prokopich, when he'd got over his coughing spell, he asked Danilushko: "What are ye doing wi' the goblets?"

"Just taking a look. Isn't it time to give them to the bailiff?"

"Ye could ha' done that long ago. They're just standing there for no good. Ye won't make them any better, however ye try."

They talked a bit, then Prokopich fell asleep again. Danilushko went to bed too, but sleep wouldn't come. He tossed and he turned, then he got up, lighted the lamp, looked at the goblets again and went over to Prokopich. He stood there by the old man and he sighed....

Then he took a sledge hammer and brought it down on the thornapple so it smashed to splinters. But that other goblet, the one the Master'd sent the drawing for, he didn't touch. Just spat in the middle of it. Then he dashed out of the house. And disappeared.

Some said he'd taken leave of his senses and died somewhere in the woods, but others said the Mistress had taken him to her mountain workshops for ever.

However, it turned out quite different.

1938

THE MOUNTAIN CRAFTSMAN

A fter Danilo disappeared his betrothed maid, Katya, remained unwed. Two years passed, or maybe three, and she was getting past the age. In our parts, they're reckoned old maids after twenty or so. The young fellows seldom send matchmakers to such, it's mainly widowers think of them. But Katya, she must have been real comely, for the lads still kept after her. But none would she take.

"I'm promised to Danilo," she said.

Folks tried to talk sense into her.

"Think what you're about! Promised ye were, but naught came of it. No use thinking of that now. He's dead and gone."

But Katya would hear none of it.

"I'm promised to Danilo. Maybe he'll come back yet."

"He's long dead. Must be."

But there was no moving her.

"There's none has seen him dead, and for me he lives."

They thought the maid was crazed and let her alone. Some even made a mock of her, called her Dead Man's Bride. The nickname stuck, and soon she was called Katya Mertvyakova,* just as though she'd never been called by any other name.

About that time there came a sickness, and Katya's father and mother both died. She'd got plenty of relations, three brothers and sisters as well, all married. But they only started quarrelling at once, who was to step into their father's shoes. Katya saw naught good would come of all this.

"I'll go and live with Prokopich," she said, "he's old and feeble, I can look after him a bit."

Of course her brothers and sisters were against it.

"It's not fitting. Prokopich is old, that's true, but all the same folks may talk."

"What's that to me?" she answered. "It's not my tongue that'll be filthy. And Prokopich isn't a stranger, he's my Danilo's foster-father. And 'father' is what I'll call him."

So she went. To be sure, her family didn't try very hard to stop her. One less, so much bother the less, they thought. And as for Prokopich, he was glad enough to have her.

"Thank ye, Katenka, for thinking of me," he said.

So they started housekeeping together. Prokopich would work at his bench, while Katya was busy in the garden, or cooking, baking and so on. There wasn't so much to do for just the two of them, and Katya was brisk and capable, she was soon through with it all; then she'd sit down with her sewing or knitting. At first it was all as comfortable as you could wish, but after a bit Prokopich began to ail. He'd work one day and stop in bed two. It was old age, he was just worn out, that was all. And Katya started

* From *mertvets*, a corpse.—*Tr.*

69

wondering how they were going to keep on. "Women's crafts won't feed us, and I know no other."

One day she said to Prokopich: "Teach me something of your craft, Father, some of the easier things."

Prokopich only laughed.

"What are ye thinking of! That's not maids' work, malachite. I've never heard tell of such a thing in all my days."

Still she began watching Prokopich when he was at work. She'd help him a bit, too, as much as she could. Filing a bit here, polishing there. Prokopich would show her this or that. Not real fine work, of course. Medallions for brooches, handles for knives and forks and such like, whatever came along. Cheap stuff. It only brought in a few small coins, but it helped.

Prokopich didn't live much longer. Then Katya's brothers and sisters got after her again.

"Now you'll have to wed, will ye, nill ye. You can't live here all alone."

But Katya cut them short.

"That's naught for you to fret over. I want none of your suiters. Danilushko'll be back some day. He'll learn all he wants to know, there in the mountain, and then he'll come."

The brothers and sisters lifted their hands, aghast.

"Are ye in your right mind, Katya? It's a sin even to say such things. Waiting for a man that's dead long ago! Ye'll be seeing spooks next."

"Have no fear o' that," she said.

"But how d'ye think you're going to live?" they asked.

"Ye needn't fret about that either," she said. "I'll manage alone."

Well, then they thought Prokopich must have left some money, and started again with their old song.

"A fool ye are, naught else! If ye've got money, ye surely need a man in the house. Or one fine day someone may come after it. Wring your neck like a chicken's. And that'll be the end o' ye."

"Soon or late, my end'll come when it's fated."

Brothers and sisters kept on a long time, some shouting, some urging, some weeping. But Katya knew her mind.

"I'll manage alone. I don't need any o' your suiters. I've a lad o' my own."

In the end, of course, they got angry.

"Keep away from us, then!"

"Thank ye," she said, "dear brothers and kind sisters. I'll remember. And you too, don't forget; when ye pass—pass by."

Laughed at them, she did. So they banged the door behind them.

Katya was left all alone. She cried a bit at first, of course, but then she said: "No! I won't give in!"

She wiped her eyes and started on her housework. She washed and scoured—a real good clean-up. As soon as she'd finished, she went to the work-bench. There too she ordered and arranged everything to her mind. What she didn't need, she put out of the way, and what she'd be wanting all the time was right under her hand. When she'd everything to her liking, she sat down to work.

"I'll try if I can make one medallion alone."

She looked round for stone, but there wasn't any that would do. She still had the pieces of Danilo's thornapple goblet, she treasured them and kept them wrapped in a separate bundle. Prokopich had had plenty of stone, of course, but right up to his death he'd always been doing big jobs. So the stone was in large pieces. The smaller ones had all been used for decorations.

"Well," said Katya to herself, "seems like I'll have to go to the dumps by the mines, mebbe I'll find something I can use."

She'd heard Danilo and Prokopich talk about going to Serpent Hill for stone. So that was where she went.

There were always plenty of folks on Gumeshky picking over the rock and ore, or carrying it away. They all turned to look at Katya when she came by with her basket. She didn't like the way they stared so she went past the dumps and round to the other side of the hill. Woods were still standing there, and Katya went through them right to Serpent Hill and sat down on a rock. Her heart ached as she remembered Danilushko and tears ran down her face. She was all alone, only the trees round, she could let them run. And so they dropped and dropped on the ground. After she'd wept a bit she looked down—and there was a piece of malachite right by her feet, half buried. How was she to get it out without a pick or crowbar? But she found she could move it a bit with her hand. It wasn't stuck very firmly. She found a stick and began digging the earth away from round it. She scraped away as much as she could, then tried to move it again. It came up quite easily, with a crack—like breaking off a dry twig. It was a flat slab, not very large—three fingers in thickness, as wide as your palm, and two hands long. Katya wondered at it.

"Just as if it was put there for me. See how many brooches I'll make by just cutting it. And hardly anything lost."

She took the stone home and set to work filing it into pieces. It wasn't quick work, and Katya had plenty to do round the house as well, so she was busy all day and had no time to grieve. But when she sat down at the work-bench, she'd start thinking of Danilushko.

If only he could see the new craftsman that's here! Sitting in his and Prokopich's place!

Of course there were scoffers, and worse. You'll always find those.

One night, just before a holiday it was, when Katya sat up late working, three young fellows climbed her fence. Maybe they just wanted to frighten her, or maybe something more, who knows. But they were all a bit drunk. Katya was filing away and didn't hear them come into the entry. The first thing she knew was when they started hammering at the inner door.

"Hey, open up, Dead Man's Bride! Here's some live 'uns come to see ye!"

First Katya tried fair words. "Go away, let me alone, lads!"

She might have spared her breath. They kept battering at the door, any minute they'd break it down. So then Katya took off the hook and threw the door wide open.

"Come in if ye dare. Who's the first to get this?"

They looked—and there she stood with an axe.

"Here, none o' your fooling," they said.

"Think I'm fooling?" she answered. "The first that sets foot inside gets this in his head."

Though they were drunk, they could see there wasn't any fooling about that. The maid was tall, with straight shoulders, and a grim look in her eye. And she handled the axe as though she knew how to use it. So not one of them dared go in. They shouted a bit, then they made off, aye, and went and talked about it too. Of course the other lads laughed at them, three of them running away from one maid. They didn't like that, so they made up a tale: Katya hadn't been alone, she'd had the dead man standing behind her.

"And so awful he looked, your feet 'ud run of themselves."

Maybe the other lads believed it, or maybe not, but anyway, talk started going round.

"Unhallowed things are in that house. There's cause why she lives alone."

The talk got round to Katya, but little she cared. Let them gossip, she thought, all the better if they're a bit scared. They won't be trying to get in.

The neighbours wondered to see her sitting at the bench, and made a mock of her.

"Trying to do men's work! We'll see how far she gets!"

That was worse. Katya had been wondering herself—will I be able to do it alone?... But then she plucked up courage again. Market wares— what craft does that take? Just so long as they're polished smooth. ... That much I can surely do!

When Katya sawed through the stone, she could see at once it had a pattern like you seldom find, and it was clear at a glance where she ought to cut it across. Katya was amazed to see how well the work went. She cut the stone at the places it showed and then started to grind it. That's not such a difficult job, but it needs practice all the same. At first it went slowly, and then she got the knack. The brooches came out real well, and hardly a bit of waste, only what was taken off in grinding.

Katya finished her brooches, wondered again at the stone being just as if it was made for her, and then started thinking where to sell them. Prokopich used to take things like that into the town and sell them to a shop. Katya had heard tell of it many a time. So she decided to go there.

I'll ask if they'll take other work I do, too, she thought.

She fastened up the hut and set off on foot. Nobody in Polevaya noticed she'd gone to town. She found out where the merchant who'd bought Prokopich's things had his shop and went straight to him. When she looked round she saw the shop was full of stoneware, and there was a whole cupboard with a glass front that had only malachite brooches. There were a lot of people, some buying, others offering their work. And the merchant stood there, stern and very dignified.

At first Katya was afeard to speak to him. But then she took heart.

"Have ye any need of malachite brooches?"

The merchant pointed at the cupboard.

"Can't you see how many I've got already?"

The craftsmen selling their wares caught up the song. "Plenty o' folks trying their hand at that stuff. Just spoiling stone. Can't even see that for brooches ye need a good pattern."

One of the craftsmen was from Polevaya, he pulled the merchant aside and said in his ear: "She's a bit lacking, that maid. The neighbours have seen her at the work-bench. A fine botch she'll ha' made."

Then the merchant turned to her and said: "Well, show me what you've got."

Katya handed him a brooch. He took one look at it, and stared at her.

"Where did you steal this?"

That made Katya angry, of course, and she spoke up boldly.

"What right have ye to say that to a woman ye don't even know? Just look here, if ye're not blind, where could I steal all those brooches, all o' the same pattern? Tell me that!" And she poured them out on the counter.

The merchant and the craftsmen saw—yes, it was all the same pattern. And a kind you don't often see. There was a tree growing in the middle, and a bird sitting on a twig, and another bird down below. It was clear as clear, and clean work. The buyers heard the talk and came crowding round to look, but the merchant covered up the brooches. Found an excuse for it.

"Can't see them properly all in a heap. I'll put them under the glass. Then ye can choose what ye want." To Katya he said: "Go in there, through that door. You'll get your money in a minute."

Katya went, and the merchant followed her. He fastened the door and asked her: "What d'ye want for them?"

Katya knew what Prokopich always got and that was the price she named. But the merchant just laughed.

"Eh? What's that? I never gave such a price but to the Polevaya craftsmen Prokopich and his foster-son Danilo. But they were master craftsmen."

"I heard of it from them," she said. "I'm from the same family."

"So that's it," the merchant marvelled. "And I suppose that's things Danilo left wi' ye?"

"Nay," she said, "it's my own work."

"You'd some of his stone left, had ye?"

"I got the stone myself too."

You could see the merchant disbelieved her, but he didn't bargain. He settled with her honestly and even told her: "If you make more o' that kind, bring them here. I'll always take them and give ye a good price."

Katya went away real glad—fancy having all that money! The merchant put the brooches under the glass and buyers came running.

"How much?"

He hadn't cheated himself, of course—he asked ten times what he'd given, and kept telling folks: "You've never seen a pattern like that before. It's by Danilo the master craftsman of Polevaya. There's none better."

Katya came home in a daze.

75

Think of that, now! My brooches the best of them all! I happened on a good bit of stone. Luck favoured me. . . . But then she suddenly thought: What if it was a token from Danilushko?

As soon as she thought of that, she lost no time but hastened off to Serpent Hill.

Now, the malachite carver who'd wanted to make a fool of her before the merchant had got home too. And real envious he was, because Katya'd found such a rare pattern. I must see where she gets her stone, he thought. Maybe Prokopich or Danilo showed her some new place.

He saw Katya go running off somewhere, and set out after her. She went round one side of Gumeshky and somewhere up Serpent Hill. He followed, thinking to himself: It's all woods there. I'll be able to creep right up to the hole.

They entered the woods. He got quite close to Katya, but she never thought of anything, never looked back or stopped to listen. He was real glad to think he was going to get hold of a new place so easily. Then suddenly there was a noise off to the side, and he waited, a bit frightened. What could it be? And while he stood there listening, Katya disappeared. He started running, he blundered about in the woods all of a maze so he hardly found North Pond, about two versts from Gumeshky.

Katya never even dreamed anyone was watching her. She climbed up the hill, to the same spot where she'd found the first slab of stone. The hole seemed to have got bigger, and at the side she could see another slab like the first. She shook it and it moved, then seemed to snap off again like a twig. Katya picked up that stone, and then she started to weep and lament. Well, the way maids and wives do when their men have died, with all the words they can think of. "Where have you gone, why have you deserted me, my beloved?" and so on.

She cried a bit and felt better; then she stood thinking, looking over toward the mines. It was a sort of glade she was on. The trees were tall and thick all round, but between her and the mines they were smaller. It was sunset time. Down the slope the glade was dark from the thick woods, but the sun was still shining over where she looked. It was like as if it was on fire, and all the stones sparkled.

That seemed strange, and she wanted to go a bit closer. She moved her foot and something cracked under it. She pulled it back and looked down —and there was no ground under her. She was standing on a high tree, right on the very top. And there were other tree-tops like it all round her. In between them she could see grass and flowers down below, but they weren't the kind she knew.

Anyone else would have been real scared, started to shout and scream most likely, but Katya, she was thinking of something else. . . . It's opened, the mountain has. If only I could get a sight of Danilushko!

She'd no sooner thought it, than she saw someone coming through an opening in the trees; he was like Danilushko and he reached up his arms as if he wanted to say something. And Katya, she didn't think twice, she just threw herself down towards him—from the top of the tree!—well, and she fell right down there on the ground where she'd been standing before. So she pulled herself together, tried to tell herself sensibly: I must be seeing things. Better get home.

It was time to be going, that was right, but all the same she kept on sitting there, maybe the mountain would open again and she'd get another sight of Danilushko. So there she stopped till it was dark. At last she went home, but all the way she kept thinking: At last I've seen Danilushko.

That man who'd tried to follow her had got back again, and seen Katya's cottage was still shut up. So he hid himself and waited to find out what she'd bring. As soon as he saw her coming he put himself in her path.

"Where've ye been?" he asked her.

"To Serpent Hill."

"At night? What for?"

"To see Danilo."

The man started back, and next day there were whispers going round all over the village.

"The Dead Man's Bride's gone right off her head. Goes up Serpent Hill at night, looking for a man that's a corpse. What if she sets the whole place afire in a mad spell?"

Her brothers and sisters heard the talk and came hurrying to Katya again to scold her and argue with her. But she wouldn't listen to a word from them. She just showed them the money she'd got.

"Where d'ye think that's come from? There's good craftsmen whose work they don't take, but look what they paid me for the first I made! Why's that?"

They'd heard of her success, of course, and they told her: "Ye just had a bit o' luck. Nothing odd about that."

"Bits o' luck like that don't happen," she told them. "It was Danilo put the stone there for me and traced the pattern on it."

The brothers laughed, the sisters shrugged their shoulders.

"She's off her head! We ought to tell the bailiff or she really might burn us all down."

They didn't tell him, of course. They were ashamed to speak ill of their sister. But when they went out they agreed among themselves. "We'll have to watch her. Wherever she goes, someone must go after her at once."

Katya saw them to the door, fastened it after them, and set to work filing down the new piece of stone. She took it as a sign, what it would be like. . . . If it's the same kind again, she thought, then I haven't been seeing things, it was really Danilushko there.

So she hurried with her work all she could. She wanted to see if there would be a real pattern. She kept on and on, right into the night. One of her sisters happened to waken, saw a light burning in the cottage, ran to the window and peeped in through a crack in the shutters. She gasped in amaze.

"Doesn't even sleep! It's awful, the way she is!"

Katya filed the slab through, and there was the pattern. It was actually better than the first. The bird was flying down from the tree, its wings spread out, and the other was flying up from the ground to meet it. Five times the pattern was repeated. And marked exactly where to cut it across. Katya didn't stop to think. She jumped up and ran out. The sister ran after her, knocking at the brothers' doors on the way—hurry, hurry, run! They dashed out, and other people came too. It was beginning to get light. They could see Katya run past Gumeshky. They all made after her, but she didn't even see folks were following her. She ran past the mine, and then went a bit slower round Serpent Hill. All the other people started going a bit slower too, they wanted to see what she'd do.

Katya went her usual way up the hill. She looked round her, and the woods seemed sort of strange. She touched a tree and it was cold and smooth like polished stone. And the grass under her feet was of stone too, and it was still dark here.... I must be under the mountain, she thought.

Everyone was running about, they didn't know what to do. "Where's she gone? She was quite close, now she's vanished!" They ran here and there, all excited, calling: "Is she over there?"

But Katya was walking through the forest of stone, wondering how she could find Danilo. She walked and walked, and kept calling: "Danilo, where are ye?"

Her call echoed through the woods and the twigs knocked together saying: "Not here! Not here! Not here!" But Katya wouldn't give in.

"Danilo, where are ye?"

Again the trees answered: "Not here! Not here! Not here!"

And again Katya called: "Danilo, where are ye?"

Then the Mistress of the Mountain suddenly appeared before her.

"Why have you come to my forest?" she asked. "What is it you want? Is it stone? Choose what you will, and go!"

But Katya answered: "I don't want your dead stone! Give me my living Danilushko! Where have ye hidden him? What right have ye to lure away another maid's sweetheart?"

She's got pluck, that maid. Set upon her right away. And it was the Mistress! But the Mistress, she just stood there quietly.

"What more have you to say?"

79

"Only one thing—give me Danilo! You've got him..."

The Mistress burst out laughing, and then she said: "Foolish maid, d'ye know who you're talking to?"

"I'm not blind," cried Katya. "I can see who ye are. But I'm not afeard o' ye, ye temptress! Not a mite! Cunning as ye are, still it's me Danilo thinks of. I've seen it myself. Ah—I've hit ye there!"

Then the Mistress said: "Let us hear what he says himself."

All the time the forest had been dark, but now it seemed to come alive. It got light, the grass sparkled all colours, and the trees—each one was more beautiful than the other. At the end of an opening there was a glade with flowers of stone growing on it, and golden bees like sparks flashing over them. It was all so beautiful, you could have looked an age and never wearied of looking. And then Katya saw Danilo come running through that forest. Straight to her. And she rushed to meet him.

"Danilushko!"

"Wait!" the Mistress commanded, and then she said: "Well, Danilo the Master Craftsman, now you must choose. If you go with her you forget all that is mine, if you remain here, then you must forget her and all living people."

"Living people," he said, "I can't forget, and her I remember every minute."

Then the Mistress smiled very sweetly.

"You have won, Katya! Take your craftsman. And for your wisdom and faith I have a gift for you. Let Danilo remember all he has learned here, only this—let him forget forever." And in an instant the glade and the marvellous flowers faded and vanished. "And now, go back to the outer world," said the Mistress, and warned him: "You, Danilo, say no word about the mountain. Tell them you went away to a master craftsman in far parts to learn his skill. And you, Katya, never dare think again I lured away your sweetheart. He came himself for that which he has now forgotten."

Then Katya bowed low.

"Forgive me my sharp words."

"Be it so," said the Mistress. "What can hurt stone? I say it for your sake, that you should not let your love cool."

Katya and Danilo walked through the forest; it was all dark and rough underfoot, with humps and holes. They looked round and found they were in the mine, under Gumeshky. It was still early, nobody was there. So they made their way quietly home. And all those who'd gone running after Katya were still in the woods calling: "Can you see her?" They searched and searched but couldn't find her, so they went back home, and there was Danilo sitting by the window.

They were real scared, of course. They got further away and started muttering prayers and spells together. But then they saw Danilo filling his pipe. Well, that settled it. A dead man wouldn't smoke a pipe, they thought.

They started coming up a little closer and a little closer, one by one. And there was Katya in the cottage, she was heating up the stove, as gay and happy as could be. It was long since they'd seen her like that. Then they got quite brave and went right into the cottage and started asking questions.

"Where've ye been all this time, Danilo?"

"I went to Kolyvan," he said, "I heard of a master craftsman, none there was with greater skill and art, folks said. I thought I'd go and learn a bit from him. Father, peace be to him, didn't want me to go. Well, so I made off without telling any. It was only Katya I told."

"But why," they said, "did ye smash that goblet o' yours?"

"Eh, all sorts of things happen," he said. "I'd just got home from the merrymaking.... Mebbe I'd taken a drop too much.... It hadn't turned out as I wanted, so I just took and smashed it. It can happen to anyone, a thing like that. Naught to talk about."

Then Katya's brothers and sisters started on her, why hadn't she told them about Kolyvan? But they didn't get much out of her either, only tart words.

"When other tongues clack, mine's still. Didn't I keep telling ye Danilo was alive! And what did ye do? Kept pushing suiters at me and trying to put me wrong. Come to table, my eggs are just fried."

So that was the end of it. They sat there a bit, her brothers and sisters, talking of this and that, and then went their ways. In the evening Danilo told the bailiff he was back. The man shouted and stormed a bit, of course, but it passed off all right.

So Danilo and Katya started living together in their cottage. Folks say they were happy, never a cross word. Danilo was always called the Mountain Craftsman because of his work, there was none could come near him. So they were well off. Only sometimes Danilo would get sort of thoughtful. Katya knew what he was thinking about, of course, but she said naught.

1939

A FRAGILE TWIG

Danilo and Katya —her that got her man out of the Mistress' mountain —had a big family of children. Eight of them, and all lads. Their mother used to complain, times—why couldn't there be just one girl among them all? But their father would just laugh. "Looks like that's the way it's got to be."

The boys grew up strong and sturdy. There was only one suffered a mishap. He fell down when he was little, maybe from the steps or maybe somewhere else, and hurt himself. A hump started to grow. They took him to wise women, but it didn't help. He just had to stay a hunchback.

Now, a child like that is apt to be cross and spiteful, I've often marked it, but this one was all right, bright as could be, full of ideas. He was the third eldest, but all the others took heed of him, they'd ask him: "What d'ye think, Mitya? What's that for, Mitya?"

And his father and mother were the same. They'd call him with "Take a look at this, Mitya—does it look right?" or "Mitya—did ye happen to see where I put the file?"

Danilo had played the horn real fine when he was young, and Mitya had taken after him. He made himself a pipe and played it so it seemed to have music and words too.

Danilo earned good money with his craft, and Katya wasn't idle either. So they lived comfortable, and never had to ask of others. Katya saw to it the children were well clothed, with warm coats and felt boots and all the rest of it. In the summer, of course, they ran about barefoot, on their own soles, not bought ones. But Mitya had topboots because he was frail and they were tender of him. The older boys weren't envious, and as for the younger ones, they'd come to their mother with "Mum, it's time to give Mitya new boots. He can't get those on, but they'll be just right for me."

Cunning, children are! There they were, eyeing Mitya's topboots, waiting for their turn at them.

So they all lived in good harmony, and the neighbours used to talk of them with wonder.

"See what lads Katerina's got! Never a fight, never a quarrel!"

But it was all Mitya. He was like a light burning in the forest, some it cheers, some it warms and some it sets to thinking.

Danilo wouldn't let the boys start early on his craft. "Let them get their growth first," he said, "time enough for them to be swallowing malachite dust."

Katya was of the same mind—early yet to start them working. She even got the idea of having them learn to read and write, and a bit of figures too. There were no schools then, of course, so the elder brothers started going to a woman who'd got skill in that sort of learning. And Mitya went with them. The elder lads were bright enough, the woman praised them, but Mitya—he was ahead of them all. They'd difficult ways of teaching in those days, but he took everything in at once. The teacher hardly had time to show him—and he'd got it. His brothers were still at their letters and simple words, and he was reading away—you couldn't keep up with him. The teacher kept saying: "Never have I seen such a lad!"

Well, his parents were proud of him when they heard that, and the next boots they had made for him were real smart ones. And it was those boots that started all the trouble.

That year the Master was living here. Played ducks and drakes with all his money in that St. Petersburg, and came to see if he couldn't squeeze out a bit more.

There'd be plenty to be found in a place like that, if you went the right way about it. The bailiff and all those clerks, it stuck to their fingers pretty thick. But that was where he never even looked.

One day when he came driving down the street he saw three children playing in front of a cottage, and every one of 'em wearing boots. Well, the Master beckoned to them.

Now, Mitya'd never seen the Master before, but he guessed who it was. The horses were sleek, the coachman had a livery, the carriage was shining and the man in it was all puffed up, so fat he could hardly move, and he held a stick in front of him with a gold knob on it.

Mitya felt a bit shy, but he took the smaller ones' hands and they went to the carriage. And the Master wheezed: "Whose brats are you?"

Mitya was the eldest, so he answered, calm as you please: "We're Danilo the Stonecarver's lads. I'm Mitya and they're my brothers."

Well, the Master, he nigh choked when he heard it, he got all black in the face and puffed and wheezed: "Ugh! Ugh! Look at that! Look at that! Ugh! Ugh!"

Then he got his breath a bit and started roaring like a bear.

"What's that?" He pointed with his stick at the boy's feet. The little 'uns got real scared then and ran in the gate. But Mitya stood there puzzling his head—what was it the Master wanted to know?

But he, the Master that is, he just kept on in a frenzy. "What's that? What's that—eh?"

Mitya was all confused with it, so he said: "The ground."

Well, the Master looked like he was having a fit, he just gasped: "Hr-r-r! Hr-r-r! What's it come to! What's it come to! Hr-r-r! Hr-r-r!"

Then Danilo himself came running out, but the Master didn't stop to talk to him, he poked the coachman in the neck with the knob of his stick —drive on!

That Master was sort of queer in the head. He'd been a bit off, like, when he was young, and when he got old it was real bad. He'd get in a rage with a man, and then afterwards he didn't know himself what he'd been wanting. So Danilo and Katerina thought maybe it would all pass off, he'd forget about the children by the time he got home. But not this time—the topboots on those children was something he didn't forget. He started right away rating the bailiff.

"Where are your eyes? What are ye here for? Your master can't afford shoes and there's serfs' brats running about in topboots! Call yourself a bailiff?"

The man tried to excuse himself.

"It was Your Honour's kindness let Danilo go on quit-rent, ye named the figure yourself, and he always pays, so I thought..."

"Not your place to think! It's your job to watch!" the Master howled. "Look what's going on there! Where else 'ud ye find that? Put him on fourfold quit-rent!"

Then he sent for Danilo and told him himself about the new quit-rent. Danilo saw it was out of all sense or reason.

"I can't withstand the Master's will," he said, "but neither can I pay a quit-rent like that. I will work as others do, on task-work."

That didn't suit the Master at all. He was short of money as it was, he'd little desire just then for carved stone. He was more like to sell what he'd got together earlier on. But to put a stonecarver to other work—no sense in that either. So he started bargaining. Danilo tried all he could, this way and that, but all the same the Master gave him a quit-rent double what it had been, and if he didn't like it he could go and work in the mine. That was what the Master threatened.

Of course it was a blow for Danilo and Katya. It came hard on them all, but worse for the children, they had to start working before they'd their full growth. So they never got learning after all. Mitya—he felt it was his fault more than anybody's—he kept asking for work. He wanted to help his parents, but they got to thinking again, the way they had before. He's frail as it is, set him working on malachite and he'll just waste away. It's bad on that job, whatever you're doing. If it's making cement, then there's the dust, if it's breaking up stone—look out for your eyes, and dissolving lead in strong spirit for polish near chokes you with the fumes. They thought and thought, and at last they made up their minds to have Mitya apprenticed to the gem cutting. He'd a keen, true eye and quick fingers, and the work didn't need much strength—just right for him.

Among all their relatives they'd got a gem cutter, of course, so they sent the lad to him. He was glad enough, you can be sure, for he knew Mitya had a head on him and was a good, hard worker.

That gem cutter wasn't one of the best or one of the worst, he'd take second or sometimes third price for his work. Still, Mitya learned all he could teach. And then the man told Danilo: "Ye ought to send the lad to town. Let him learn the fine craft. He's got a real good hand."

So that was what they did. Danilo knew plenty of folks in town doing that sort of work, he found the man he wanted and settled for him to teach Mitya. This was an old master craftsman who made berries. It was the fashion then, you see, to have berries made of all kinds of stone. Raspberries, and grapes, and currants, and all the rest. And it was all worked out, what each was made of. They used agate for black currants, and crystal for white, they made strawberries out of red jasper and for blackberries they stuck together tiny balls of black tourmaline. Each berry had its own stone. And the same for the stalks and leaves—some of ophite, some of malachite or coloured quartz and other kinds of stone.

Mitya learned the rules, all right and proper, but then he started thinking things up for himself. His master scolded at first, but then he praised the boy. "Aye, it does look more lifelike that way." And a bit later he said right out: "I can see, lad, ye've got a real gift for this sort o' work.

Even an old man like me can learn from ye. You're a real master craftsman, and with ideas in your head, too."

He thought a bit, then he added: "Only see you don't let them run away
with ye—those ideas o' yours! Or they may get ye into trouble. That's
happened to folks too."

Mitya—well, he was young, so of course he didn't listen to any of that.
He just laughed.

"So long as the ideas are good 'uns. How'd those get me into trouble?"

That was the way Mitya became a master craftsman, and quite young
still, with the first down on his lip. He'd plenty of orders, and the work he
could do. The merchants who sold those kind of wares soon saw they could
make good money on the lad's work, and they kept ordering this and
that, he'd hardly time to turn around.

Then Mitya thought to himself: I'll go back home. If folks want my
work, they'll come there for it. It's a short road and a light load—to bring
me the stone and take away my work.

So that's what he did. And glad his parents were, of course—Mitya had
come back. And he liked to see them merry, too, but he wasn't so merry
himself. Seemed like the whole house was just one malachite workshop.
His father and two elder brothers were always at the bench with malachite all round them, and the younger ones were there too, filing or grinding. His mother had the baby girl she'd wanted so badly, but there was
no joy in the family. Danilo was looking old, the elder boys coughed and
the little ones were sickly. All day they toiled, just to pay the Master's quit-
rent.

Mitya thought to himself: It's all because of those topboots. He wanted to
get his own work going quickly. It was small, finicking work, but all the same
he had a number of wheels and instruments, and a work-place had to be
found. He chose a spot by the window and started. And all the time he kept
thinking: How could he make berries out of the stone found hereabout?
Then he could get the younger lads to help him. He thought and thought,
but he couldn't see a way. It's mostly chrysolite and malachite round our
way, you know. Chrysolite isn't so cheap, and it wouldn't do either, while

malachite would only do for leaves, and not always for them, even, without a lot of setting or cementing.

One day he was sitting at work. It was summer and the window was open. There was nobody else at home, his mother had gone out somewhere, the little ones too, and his father and the older lads were at the wheels in the workshop. Not a sound from them. You don't feel much like talking or singing when you're grinding malachite.

Mitya sat there carving his berries out of the merchant's stone, thinking and thinking of the same thing all the time—where could he find some cheap kind of stone to make things like that?

Suddenly a hand came in through the window, a woman's or a girl's, he couldn't tell, with a bracelet on the wrist and a ring on the finger, and put a big slab of serpentine on the bench, with a bit of slag, like they used for roads, lying on it.

Mitya made a jump for the window—no one there, and the street was empty, not a soul passing.

What could it be? Was someone having a joke with him, or was it a vision? He took another look at the serpentine and the slag lying on it and nearly jumped for joy. You could get that sort of stuff by the cartload, and you could make things of it too, if you chose it with care and worked with skill. But what?

He started thinking what sort of berry it suited best, and all the time he was staring at the place where the hand had appeared. And suddenly it came in again and put a burdock leaf on the bench, and on the leaf were three twigs with berries on them; one was bird-cherry, the second ordinary cherry and the last was ripe gooseberries, so ripe they seemed near bursting.

Well, Mitya didn't wait, he ran right outside into the street to see who was playing tricks. He looked and looked all round, but not a soul was in sight, it was just like a dead place. It was the real heat of the day, who'd be outside at that time?

He stood there a bit, then he went to the window, picked up the leaf and the twigs from the bench and looked at them every way. They were real berries, live ones, but the wonder was, where the cherries had come from.

89

Easy enough to get bird-cherry, of course, and there were plenty of goose-berries growing in the Master's garden, up at the Big House. But where could the cherries have come from when they don't grow in our parts and they seemed like they'd just been picked from the tree?

He looked and looked at those cherries, but all the same it was the gooseberries he liked best, and they were the best for the material he'd use, too. And he'd barely had the thought, when he felt a hand stroke his shoulder, like someone saying: "Good lad! You understand your work!"

Of course, even a blind man would have known now whose hand that was. Mitya had grown up in Polevaya and he'd heard plenty about the Mistress of the Mountain. And he thought—if only she'd let me see her. But she didn't. Maybe she pitied the hunchback lad, and didn't want to craze him with her beauty—anyway, she didn't show herself.

Mitya set to work at once with the slag and serpentine. He hunted and hunted for a bit he could use. Well, he found it and then set wits and hands to work. He sweated over that job. First he cut halves of gooseber-ries, then he made a hole in the middle and grooves here and knots there, then he cemented the halves together and ground and polished it all smooth and fine. Looked real enough to pop in your mouth. He cut deli-cate leaves out of serpentine and he even managed to make fine thorns on the stem. It was real first-class work. Each berry—you could almost see the seeds inside, and the leaves looked alive, there were even little flaws, a caterpillar hole on one or a speck of rust on another, just like real ones.

Danilo and the other sons worked on a different kind of stone, but they could understand that craft. The mother had once worked with stone too. And all of them, they didn't know how to admire Mitya's berries enough. And the thing that amazed them was, that he'd done it all out of common serpentine and roadside slag. Mitya himself was pleased with it. It was real fine work. Delicate. For them as could understand, of course.

Mitya made a lot more things out of slag and serpentine after that. It was a big help to the family. The merchants snatched at that work, paid for it the same as they did for things made of real stone, and buyers always took Mitya's things first. It was something new, you see. So Mitya worked away at his berries. He made bird-cherries too, and garden cherries, and ripe gooseberries, but that first bit he never sold, he kept it by him. There was one maid he thought to give it to, but he couldn't bring himself to it.

And the maids, be sure, didn't turn their backs on Mitya's window. He was a hunchback, but all the same he'd a lively tongue and a quick wit, and the sort of trade to make a maid look twice. And he wasn't grudging, he'd give them beads in handfuls. So they would be round all the time, but that one, she found more errands past his window than any other, and as she went she'd flash her teeth and toss her plaits. Mitya wanted to give her the twig, but he felt awkward about it.

"They'll laugh at her, a gift like that, and she'll likely take offence."

Now, that Master who'd caused all the upset in Danilo's family was still puffing and gasping on the earth. He'd betrothed his daughter to some prince or merchant that year and had to get her a dowry. Well, the Polevaya bailiff thought he'd curry favour; he'd seen Mitya's twig with the gooseberries and he understood a bit about such things. So he sent his men for it. "If he won't give it ye, then take it."

What did they care? Naught out of the way, that. They took the twig from Mitya, brought it to the bailiff, and he had it put in a velvet box. Next time the Master came to Polevaya, the bailiff lost no time.

"Be so gracious, accept this gift for the bride. A fine piece!"

The Master looked at it and first he praised it every way, then he asked: "What stone s it made of, and how much does the stone cost?"

"That's what's wonderful," said the bailiff, "it's made of common stuff, serpentine and slag.'

Then the Master started gobbling. "What? How? Slag? For my daughter?"

The bailiff saw it looked bad for him, so he blamed Mitya.

"It was that rascal pushed it at me, gave me no peace: I'd never ha' dared else."

But the Master, he just went on snorting and wheezing: "Get him here! Get him here!"

They dragged Mitya in, of course, and the Master knew him at once.

"It's that one! The one as had topboots—!"

Then he started belabouring Mitya with his stick. "How dare ye?"

Mitya didn't know at first what it was all about, then he guessed the whole thing and told the Master: "Your bailiff took it from me by force, let him answer."

But it was no good talking, the Master didn't even listen to him, he just snarled: "I'll show ye! I'll show ye!"

Then he snatched up the twig from the table, flung it down on the floor and started stamping on it. There was only dust left, of course.

That really did sting Mitya, he fell into a fury. Well, what do you think, who's going to stand smiling when the dearest work of his hand and brain is crushed underfoot?

So Mitya, he snatched away the Master's stick by the thin end and smashed the knob down on his head, and the Master fell down sitting on the floor and his eyes rolled up.

And here was the strange thing—the bailiff was there and serving men, as many as you want, and they all stood like stuck images, while Mitya went out of the room and disappeared. And after, nobody could find him. But people saw his work, and those that understood such things always knew it.

There was another token, too. That maid who used to smile in front of Mitya's window, she disappeared too, and didn't come back.

They searched a long time for the maid. They maybe thought it would be easier to find her, a woman won't usually go far from her own parts. They kept harrying her parents: "Tell us where she is!"

But naught came of it.

They plagued Danilo and his other sons, too, for a bit, but then they likely remembered the big quit-rent, so they left them alone. And as for the Master, he puffed and wheezed a bit more till he choked with his own fat.

1940

THAT SPARK OF LIFE

It was my old parents told me this tale. So it must all have been a long time ago. But still it was after serfdom ended.

There was a man lived in our village those days, Timokha Smallhand, they called him. He got the nickname when he was well on in years.

There was no fault to find with his hands really. God give everyone no worse, as they say. With hands like his you could go hunting bears with a knife. And the rest of him was made after the same pattern—broad shoulders, a deep chest, strong legs and a neck you'd have a job to bend even if you took a pole to it. In the old days when they had fist-fights on holidays, one close row of men against another, they called that sort strikers, because wherever they struck they made a break. But the best fighters tried to keep clear of Timokha, lest he get too hot. It was lucky he wasn't very fond of it. It's a true word they say—if a man's strong he doesn't go looking for fights.

Timokha was a good worker, got through a lot and used his head with it. Show him a thing once and he'd do it right away, and no worse than you did.

Now, in our parts there's all sorts of trades.

Some get ore out of the mines, others smelt it. Folks wash gold, pick out platinum, dig for coloured stone and work in quarries. Others look for gems and polish them. Then there's a lot of trees cut and floated down rivers. Folks make charcoal for the smelting, they hunt and trap and catch fish. You could go into a hut and find one by the stove hammering patterns on knives and forks, another by the window polishing gems and a third at the bench weaving bast matting. And of course there were the fields and the beasts. There'd be a field or a meadow wherever the hills allowed. A real patchwork, it was, and for each job you had to have the knack, and a spark of life to put in it, too.

That spark's something not everyone understands about properly even now, but with Timokha a funny sort of thing happened. A lesson to all.

This Timokha, whether it was just that he was young, or whether he'd a bee in his bonnet anyway, he got the idea he wanted to try every kind of work and craft hereabouts; he even boasted: "I'll be master of all trades."

His family and his friends tried to talk him out of it.

"What's the sense of that? Choose one trade and know it inside out. Why, life's not long enough to get your hand in at every craft."

But Timokha stuck to it, he argued and reckoned it all out his own way.

"Wood-cutting—two winters, rafting two springs, gold prospecting two summers, mining a year, smelting—that'll take ten years. And then there's charcoal burning and ploughing, hunting and fishing. That'll be just play. When I get old I can do stone carving, or be a moulder, or a saddler at the fire station. Sit there in the warm, turn my wheel, work my polishing stone or prick holes with an awl."

Of course the old folks just laughed at him.

"Less of your brag, ye long-legged stork! Wait till you've racked your bones a bit."

But Timokha paid no heed to them.

"Every tree I'll climb," he said, "and grasp its topmost branch."

The old folks tried to talk sense into him. Branches are no sure measure, what was the top can become the middle, and tops are different too—some higher, some lower.

But it was no good, they couldn't make him see. So they gave it up. "Have it your own way. But don't say we didn't warn ye."

So Timokha started learning all the crafts practised in our parts.

He was a stout lad and a hard worker, the kind anyone would be glad to get. Whether it was felling trees or breaking ore—come and welcome. And he'd no difficulty getting taken on for the finer work, either, for he'd good wits in his head and good fingers on his hands—not wooden, but with cleverness in each of them.

Timokha tried many a handicraft and everywhere he made a good job of it. No worse than anyone else.

By this time he was wed and had a houseful of children, but still he didn't change. He'd learn one job inside out and right away he'd start learning another. He earned less, of course, but he didn't bother about that, just as if it was the right and natural thing.

Folks in the village were used to his ways, when they met him they'd say: "Well, Timofei Ivanovich, are you still a locksmith, or have you gone over to the fire station to be a saddler yet?"

Timokha didn't mind their jests, he'd answer the same way.

"The time will come when there's not a craft that escapes my hands."

Then one day he told his wife he was going to try the charcoal burning. She nearly wept.

"Are you crazed, Husband? Can't you think up something worse? The whole hut'll stink of smoke. And I'll never be able to get your shirts clean. Aye, and there's naught in work like that, what's there to learn?"

She said that because she didn't know. Nowadays with the furnaces it's easier, but in those times when they still burned charcoal in kilns, it took understanding and knack. Many a one tried all his life but never got the real good charcoal. His family would say: "Our old man keeps us at it, gives us no rest or peace, and all he gets is charred, rotten wood. And our neighbours, they sing all the time and the charcoal has a fine, clear ring, naught unburned, naught overburned, and hardly a bit of low-grade."

Timokha's wife could lament all she liked, but she couldn't talk him out of it. He'd only one comfort to give her.

"I won't go about black for long."

Timokha knew his own worth, and when he wanted to change his job he looked about first of all for someone to teach him the next one. And he saw he picked the best man.

In charcoal burning, Grandad Nefed was well known all round about. His charcoal was reckoned the best. Folks called it Nefed's Charcoal and it was always kept separate from the rest in the sheds, and given out only for the finest work.

So Timokha went to Grandad Nefed. Of course the old man knew all about Timokha and the bee he'd got in his bonnet.

"I'll take ye on as my apprentice," he said, "and I'll teach ye all and hold naught back—but on one condition. Ye don't leave me until you can make better charcoal than mine."

Timokha had no doubts about doing it.

"I give ye my word," he said.

So they agreed on it, and soon went off to the charcoal kiln.

Now Grandad Nefed was the sort that thinks out every little thing, how to do it the best way. Even about a simple thing like chopping logs into billets he'd something to say.

"Look ye here, now. I'm an old man, at the end of my strength. But I chop no worse than you. Now why d'ye think that is?"

"A sharp axe and a trained hand," Timokha answered.

"It's not only the axe and the hand," said the old man, "I look for the best place to strike."

So Timokha started looking for the best place too.

Grandad Nefed explained all the ins and outs of it, and Timokha saw he was right, and found a joy in the work too. Some logs would fly apart so it was a pleasure to see, but then he would think—maybe hewing another way would have been better still.

This idea of getting the exact right spot caught Timokha right off.

When it came to putting the billets in the kiln, there were dozens of things to think of. It wasn't just that each kind of wood had to be laid a certain way, even with the same kind you had to use your head. Pine wood from a wet place had one slant, from a dry place another. For wood earlier felled there was this way, later felled—there was that. For thicker billets this draught, for thinner ones another, for split poles different again. Get all that right! And the same in covering it with earth.

Grandad Nefed explained it all honestly and plainly, and now and then recalled where he'd learned this or that.

"It was a hunter taught me to sniff the smell of the smoke. They've keen noses, hunters have. And it's stood me in good stead. Soon's I get that sour smell I make the draught stronger. And everything's all right.

"Then one day there was a woman passing by. She stopped by the kiln to warm herself a bit, and she told me: 'It's burning hotter this side.'

" 'How d'ye know? I asked her.

" 'Go round it,' she said, 'you'll feel for yourself.'

"I went round it and sure enough, it was. Well, I put on some more wood and made it right. I've never forgotten that woman's word. They're always at the stoves, women are, they're used to noting the heat."

He talked of this and that, but he always came back to the spark of life.

"Through all these draught-holes our spark jumps about in the dark, take heed it doesn't turn into destroying flame or sink into useless smoke. If ye make a mistake then ye'll find the wood over-burned or under-burned. But if all the vents are well made, your charcoal will have a good, clear ring to it."

Timokha was real taken with it all. He saw it wasn't such a simple job, he'd have to work at it, but all the same he didn't think much about that spark.

The charcoal they made was all first-grade, of course, but when they came to sort the piles, they were never alike.

"Now why is that?" asked Grandad Nefed, and Timokha himself kept puzzling his head––where had he made a mistake?

Timokha learned to do the whole job alone. And sometimes his charcoal was better than Nefed's, but all the same he didn't leave the work. The old man laughed at him.

"You'll never go anywhere else now, lad. You're caught wi' the spark of life, and it'll keep ye till your death."

Timokha himself couldn't understand it. Why had it never been that way with him before?

"It was because you always looked down," Grandad Nefed explained, "looked at what ye'd done; but when you started to look up, to look for ways to do it all better, then that spark caught ye. It's there in every sort of work, it runs ahead of skilled mastery and beckons a man after it. That's the way it is, my friend!"

And that's the way it was. Timokha went on being a charcoal burner, and he found himself a nickname, too. He liked to give good counsel to young folks and always told them about himself, how he'd wanted when he was young to learn every trade, but in the end had stopped at charcoal burning.

"It's this way," he said. "I can never catch up with that spark in my work. It's over quick for me. My hands are too small, that's what it is." And he'd spread out those great hands of his. Folks laughed, of course. And that's how they came to call him Smallhand. Just as a joke, because he was well thought of everywhere.

After Grandad Nefed died, Smallhand was the best charcoal burner, and it was his charcoal that was kept separately in the sheds. He was a real master at his trade, no denying it.

His grandchildren and great-grandchildren are living in our parts yet. And they look for that spark too, each one in his own job. Only they don't complain of their hands. They know well, you see, that learning can add so much to a man's hands that they will reach up higher than the clouds.

1943

ZHELEZKO'S COVERS

It was a bit after nineteen-five. Before that war with the Germans.

Work was very slack for stone carvers in those years. And especially with malachite. Good stone was hard to come by. The Gumeshky mine where the best malachite used to be found was worked out, and the dumps had been picked over again and again. At the Tagil copper mines a piece might turn up now and then, but not very often. And those that needed them hunted for bits like that as if they were rare pelts. There was some sort of office in town just to buy them when they appeared. It was foreign, and of course it wasn't for our craftsmen it bought them. What did come to light went to other lands.

Then again, malachite wasn't the fashion any more. That happens with stone too. There's old men have worked on some kind all their lives, and when their grandsons grow up nobody'll look at it, even. Jasper and coloured quartz were wanted now and then for decorations in churches and palaces, but the shops for stoneware only took the cheap stuff. Any kind of trash would do, so long as the stone had colour and the setting was gold or silver. No joy in that for a skilled craftsman. He'd finish a job, smoke a pipeful, spit and start another. Just market stuff. Not worth looking at, if you've any understanding.

All the same, the old men who'd got malachite and its patterns in their blood, like, they didn't give up their craft. Somehow they managed to find stone and customers who knew good work when they saw it, too.

There was one like that in our village, Yevlakha Zhelezko, they called him. Folks said he'd found some secret place where he got malachite. Whether it was true or not I won't try to say, but there is one tale folks tell about him.

It was this way. There was to be some big festival for the Tsarina. Not just a name-day or birthday, it was the sort of thing they call a jubilee nowadays. The birth of a seventh daughter, maybe, or something else of the kind. But that doesn't matter. The thing was, the royal family council wanted to give the Tsarina a very special sort of gift.

Of course you know how it is with Tsars—a handkerchief waiting for every sneeze. If the Tsar wanted something special to drink, a merchant rushed up with it, if he wanted a rare dish there'd be another right there. And for gifts they'd a Frenchman called Faberger. He knew all about things of that sort. He'd got his own big workshops for jewels and gems and stone carving, his craftsmen were the finest, and he had a big trade in St. Petersburg and Moscow too.

The Tsar sent for this Faberger and told him there had to be some very wonderful gift for the Tsarina by such-and-such a day, the sort that would make everyone open their eyes and stare. Of course Faberger bowed and said: "It shall be done," but inside himself he thought—that's a hard nut to crack. He knew of things to please all, but this wasn't so simple. You couldn't amaze the Tsarina with diamonds or emeralds or other precious stones when she'd got coffers full of them, all the very best. And intricate design and fine craftsmanship were lost on people like that, they didn't understand it. Then, too, there was another thing—that Frenchman knew that ever since nineteen-five the Tsarina couldn't stand the sight of any stone that had red in it. Maybe it made her think of those red flags, or maybe it was something else. Well, for instance, it might have reminded her of pictures on the leaflets folks handed round secretly, showing her and the Tsar feeling about on the ground with hands all red with blood. What it was I don't know and it's not worth bothering about, but certain it is that after nineteen-five you'd better not bring any red stones to the Tsarina, she'd scream her head off, forget all the Russian words she knew and storm at you in German. And then you'd be had up for questioning and cross-questioning, what was your intent in showing the Tsarina those stones, who was behind you, who was with you and all the rest of it. Now, who'd want to get into that sort of trouble!

The Frenchman Faberger racked his brains trying to find something to amaze the Tsarina, and with no sign or hint of red in it. He thought and thought, and then he went to his best craftsmen to see if they could think of something. He told them all about it and said: "Well, what do you suggest?"

Each one had his own ideas, of course, his own way of looking at it all; but there was one old man who said: "To my mind, malachite is the stone ye want. It gives joy to the eye, and there's a power of beauty in it. Show it to the dreariest dullard and he'll brighten up."

The Master chided the old man, of course—that was no way to talk, about dreary dullards, when it was a question of a present to the Tsarina, it would get him into trouble. But about the kind of stone he agreed.

"You're right. Malachite might do very well."

The other craftsmen were doubtful.

"There's no real good stone to be found these days."

Well, the Master put his trust in money. "Any kind of stone can be got," he said, "if you don't haggle over the price."

So they settled it all—they'd make an album with malachite covers. And they settled all the ornamentation for it, too, there and then.

Faberger got to work at once, sent his agent off that very same day to our parts.

"Don't stint money," he said, "so long as you get the real stone with a good colour."

So that agent of Faberger's came and began searching. He tried Gumeshky first, of course. But the stone carvers there had naught to give him—no good stone to be had. He went to Tagil—there he found bits and pieces, but not the right kind. He had a man who sniffed round the office that bought for foreign lands; but they'd not sell anything when they could only scrape up a bit here and there themselves. He was getting low-spirited about it all when a miner—and thankful he was to the man—told him what to do.

"Go to Yevlakha Zhelezko. He's got stone for a certainty. He gave a job to a customer not long ago, it was such work, all the merchants here and that foreigners' office too just shook their fists and stamped about and said: 'Yevlakha had better not show himself here with his stuff. We won't take it no matter how cheap!' But Yevlakha just laughed and gave them back as good. 'Glad enough to be quit of thieves. Time was when I had to stand wi' my hat off in front of 'em. I've not forgotten it, either. Those times won't come again. If anyone wants my stone they can come to me for it, and I'll see who I'll oblige and who I'll show the door to. But those merchants of yours—they needn't bother to come round at all. I'm an old man, but I can land a buffet that'll send one with a conscience weighing a ton flying out like a bird. "

Faberger's agent was a bit worried at all this.

"That Yevlakha doesn't need any money, seemingly. Is he very rich?"

"No," the man told him, "there's not much riches to be seen about him, but he knows the worth of his craft. That means more than any money to him. If he doesn't want your order, then you won't tempt him with rubles, but if you can get him interested, he won't charge ye high. And the work

—it'll be good enough for an exhibition, good enough for the Tsar's palace. Good enough to show anywhere."

The agent felt a bit easier.... I've got something to tempt this Yevlakha, he thought, I'll tell him the stone's needed for the Tsar's palace.... And he was right, as soon as Yevlakha knew what the stone was for he agreed to sell it. All he said was: "What size stone d'ye want, and what design?"

The agent told him each slab should be at least fourteen inches long and a bit over five wide, and with a pattern of its own, so they didn't both look alike.

"Well and good," said Yevlakha, "I'll find it for ye. Come back in a week."

He named his price—two hundred rubles each slab. And the agent didn't bargain, of course. He wanted to say something more, but Yevlakha wasn't one for idle chat and cut him short.

"I told ye to come back in a week, we'll settle it all then, what's the good of talking when there's naught in our hands?"

The agent came back in a week and the covers were ready, and not just two, but four of them. They were like grass in springtime when the sun shines on it and the wind sends it rippling-green. And each one had its own design. Not a tendril of pattern on one was exactly like another, but they were chosen so that even one who' had no knowledge of carving could tell which ones belonged together. Real skilled work, it was.

Yevlakha laid them out.

"Choose which ye want."

Faberger's agent understood stone, of course. He looked them over, couldn't find a single flaw, and admired the design.

"I'll buy them all," he said.

"As ye will," said the old man. "Take 'em if ye want 'em. Hand over the money."

The agent made haste to pay the price agreed on and went back to St. Petersburg again. Faberger's workmen all praised the covers to the skies, but that old craftsman who had advised trying malachite had a few doubts.

"It looks a bit like stone that's been made, not the natural stone," he said. "Stone that's been put together."

The other men laughed—the old 'un's being clever, trying to show off all he knows. And the Master said right out: "If it's artificial, it's no worse than natural stone, and that makes the skill of it worth even more."

Well, they prepared the album and all wondered at it. And the Tsar, as soon as he heard there was another pair of covers, gave orders that nothing was to be done with them without his orders. So they lay there in Faberger's workshop until some very great people came from France to visit the Tsar. And with these great ones came a man skilled in making artificial diamonds. The diamond cutters and stone carvers at Peterhof, and Faberger's men too, were all agog to ask him this and that. They followed him about like lads after a pretty maid, trying to find ways to please him. Someone thought of showing him the stone carving in the Tsar's palace. They got permission. And there with all the other things he saw Yevlakha's covers. He wondered at the beauty of the stone, sighed and said: "Eh, but they're well off, those craftsmen of yours! Just cut the stone without taking any thought, and there's a miracle all ready and waiting for you."

Our men explained it wasn't always as simple as that, the pieces of stone had to be fitted together.

"That I know," he said, "and tedious work it is, but all the same there's no great art in it when you've got stone with any pattern ready to your hand."

Then one of the craftsmen told him: "We've been arguing about those covers at our workshops, whether they're real stone or artificial."

That made the Frenchman jump as though he was stung, he forgot all his airs, he ran and fussed round them and kept asking who'd said it and why, what were the signs? And how had it all ended? But what he most wanted to know was where the craftsman lived who'd made them. Of course he was surprised to find nobody could tell him anything much about it. All they could say was that the agent had brought them from some village or other. They'd heard the craftsman was a crotchety sort, if you didn't take him the right way he could deal you a good buffet, but what his name was they'd never been told. The agent could say, of course, but he was away on some business for the Master.

Next day the Frenchman went to Faberger at his workshops and started asking more about the covers. The old malachite carver made no secret of it, he said why he had doubts and the others started arguing again, each one trying to show he was right and the rest wrong. Then Faberger himself came in, listened to it all, jabbered something to the Frenchman in his own tongue, and told some of the men to bring in the spare covers.

"Why waste time in talk," he said, "we'll saw off the corners on the right-hand sides and test them. It won't hurt the covers, we can round them off or cover the place with some sort of ornament; and then we'll know for certain whether the stone's real or made."

They soon had the corners off and began testing them with acid, and grinding them down, and weighing them. They did everything they could think of, but still they got nowhere. The composition was like malachite, and yet not exactly the same. Most were inclined to think the old man hadn't been so far out when he said there was something not quite right about that stone.

The French craftsman was more eager than any, he brought all sorts of books along and kept looking in them. And when they decided the stone was hand-made, he went straight to the office. They must have the name of the maker somewhere there. And sure enough, a receipt turned up—for two thousand rubles, paid for four malachite slabs of such-and-such a size, and then a sort of hook instead of a signature because Yevlakha could not write; underneath was a clerk's signature and the district seal. The agent had stolen a good bit for himself the usual way—paid Yevlakha eight hundred, slipped a hundred or two to the clerk, and dropped the rest into his own pocket.

They sent a telegram to the agent asking for the full name and address of the man who'd made the covers for the Tsarina's album. The agent must have thought his swindling had come to light, because he didn't answer. They sent a second telegram and a third, and still no answer. So the Master himself sent a letter, a real angry one—what are you thinking of?

How dare you make a fool of me in front of guests from abroad? Then the agent wrote back—such-and-such a village, everybody there knows him, I can't remember his full name but the villagers call him Yevlakha.

As soon as that letter came, the Frenchman packed in a hurry and took the train. In town he hired a troika and drove to the village, put up at the inn and asked right away where the malachite carver lived. The first person he asked told him—in Penkovka Lane, the fifth or maybe the ninth gate after the big lane, on the right.

Next day he took the way he'd been told. He was dressed French fashion, of course, with yellow boots and green summer gloves and a hat like a bucket, all white with a black satin ribbon round it. Nobody'd ever seen the like in our village, and of course all the children came running to look at the fine gentleman in the white hat.

The Frenchman went along to Penkovka, and saw at once it wasn't one of those streets where the good houses stood. He began to think he'd missed the way. So he asked the children.

"Whereabouts does the man live who carves malachite?"

Of course they were quick and willing to help, they all started shouting at once and pointing—there, that hut, that's where Grandad Yevlakha lives.

The Frenchman looked, he was a bit surprised, but he went to the fence. There he saw an old man sitting in the porch. Tall, he was, but thin in the face and sick-looking. He'd a thick grey beard cut like a spade, with a greenish tinge to it. He was in his old house clothes—trousers of cotton ticking, his bare feet in galoshes, and an old waistcoat all stained with acid on top of his shirt. Just then he was busy whittling something out of pine bark, and a little boy who might be his grandson was saying: "Make me a better float than Mityunka's, Grandad, won't ye?"

Some of the old man's household were outside and when they saw the visitor they started whispering. But Yevlakha just sat there as though none of it concerned him. It wasn't his way to bow and scrape before customers from town, he kept them in their places.

That foreign craftsman stood by the gate looking round, then he went up to the porch, took off his white hat and asked with all his French politeness—might he inquire if you please whether he could see Monsieur the Craftsman Yefliaque who made the things of the malakeet.

Yevlakha could hear from his talk he was from some other land so he answered him friendly-like.

"Look your fill, if it pleases ye. I'm that malachite craftsman. There's only one left now in our village. The old 'uns, they've all died off and the young 'uns aren't ripe yet. Only my name isn't Fliaque, but plain Yevlampy Petrovich, known as Zhelezko, and in the book I'm written Medvedyev."

The Frenchman didn't understand a half or a quarter of it all, but he kept nodding, and pulled off his green gloves and shook hands with Yevlakha, and said something like—he was glad to know him, and please excuse him and accept his apologies for any lack of courtesy, for not knowing his proper name. And he tried to explain who he was, and that he was a master craftsman working in diamonds.

Yevlakha had a good word to say for that.

"There's naught ye can say against stones like those," he said. "It's right they should cost the most of all, for they give joy to the eye. To each stone its own virtue. Ours is much cheaper, but it wakens spring in the heart and makes a man glad."

The Frenchman kept nodding and nodding, and jabbering in his queer way—glad to be able to have this talk, he'd come specially from the French land for it. But Yevlakha joked it all off.

"If it's a good word ye've brought ye're welcome, and if it's a bad one, the gate's open and the way out's clear."

Then Yevlakha led his guest inside. He told his daughter-in-law to light the samovar, and put a bottle on the table. Made the visitor welcome, that is. They talked a bit, but all the time that foreign craftsman kept wanting to take a look at Yevlakha's workshop. The old man found that a bit fishy, but he didn't show it.

"Why not?" he said. "I don't make false money there. Come and look all ye want."

So out they went. Yevlakha took the visitor through the kitchen garden to the workshop. It was just a shed, not very big. The door was wide enough, but you had to bow your head to get in. That wasn't stopping the Frenchman, though, he didn't bother about dirtying his fine white hat but pushed in ahead of his host. Yevlakha wasn't too pleased. ... Look at that, all in a rush! Thinks I'm going to tell him the lot!

Inside the workshop there was the usual wheel and turning stones, and an iron stove. It wasn't specially clean, of course, but everything was laid out tidily, stone here, mountain-green there, crushed slag, powdered coal and so on. The Frenchman looked at it all, picked up this and that, and seemed to be searching for something he couldn't find. Yevlakha just laughed.

"There's no cement here. I don't use it."

He kept peering about, that Frenchman did, but his eyes didn't help him. Then Yevlakha went to the bench, pulled out a box and tipped out at least a hundred slabs of malachite.

"Take a look, Master, at what I make of that dirt."

The Frenchman began turning over the slabs and saw they were different colours and different patterns. He marvelled how they came that way, but Yevlakha laughed at him again.

"I look out of my window on to the meadow there. It gives me colour and pattern. Ye see it this way when there's sun, and that way when there's rain. In spring it's one thing, in summer another, in autumn it's different again, but always it's got beauty. And of that beauty there's no end."

The visitor tried to get out of him how the stone was made, but Yevlakha wasn't being caught like that, he put him off with words that told naught.

"There's all sorts of ways. Times ye take more of one thing, times more of another. Ye can bake it or boil it and sometimes ye just mix it."

"But what tools do you use?" asked the Frenchman and Yevlakha answered: "The usual ones—hands."

The foreigner shook his head and smiled all over his face and started flattering Yevlakha.

"Magic hands, Yefliaque Petrosh! Magic hands!"

"Nay, there's no magic about it, but I don't complain."

The Frenchman saw flattery wouldn't help him any more than cunning; so he pulled two banknotes out of his pocket, a thousand rubles each they were, with Peter the Great's head on them, and put them on the bench.

"I'll pay a thousand if you'll tell me honestly all about it," he said, "and if you'll show me I'll give double."

Yevlakha looked at Peter's picture on the notes.

"A good ruler he was, none other like him, but one thing he didn't teach us—to sell our souls. Pick up your money, Master, and go your ways back where ye came from."

The Frenchman kept arguing and persisting, of course—what was the matter? Was he offended at something?

Well, then Zhelezko lost his temper and gave his visitor some straight words.

"You, with your white hat, calling yourself a craftsman! Tell you— why, ye'd sell it to the first that gives you a hat and gloves. Ye'd put snot in a gold setting and sell it as malachite for five rubles. D'ye understand that? Snot instead of our stone that holds the joy of the earth! But ye won't, never! We can use that stone ourselves. And we won't only make things like those covers for the Tsarina's album, we'll make things of such beauty, folks'll come from all ends of the world to set eye on them. And it'll be our work! Made wi' these hands!"

So the foreign craftsman got naught out of Zhelezko. But he did get the covers from Faberger. The great folks he was with talked the Tsar into making a gift of them.

Zhelezko died during the Civil War. There were still some who weren't sure how it would all end, but Zhelezko kept on saying: "Never you doubt it—workers' hands can do all! Some they'll grind to powder, some they'll gather up grain by grain and smooth them out carefully, and then ye'll have a whole stone of joy and beauty like none have ever seen. For the world to wonder at. And to learn from, too."

1940

THE BAILIFF'S BOOT-SOLES

There was a bailiff in Polevaya once called Severyan Kondratych. Eh, what a ruffian he was, what a ruffian! They'd never known the like since there'd been mines and mills there. A hound, he was, and worse. A wild beast.

He knew little enough about the work, but when it came to knocking folks about, that he was real good at. He came from the gentry, he'd had villages of his own but he'd lost them. And all because of his savage ways. He beat a lot of men to death, and some of them were from other estates. So then it got known, couldn't be hushed up. He was tried and the judge gave him his choice—either Siberia, or else our mines here. And the Turchaninovs, our masters—a butcher like that was just right for them. They put him over Polevaya at once. "Be so good and be so kind, put a strong curb on the folks there. And if you happen to kill any, no one'll try ye for it in those parts. So long as they're quietened down a bit; for you see the sort of thing they've been doing."

Just before that some of the men in Polevaya had sat the old bailiff down on a red-hot ingot—and done it so he died within the hour. Of course there'd been plenty of floggings for it, but it never came to light who'd done it.

"No one put him there. He sat down himself. Got dizzy with the fumes, mebbe, didn't rightly know what he was doing. We took him off as quick as we could, but all his bottom was burnt right to the inside. God's will, it must ha' been, that he got his death from the bottom."

After that the Master looked for a proper hell-hound to strike fear in folks.

So that butcher Severyan was made bailiff. He was bold enough, but all the same, he knew a mining village isn't like an ordinary village, he'd have to take care. Folks are always close together, not much room, and there's the fire in the workshops. And every man with something in his hand.... Crack you over the head with the tongs, give the hammer a bit of a swing, come down crash with the rake or a log. Easy enough. Push a man's head between the rollers, or into the furnace. He got dizzy with the fumes, went too close and fell in. They'd roasted the other bailiff.

So Severyan hired body-guards. Where he dug them up I don't know. Each one stronger and fiercer than the other. And real vermin. Brigands from lawless parts. Well, he took that band with him when he went to the workshops. He'd stalk along in front of them all. In his hand he'd have a whip two fingers thick, knotted at the end. In his pocket a pistol with four barrels loaded and primed—naught to do but pull it out. And then came that band after him. Some with clubs, some with sabres, and some with pistols too. Just like they were going off to battle somewhere.

First of all he'd ask the foreman: "Who's working badly?"

The foreman knew if he spoke well of all he'd get a taste of the whip himself for going easy with folks. So he'd start looking for something wrong. He'd name one and name another, it might be for something real or it might be for something that didn't just suit himself or it might be for nothing at all. So long as the whip fell on other backs, not his. He'd speak bad of this one and that, and then the bailiff would start raging about. Flog them himself, he would. He really enjoyed tormenting folks, it was better than meat and drink to him. That's what he was like. A butcher.

He didn't go down the Copper Mountain mine at first, though. It's fearsome underground for one not used to it, whoever he is. First there's the darkness, and you can't get more light. If the Master himself came down he'd have only the same lamp. You don't know whether it's really burning or only looks like it. And then there's the wet, too. And the folks working down there, they care for naught, it's the same to them whether they live or die. Ready for anything, they are, and they're the ones that bother the masters the most. Then too, Severyan had heard the Copper Mountain had its Mistress. And that she didn't like it when folks were treated ill underground. So Severyan was a bit afraid. But at last he plucked up courage and down he went with all his band following. Well, then it started. Seemed like he'd got twice as savage. Before that the bailiffs waited till the miners came up to flog them. But now he started a new style. He'd lay on right there at the face with his whip or whatever came to hand. He'd go down every day, and it was always the same—he tried to see how many men he could ill-treat. If he'd beaten plenty, then he'd feel real gay. He'd stroke his whiskers and growl at the overseer: "Well, old bag o' bones, get the cage ready. Swung my arm a bit, time for dinner."

He raged about the mine like that for a week. And then something happened. He'd just told the overseer to get the cage ready when he heard a voice, clear and ringing as though it were quite close.

"Take care, Severyan, that you don't leave your boot-soles as a remembrance for your children!"

The bailiff jumped.

"Who said that?" He turned towards the voice, and fell down so he nearly broke his legs. Because they were fixed as though they'd been nailed. He could hardly pull them up. And the voice had been a woman's. That made the bailiff a bit bothered, but he didn't show it. He just went on as if he hadn't heard it. And his band of ruffians kept quiet too, but you could see the heart was out of them. They'd guessed at once—it was *she* who'd warned the bailiff.

Well, all right. He stopped going down the mine. The men had a chance to breathe easy for a bit. But not for long. Severyan was ashamed, you see. What if the workers had heard that voice and were laughing at him? Saying Severyan was afraid? That was sharper than a knife for him, for he'd always boasted he feared naught.

One day he went into the rolling shop and someone shouted: "Watch your boot-soles!" That was a saying they had, to warn folks to look out. But the bailiff thought: They're making a mock of me. It got him real mad. He didn't try to find the man who'd spoken. He didn't even beat anyone that day, he stopped there in the middle of the shop and said to his men: "We haven't been down the pit for a long while. Time to pull things up there."

So they went down. And the bailiff, he was in such a fury as he'd never been before. Beat up everyone he saw. He wanted to show there was naught could scare him. And then came the same voice again.

"For the second time, Severyan, I warn ye. Think of your children. Only the soles of your boots will be left them."

The bailiff turned round and fell, just like the other time. He couldn't get his feet off the ground. He looked down, and there they were sunk nearly an inch in the rock, looked like it would take a pick to get them out.

He did manage it all the same, but his topboots were gaping in front, with the soles hanging loose.

The bailiff got a bit quiet, but when he came out on top he plucked up heart. He turned and asked his men: "Did ye hear aught? Down there in the pit?"

"Aye, we heard it," they said.

"And did ye see how my feet got stuck?"

"Aye, we saw that too."

"And what d'ye think—what does it mean?"

Well, they hemmed and hawed, then one of them came right out with it.

"It looks like the Mistress of the Copper Mountain was giving ye a kind of hint. Sort of threatening something, but what it is, I don't know."

"Well then, harken to me," said Severyan. "Get ready to go down tomorrow as soon as it's light. I'll teach them to try and frighten me, and hide some wench in the mine. I'll go through every gallery till I catch her, and then I'll drive the soul from her body with five strokes of this whip. Ye hear me?"

He started bragging the same way to his goodwife when he got home. Well, she was a woman so she started to weep.

"Eh dear, eh dear, take care of yourself, Severyan, husband! Let's send for the priest, so he can arm ye against uncanny powers."

They did send for the priest. He sang and he prayed and he hung a holy medal round Severyan's neck and sprinkled holy water over his pistol.

"Have no fear, Severyan Kondratych," he said, "and if anything should happen, then say the prayer: 'O Lord our God, arise.' "

The bailiff's band of ruffians were at the pithead the next morning at dawn. They were all white in the face, only the bailiff strutted about like a cock. He'd got his shoulders back and his chest thrust forward, and new topboots on his legs shining like mirrors. And he kept slapping those boots with his whip.

"If the soles are torn off again," he said, "I'll give the overseer something for not having the muck cleared away. He may have been working twenty years, but I'll flay the hide off him all the same. And you try to get a sight o' that wench. There's fifty rubles for whoever catches her."

Well, they went down and started poking about everywhere. The bailiff was in front as usual, with his band following. But the galleries were narrow, so they had to go one after the other. All of a sudden the bailiff saw a figure in front of him. It was moving lightly, waving a lamp. At the turn of the gallery he saw it was a woman. The bailiff shouted to her to stop.

but she went on as if she hadn't heard him. He started running after her, but his faithful men weren't in any great hurry to follow. They were all shaking. Because they saw this was bad—it was *she* herself. But they didn't dare go back either, Severyan would have them beaten to death. The bailiff kept running, but he couldn't seem to catch that woman. He bawled, of course, and threatened, but she didn't even look round. There was nobody working in that gallery, not a soul.

Suddenly the woman turned, and at once it got light. The bailiff saw a maid of amazing beauty standing before him, and her brows were drawn together in a line and her eyes blazed like burning coals.

"Well," she said, "now let us settle accounts, butcher! I warned you to make an end, but you—what did you do? Boasted ye'd drive the soul from my body with five strokes of your whip! And what d'ye say now?"

But Severyan bawled: "I'll do worse than that. Hey, Vanka, Yefimka, seize that wench, drag her out of here, the hussy!"

He shouted for his men, he thought they were close by, but then all of a sudden his feet were stuck again.

He yelled in a frenzy: "Hey, come here!"

"You can spare your voice," said the maid. "There is no way here for your men. In a moment many of them will not be with the living."

She gave a bit of a wave with her hand. And then he heard the gallery collapse behind him and the wind roared past. The bailiff looked behind him and saw a solid wall, just as if there'd never been a gallery there at all.

"Now what do you say?" asked the Mistress again.

But the bailiff was in a rage and the priest had made him feel secure, so he pulled out his pistol.

"This is what I say!" And bang!—he fired one barrel—right at the Mistress! But she just caught the bullet with her hand, tossed it against the bailiff's knee and said quietly: "To that place he is no more." She said it like she was giving an order. And the next moment the bailiff was covered with green stone right up to his knees. Well, then of course he started to howl.

"Oh kind, sweet maid, forgive me, have mercy! I'll teach my grand-children and great-grandchildren to bless you! I'll go away from here. I'll repent all my sins!"

He kept on roaring and howling, and tears ran down his face. The Mistress was so disgusted she spat.

"Ugh, you foul insect, worthless trash! Can't even die decently. It turns my stomach to look at ye."

She stretched out her hand and the stone rose right over the bailiff's head. There was just a great green block standing in his place. The Mistress went up, gave it a little push and it tumbled over. And then she melted away like mist.

There was a great running about in the mine. After all, a whole gallery had fallen, and one where the bailiff and his men had gone. No joke, that. All the folk were driven down and started digging the rock away. There was plenty of fuss on top, too. A message was sent to the Master at Sysert, and the next day a lot of mining officials came from the town. Two days later they dug as far as the body-guards. And here was a strange thing— the ones that had been the worst of all were dead, but the ones that had had even a mite of decency, they were only hurt.

They found all those men, but they couldn't find the bailiff. Then they came to some place nobody had ever seen before. And there in the middle was a great hunk of malachite lying on its side. They started looking at it and saw one end was polished.

Here's a marvel, they thought. Who's been polishing malachite in this place?... They took a better look and saw two boot-soles, in the very middle of the polished part. Quite new, they were, you could see all the nails. Three rows of them. They told the Master about it. Now, he was an old man and hadn't been down for many a year, but he wanted to see this. So he ordered them to get the malachite out just as it was. What a job they had with it! But they got it up in the end. And the old Master—when he saw those boot-soles, he burst into tears.

"What a faithful servant he was to me!" he cried, then he said: "The body must be freed from the stone and buried with honour."

They sent off at once to Mramor for the best stone cutter. Kostousov was famous then. They brought him alone and the Master asked him: "Can ye get the body out of this stone, and without spoiling it?"

The stone cutter examined it.

"And who'll get the stone?" he asked.

"You can keep that for yourself," said the Master, "and I'll pay for the work, I won't stint the cost."

"Well," said Kostousov, "I can make a try at it. It's real good stone, ye don't often see stone like that. The only thing is, our work takes time. If I cut through to the body at once, it'll stink. I'll have to start by taking off the outside, but that'll mean malachite going to waste."

When he heard that the Master flew into a rage.

"It's not malachite ye've got to think of," he said, "but how to get the body of my faithful servant out undamaged."

"Well, that's how ye look at it," said Kostousov.

You see, he was a free man, so he could talk free too. He started getting out the body. First he took off the outside and carried the malachite home. Then he started cutting through to the body. And what do you think? Wherever there had once been body or clothes, there was just plain rock, and round it was first-class malachite.

All the same, the Master had that dirt buried like a man. But Kostousov was real disappointed.

"If I'd known," he said, "I'd have sawn through the hunk at once. All that good stone lost because of the bailiff, and see what's left of him! Just the soles of his boots."

1936

SOCHEN'S GEMS

After Stepan's death—he was the one that got the malachite columns—a lot of folks came around Krasnogorka. They wanted to find the kind of stones that had been in Stepan's dead hand. But it was autumn, just before the snow. Not much to be done then. As soon as the snow melted, though, they all came back, swarms of them. They grubbed here, dug there, found iron ore, saw that was all there was and gave it up. Only Vanka Sochen kept at it. Other folks were getting ready for the mowing and there he was, picking away round the ore mines. He wasn't a real prospector, either, he'd just drifted into it. In his young years he'd been a sort of lackey for the Master and got thrown out for something he'd done amiss. But the taint stayed with him—a lickspittle, that's what he was. Always trying to put himself forward, anyway. To curry favour. But what could he do? Of learning he'd but a mite. Not enough to be a clerk. He was no good for the furnaces, and in the mines he wouldn't last a week. So he tried prospecting for gold. Thought that would be sweet as honey. Tasted it and found it bitter. But then he got a job after his own heart. Pushing his snout in among the prospectors, sniffing and listening, and carrying all he picked up to the office. He didn't put away his prospector's pan, though. He still washed sand, but his only thought was—what he could spy out. And those in the office, they saw he was crafty and useful to them. So they'd make it worth his while, give him a good place to work, and money, and clothes and boots too. The prospectors settled their own accounts with him as well— one with a box on the ear, another with a buffet over the head, and some everywhere at once. Whatever he'd deserved. But Sochen was used to blows, after all, he'd been a lackey. He'd lie up a bit and then start all over again. And that was how he went on, from one to the other. And he'd picked a woman to fit him. I don't mean she was light in her ways or a trollop, but just—well, they all called her Sup-Abroad; she liked to get something for nothing. They'd no children, of course—what would they want with children?

So when the talk went round about Stepan's stones and all the folk started swarming over Krasnogorka, Sochen was there too.

I'll try my luck, he thought. I'm no worse than Stepan. Anyway, I wouldn't be such a fool as to crush wealth to powder in my hand.

Now, prospectors know the signs, whether it's worth looking here or there. They scratched a bit on Krasnogorka, saw it wasn't the right kind of rock and let it alone. But that Sochen, he thought he knew better, and he stopped there.

If I don't get rich. he thought, my name's not Vanka Sochen! He'd an opinion of himself, he had!

One day he was digging in a gallery of the mine. He'd turned over ore in plenty and got naught for his pains, when suddenly a rock broke away. Twenty poods weight. it must have been, maybe more. Nearly crushed his feet. He jumped back, then he took a look in the hole it had left and right in front of him he saw two green stones. Sochen was all cock-a-hoop, thought he'd lighted on a pocket. He reached out to get them, when there came a hiss—Vanka nearly lost his senses with fright. And then he saw a cat jump out. Brown all over, it was, without any markings, only its green eyes and white teeth shining. It was bristling, back up, tail like a poker—looked ready to fly at him. Vanka ran for his life. He covered a verst or maybe two without looking back till he'd no more breath and was half-dead. Then he eased off a bit. He went home and shouted to his goodwife: "Heat the bath-house quick! Something's happened."

When he'd finished steaming himself, what must the fool do but go and tell the whole tale to his wife. And of course she had her word to say.

"You'd better go to Granny Cartwheel, Vanyushka. Beg her to help. She'll give ye the right counsel."

That was an old woman folks tell of. She'd make steam baths for women whose time had come, and sometimes rid maids of the fruit of their foolishness. She'd got legs bowed like a hoop, so her body seemed set on a wheel. That's why they called her Cartwheel.

Vanka wanted no more to do with it all.

"I won't go anywhere, and there's no gold in the world would get me down that mine again. Not wi' things like that there! Nay, I'll have naught to do with it!"

He even wanted to send someone else to get his tools. He was real scared. But when a day had gone, and another, and a third, he got over it a bit. And his wife kept on nagging at him.

"Go to Cartwheel, go to her! She's a witch. She'll tell ye how to get the stones." The woman was greedy for wealth too, you see.

So Vanka went to Cartwheel. He started telling her about it, but what could that old crone understand about wealth underground? She just sat there muttering: "Dyrr-gyrr-byrr. The snake fears the cat, the cat fears the dog, the dog fears the wolf, the wolf fears the bear. Dyrr-gyrr-byrr! Avaunt! Begone!" All that sort of witches' jabber. But Vanka, he just stood there thinking: That's a real wise woman!

He told her the whole tale, and the crone asked: "Have ye a coat of dog-skin, my son?"

"Aye," he said, "but it's a bad one, all torn."

"No matter," she said, "so long as it's got the stink o' dog."

"It's got that a-plenty," said Sochen, "it was taken from starved curs."

"That'll do, then. Put on that coat and mind ye don't take it off till ye bring the stones home. And if ye're still afeard, I'll give ye a wolf's tail to hang round your neck or bear's fat to sew inside your shirt. Only ye'll have to pay for them, and pay well."

Sochen bargained with the crone, then went home for the money.

"Here you are, Granny, now give me the tail and the fat." The crone was real glad—what a fool God had sent her!

Sochen hung the tail round his neck, and his wife sewed the fat into the collar of his shirt. Then he put the dogskin coat on top of it all and set off for Krasnogorka. Folks that met him stared to see him wearing a dog-skin coat in that heat. But he groaned a bit and said he was shaking with fever, though the sweat was running down his face.

He came to the mine and there were his tools lying about, just as he'd left them. Only the shanty he'd made of branches had been pushed crooked by the wind.

Clear enough, nobody'd been there. Sochen looked about a bit, and then started breaking out the ore again, and getting naught for his pains. The day wore on to evening. Sochen was afeard to stop there, but he got tired. Try to swing a pick wearing a dogskin coat in summer time! A strong man'll soon have enough of it, and Sochen was puny. So he just lay down to rest where he stood. Sleep's not like us, it takes all the same. The coward snores as hearty as the brave man.

When Vanka wakened, he felt fine and as bold as could be. He had a bite to eat and back he went to work. He kept on striking with his pick, and then, just like that other time, a great rock fell down, nearly took his feet with it. Now the cat'll jump out, he thought. But no, nothing came. Seemed like the wolf's tail and the bear's fat had virtue in them. He went up to the hole and saw the rock in the back was a different kind. He cleared everything away all round, got to that place and started picking out the new rock. It was bluish, like the kind they call lapiz lazuli, and lay light and loose. He picked at it a bit and came on a pocket. Six green stones he found, and all of them lying in pairs. Somehow or other Sochen found strength to go on hewing. But no matter how much he tried, he saw no more. Not a sign. Not even that kind of rock. Just as if it had been put there to show him.

Vanka didn't give up for a long time. He'd take another look at those stones and set to work with his pick again. But it was no good. He got tired out, his bread was all eaten, time to go home.

There was a path straight to the spring by the bridge over the Severushka. That was the path Vanka took. The trees grew high and thick there, and the path was easy to see. Sochen walked along thinking how much he'd get for the stones. And then suddenly he heard something behind him.

"Miaaw! Miaaw! Give us our eyes!"

He turned round. There were three cats running after him, all of them brown, and with no eyes in their heads. Looked just ready to spring. Vanka dashed into the wood on one side and the cats after him. But what could they do, blind? Even with sight to help him, Sochen scratched his face till it bled and tore that dogskin coat to tatters. He got stuck in a swamp and fell down more times than he could count before he managed to get out on the highroad, more dead than alive. By good fortune some of the men from Severnaya were passing with five carts. They saw a man dash out, all frantic, so they just put him on one of the carts and took him to Severnaya, and from there Sochen made his way home himself. It was night, his wife was asleep, but the hut wasn't fastened up. She was slipshod too, Sochen's wife was. She'd lie and sleep, and let the household look after itself. Sochen blew the fire to a blaze, made the sign of the cross at all the corners and pulled out his wallet to take a look at the stones. But what d'you think?—there was naught but a pinch of dust inside! He'd crushed them all. Well, Sochen set up a howl and started cursing Cartwheel with all the words he could think of.

"With all your mummery, you this and you that, you couldn't keep the cats off me! What did I give ye money for, what did I wear that coat for?"

He wakened his wife, gave her a buffet and plenty of abuse. She saw he was beside himself and thought soft answers better. So she let him shout and kept saying: "Vanyushka, shall I heat the bath for ye?"

She knew the way to smooth him down, you see. Well, Vanka shouted some more, but after that he quieted a bit and told the woman the whole story. Then it was she who started crying and screaming. She took a look at that dust in his wallet, picked up a bit, licked it and back to her crying. So they both howled together. And then the woman started off with her counsel again.

"Cartwheel's not strong enough, seemingly," she said. "You need to go to the priest, that'll make the spell more powerful."

At first Sochen wouldn't hear a word. He shook at the very thought of going back to that mine. But the woman kept at him like a fly. She buzzed round him one whole day, and a second, and at last she got her way. And Vanka himself began to take heart a bit.

I needn't have been so scared of the cats, he thought. They'd no eyes, after all!

So off he went to the priest, and told him the whole tale.

The priest thought and thought, and then he said: "You must promise the first stone you get for the Virgin's crown, my son, and after that give as many more as ye can."

"That I'll do," said Sochen. "If I get a couple of dozen, I won't grudge five or six of them."

Then the priest got down to praying over Sochen. He read prayers out of one book, then out of another, and a third; he sprinkled water and blessed Sochen with a cross, and took half a ruble from him.

"It would be good, my son," he said, "if you took a cross of cypress from Mount Athos. I have one but its cost is high. However, as it's a special occasion, I'll let ye have it for what I paid myself." And he named a sum twice as big as Cartwheel's. Well, you can't bargain with the priest; so Vanka went home, and he and his wife scraped up the last money they could find. Then Sochen bought the cross and started bragging to his wife. "Now there's naught I fear."

The next day he set off for the mine again. His wife had washed the shirt, the one with the bear's fat, and mended the dogskin coat as well as she was able. Vanka hung the wolf's tail round his neck and the cypress cross with it. When he came to Krasnogorka, it was all just the same as it had been. Everything lying as he'd left it. Only the shanty was a bit more crooked. Well, Vanka wasn't bothering himself about that. He went straight into the gallery. But as soon as he began to swing his pick, he heard a voice.

"So you've come again, Vanka. Have ye no fear of cats without eyes?"

Vanka turned round, and there *she* was, sitting quite close. He knew her at once by her dress of malachite. His arms and legs went all weak and his tongue could only stutter: "Oh aye—oh aye... Dyrr-gyrr-byrr... Holy —holy.... Avaunt!

She burst out laughing at him.

"Now don't be so scared. I'm not a cat without eyes. Tell me, better, what you want here."

But Vanka just kept on stuttering: "Oh aye, oh aye... Dyrr-gyrr-byrr...." Then he got a bit of a hold on himself. "I'm looking for gems.... Like the ones folks saw in Stepan's hand...."

At that she frowned.

"Keep that name off your tongue. But gems, I'll give ye those. I can see what kind of prospector ye are, aye, and I've heard the gold miners talk of ye. Ye do them many a good turn."

"Aye, that I do," said Vanka, quite cheerful now. "I always do as my conscience bids me."

"And by your deeds you shall be rewarded. Only one thing, beware, see ye don't sell the stones. Not a single one. Look to it! Take them straight to the bailiff. And he'll reward ye with his own hands. And add more from the treasury. Enough for your whole lifetime. He'll give ye so much you won't be able to carry it home without help."

That's what she said, and then she led Sochen inside the hill. They went down, and she gave a kick to a great boulder. It rolled away, and underneath there was something like a hidden pocket. The rock was blue, and on it lay green stones, no end to them.

"Take all you will," she said, and stood there watching.

Vanka may have been a poor sort of prospector, but his pouch was a good stout one, bigger than any of the other men's. He stuffed it full and still lusted for more. He thought of filling his trousers pockets, but feared to do it, for the Mistress was looking angry, though she said no word. So all he could do was say "thank you." He looked up again—and saw no one. He looked down at the pocket and it was gone. Just as if it had never been there. A boulder lay on the spot shaped like a bear. Vanka felt his pouch—it was stuffed so full it was like to burst. He looked again at the place where he'd got the stones, and then set off for home as fast as he could go. And as he ran he kept feeling at his pouch to make sure it was still there. He'd wave the wolf's tail over it, and rub the cross against it and then run again. He got home long before evening. His wife was quite scared.

"Shall I heat the bath-house?" she asked. But he was like a man in a frenzy.

"Hang something over the street windows," he said. So she covered them both with the first things she found. Then Sochen put the pouch on the table.

"Look!"

She did look, and saw the pouch stuffed full of some kind of green grains. First she rejoiced and crossed herself, but then she said: "Mebbe they're not real?"

That made Vanka angry.

"Fool! I got them in the mountain. Who's going to put false ones there?" But he didn't say it was the Mistress herself who'd shown him the stones. And given him strict orders about them, too. And the woman kept on with her nagging.

"If there's so many you got your pouch full at once, then what if the muzhiks with horses hear of it? They'll be taking them away in cartloads.

And what use'll they be then? Necklaces for the maids and toys for the children."

Sochen went purple in the face.

"You shall know the price of these stones at once!"

He tipped five of them into his hand, slung the pouch round his neck and hurried to the mine foreman.

"Kuzma Mironych, take a look at these stones."

The man looked at them. Then he took that glass of his and peered through that. Then he tested them with acid.

"Where did you get them?" he asked.

Well, the office spy Vanka told him at once, of course.

"On Krasnogorka."

"What place?"

But here Vanka turned sly and described the spot where he'd been working at first.

"Something queer about it," said the foreman. "Iron ore doesn't have copper emeralds. Did ye get many?"

Vanka put the pouch on the table. The foreman looked inside and stood there in a daze. When he'd got his breath back a bit, he said: "I congratulate ye, Ivan Trifonych! Luck's smiled on ye. Don't forget us small folks." And he kept shaking hands with Vanka and making much of him. A marvel, it is, what money does! "Come right along," he said, "to the bailiff."

Vanka held off a bit.

"I ought to get a wash first, steam myself in the bath-house, put on other clothes."

What he really wanted was to put some of the stones aside. But the foreman kept on at him.

"With a pouch like that you could go to the Tsar himself, let alone the bailiff. He'll not look askance at your clothes, he'll let ye in any time."

No way out. The foreman took Vanka straight to the bailiff. And there was the room full of folks. The Old Master himself had just come. He

126

was sitting in the maddle holding a horn to his ear, and the bailiff kept boom-booming into it, telling him all about everything.

The foreman went in and said why he'd come, and the bailiff poured it into the Master's horn.

"We've found copper emeralds at last. A good, faithful man's grudged no trouble to get them. We must give him a proper reward."

Then Sochen was brought in. He took out his pouch, gave it to the Master and smacked a kiss on his hand, too. The Master was surprised.

"Where's he come from? He knows his manners."

"He was once a lackey," the bailiff boomed.

"Ah, so that's it," said the Master. "You can see it at once. And then they say house serfs make bad workers. Look how much he's got."

All the time he was sort of weighing the pouch in his hand. All the important folks of the place had crowded round to see. And the wives of the biggest officials were there too. The Master wanted to unfasten the pouch, but he hadn't the knack, so he gave it to Sochen. And Sochen was glad to oblige. He pulled the strap and opened the mouth.

"By your leave, Master."

And then out came a stench, enough to turn your stomach. Like a horse or cow that had died and rotted. The fine ladies standing nearest clapped their handkerchiefs over their noses and mouths, and the Master roared at the bailiff: "What's this? Will you make a mock of me?"

The bailiff pushed his hand into the pouch, but not a thing was inside. Only the stink kept getting worse. The Master clapped his hand over his mouth and rushed cut of the room. The rest made off all ways. Only the bailiff was left, and Sochen. Sochen was white, and the bailiff was shaking with rage.

"What's this ye've done! Eh? Where did ye get all that stench together? Who taught ye the way?"

Sochen saw it looked bad for him, so he came out with the whole story. Kept none of it back. The bailiff listened to it all. Then he said: "She promised you a reward, you say?"

"Aye, that she did," sighed Sochen.

"And from me?"

"That's what she said—you'd reward me with your own hands, and add more from the treasury."

"Here's the first of it, then," roared the bailiff, and smashed his fist into Sochen's face so his head nearly went through the wall.

"That's just to be going on with," he shouted. "You'll get your reward at the whipping post. And ye won't forget it to your dying day."

He got it. He got so much he couldn't get it home without help, he had to be carried on bast matting to the sick-house. Even those who'd given Sochen many a buffet felt a bit sorry for him.

"The spy's got his portion!"

The bailiff too had a bitter mouthful to chew. The Master sent for him the same day.

"How dare you serve me a trick like that?"

Of course the bailiff twisted and turned every way. "It was none of my doing, it was all that knave."

"But who," said the Master, "let the knave into my presence, and with the pouch in his hand, too?"

Well, there was no way out for the bailiff, he could only say: "The fault was mine."

"Then take your deserts. And well earned. Instead of bailiff, you'll be plain overseer at Krylatovskoye," said the Master, and then he turned to the officials who were there. "Let him get about in the fresh air a bit. He's got a bad smell. No wonder they call him the goat. As for me, I can't stand the sight of him. He turns my stomach, after yesterday."

In Krylatovskoye that bailiff was buried. After the way he'd been living, he found it hard fare there.

Seems like the Mistress had played a trick on him too.

1937

CAT'S EARS

In those times there were no Verkhnevo and Ilyinskoye iron works, not a sign of them. Only our Polevaya and Sysert. And iron was worked a bit in Severnaya too. But naught to speak of. Sysert was most in touch with the world. It was on the highroad that went to Cossack parts. There were folks passing all the time, afoot or with horses. And Sysert folks went to the Revda wharf with iron. You'd meet all sorts on the road, and hear all sorts of news, too. And villages thick all round.

In our Polevaya it was different. We were right out of the world. We didn't make much iron those times, it was mostly copper. And that was always taken to the wharf in convoys, so it wasn't easy to stop and talk to this one and that. Try it when you've got a guard watching you! And only one village our way, Kossoi Brod. Just woods and hills and bogs all round. In those days folks here lived in a hole like blind moles. Of course that just suited the Master.

Aye, here it was quiet, but he had to keep an eye on Sysert.

So he went over to live there. Made it his main works. He sent more guards to watch the folks here, and gave all his men strict orders: "See no strangers come, and keep the folks on a tight rein."

Now, what strangers would there be when our village was out of the way like that? There was a road to Sysert, of course, but they say it was a real bad one in those days. Through the bogs, it went, and for verst after verst it was just a log track. Enough to give anyone the belly-ache rattling over it. And there were few that used it. Not like now, when there's a constant coming and going. Only the Master's servants and the guards used it then. And they were mostly on horseback, so it mattered little if the road was a bad one. The Master himself came only when he could use runners instead of wheels.

As soon as there was a sledge track he'd be here, making up for time lost in the summer. And he'd a way of turning up unexpected. He'd leave in the evening, say, and next day at dinner-time he'd be back again. Hoped he'd catch someone. So in winter-time all knew the Master could be here any minute. But when it meant coming on wheels, there'd never be sight or sound of him. Rattling and bumping over logs didn't suit him, and he'd no liking for horseback. He was getting on in years, they say. How could he sit a horse? So till winter came round again, folks had it a bit easier. Because no matter how the bailiff drove them, the Master would find something wrong as soon as he came.

But one day the Master suddenly turned up in the autumn, when the road was at its worst. He didn't go to the works or the mine as his way was, but to the bailiff. And he had all the officials and clerks called and the priests too. They were there till evening. On the morrow the Master went to Severnaya, and then the same day to the town. Rushing about in all the dirt and mud. And he'd got an extra lot of guards with him, too. Folks started asking: "What's happened? How can we get to know?"

That would be easy enough nowadays—walk or ride into Sysert. But then they were serfs. A man had to find some excuse, aye, and then they wouldn't always let him go. And you couldn't slip off in secret, either, because folks were watched, held in a tight grip. But all the same, there was one lad said he'd try it.

"Saturday evening, when we come up from the mine, I'll get off quick to Sysert, and Sunday evening I'll be back. I've got friends there. I'll soon find out what it's all about."

Off he went, but he didn't come back at all. After a bit they told the bailiff he wasn't there, but the bailiff didn't seem to care, he didn't even have a search made. Then folks got burning eager to know what it all meant. Two more went off, and they didn't come back either.

There were new ways in the village, too—the guards started going round the houses three times a day, counting the men to see they were all at home. If a man wanted to go to the forest for wood or to cut hay, he had to ask leave. They weren't allowed out of the village, except in parties, and a guard went with them.

"I'm letting none go alone," said the bailiff. "There's three run off already."

The wives and children weren't allowed into the forest either. The bailiff set a watch on all the roads. And he'd found men that were close-tongued, you couldn't get a word out of them. Well, it was clear as daylight something was going on Sysert way, and something that had the Master's overseers on the jump. Folks whispered at the iron works and in the mine.

"We've got to find out somehow."

Then a maid, a miner's daughter, spoke up.

"Let me try. They don't count the women when they make their rounds. And they don't come to us at all, they know I'm all alone with Granny, and no menfolks. Mebbe it's the same in Sysert. It'll be easier for me to get to know."

She was a clever, fearless maid. Well, a miner's lass, with a head on her. But all the same it took the men aback.

"But how'll you go forty versts through the woods all alone, Dunyakha, ye fledgling? It's autumn, the wolves are out. There won't be even bones left of ye."

"I'll get off on Sunday," she said. "The wolves won't venture out on the road in the daytime. And I'll take an axe, to be sure."

"D'ye know anyone in Sysert?" they asked.

"Aren't there women enough there?" she said. "I'll learn it all from them."

Some of the men doubted.

"What do women know?"

"All their men know, and sometimes more."

The men argued this way and that, then they said: "It's true, Dunyakha Fledgling, it's easier for you to get away, but still it would be shameful to let a maid go on such a journey alone. The wolves'll eat ye."

Just then a young fellow came up. He heard what the talk was about, and he said: "I'll go with her."

Dunyakha went red, but she didn't say him nay.

"It 'ud be pleasanter, two of us, that's right, but what if they catch ye in Sysert?"

"They won't," he said.

So Dunyakha set off with that young fellow. They didn't leave by the road, of course, they slipped away behind the houses, and then kept on through the woods, so they couldn't be seen from the road. They'd no trouble till they came to Kossoi Brod, and there they saw three men on the bridge. Guarding it. The Chusovaya wasn't frozen yet, but it was too cold to swim it higher or lower.

Dunyakha looked at it all from the woods, and then she said: "Matyukha, lad, seems like ye won't be able to go with me after all. Ye'll only bring misfortune on yourself for no good, and spoil it for me too. Better get back quick before they miss ye, and I'll see what woman's wits can do."

Matyukha tried to talk her out of it, of course, but she wouldn't give way. They argued a bit, and then they settled that he'd keep watch from the woods. If she wasn't stopped on the bridge, then he'd go home, but if she had any trouble, he'd come out and fight them off her. Then Dunyakha crept up closer, hid the axe well, and suddenly dashed out of the woods. Ran straight to the men crying and screaming: "Help! Help! A wolf! Oh, a wolf!"

The men saw a maid all frightened, and they just laughed, one even put out a foot to trip her, but Dunyakha had quick eyes, she flew past still screaming: "Oh—a wolf! A wolf!"

The men shouted after her: "Look, it's got ye by the skirt! It's got your skirt! Run quick!"

Matyukha watched it all... The fledgling's flown clear through them. What a maid! Slips through danger herself and keeps a friend out of it, too. She'll have it easy the rest of the way, just going through the woods along by the road. If only she gets there before dark, before the wolves come out.

Matyukha got home before the watch made their rounds. They hadn't missed him. The next day he told the miners about it. So now they knew what had happened to the first ones, they'd been caught at Kossoi Brod.

"They're locked up somewhere, and in chains too, very like. That's why the bailiff didn't seek them—he knows well enough where they are. If only our Fledgling doesn't get caught coming back."

They talked a bit more and then they went home. And Dunyakha? She went quietly through the woods till she got to Sysert. Once she saw some of the Polevaya guards riding home. She hid herself till they'd gone, and then went on. There were more guards along the road, but to slip past was as easy as eating pie. She turned into the woods and went through the vegetable patches, and there she saw a well quite near, with women round about it. Dunyakha slipped in among them.

"Whose maid are you?" asked one old woman. "I don't mind seeing ye about here before."

Dunyakha felt she could trust the old woman.

"I'm from Polevaya," she said, and the woman stared, amazed.

"How did ye come? There's guards everywhere. Our men can't get through to you. All that tried never came back."

Dunyakha told her all about it. Then the old woman said: "Come to my hut, young maid. I live alone. They never come searching. And if they do come, I'll tell them ye're my granddaughter from over the river. She's a bit like you to look at. Only your nose turns up more. What do they call ye?"

"Dunyakha."

"There ye are. My maid's called Dunya too."

From that old woman Dunyakha learned it all. The Master, it seemed, had run away somewhere far off, and every week messengers came from him and rode back again. The Master would send orders, and the bailiff Vanka Shvarev read them out to all the folks. The iron works were shut up, and all the men had been sent out on the Shchelkunskoye road to dig deep trenches and pile up barriers. Something was coming from that way. Folks had been told the Bashkirs had risen, but it wasn't that at all. All the people had risen—the far-away iron workers and the villagers and the Cossacks too, and the Bashkirs had risen with them. They'd got the masters and gentry by the throat, and the people's leader was Omelyan Ivanych.* "Some say he's the real Tsar, others say he's a common man, but however that may be, it's freedom for the people and death to the gentry with him. That's why that fox of ours slunk off as far as he could get! Scared!"

Dunyakha learned the guards made the rounds in Sysert three times a day and counted all the men, just like in Polevaya. But in Sysert it was even stricter. If a man couldn't be found, his wife and children, his whole family, were taken and pushed into prison. He'd come running up: "I'm here, I'm a bit late, that's all." But they'd tell him: "See you're not late the next time," and keep his family two days or maybe three.

They'd got the folks muzzled all right, and the bailiff, he was as savage as a chained dog.

* Emelyan Ivanovich Pugachev—leader of a peasant uprising.—*Tr.*

But all the same, as soon as the evening rounds were over, the men all came to the old woman's hut, and started asking Dunyakha how things were her way. She told them all about it.

"And we kept sending folks over," they said, "and not one ever came back."

"The same with us," said Dunyakha. "A man 'ud set off and just disappear. They must all have been caught at the Chusovaya."

They talked and talked, and then they started thinking—how was Dunyakha to get back to Polevaya? They'd be looking out for her at Kossoi Brod, how could she get past?

Then one of them said: "She might go through Tersutskoye Bog to Galyan. That 'ud be safe enough, but she doesn't know the path and there's none to show her."

"And haven't we brave maids too?" asked the old woman. "They aren't counted here either, a lot of them have been on Tersutskoye getting berries. They'll set her on her way. Only tell her how to go on after, so she'll not get lost, and be home before nightfall. Or the wolves may get her."

Well, so the man told her how to go. First through Tersutskoye Bog, then along the River Mochalovka to Galyan Bog and that would take her to the Chusovaya itself. It was narrow there, she'd get across somehow, and after that there'd be the Polevaya mines quite close.

"If it should be getting late, there's less danger that way," he said. "The Earth Cat* roams from Galyan to Dumnaya Hill. She doesn't hurt folks, but the wolves are scared off if she shows her ears. They don't run in those parts much. But don't put too much trust in that, all the same, go as fast as your legs'll carry ye and try to get home while it's light. Mebbe it's just talk about the cat. Who's ever seen her?"

Brave maids were found, of course, ready to set Dunyakha along the way to the Mochalovka. Early in the morning, while it was still dark, they slipped past the guards.

"The wolves won't touch us if there's a lot of us. They'll be afeard. We'll get home earlier and it'll be better for her, too."

* A mythical creature living underground, which sometimes showed fiery ears.—*Tr.*

So they set off, a whole flock of maids, chattering away. And then in a little while someone started a song. It was a road they knew well, they often went berrying on Tersutskoye, why shouldn't they sing?

They came to the Mochalovka and took leave of Dunyakha. It was still quite early and a sunny day. All going well. That man had told her it wouldn't be more than fifteen versts from the Mochalovka across Galyan to Polevaya. She'd get there before dark, and they'd seen no wolves at all. She needn't have feared.

So they took leave. Dunyakha went on alone, and right away it was worse. The parts were strange and the forest fearsome. She wasn't a timid maid, but she kept looking behind her. Well, and then she got off her way a bit.

While she was looking for the path again, dusk fell. And then a howling started all round. There were a lot of wolves in our parts then. Even now in autumn they'll howl right by the very works, but in those days—no end of them! Dunyakha saw it looked bad. To find out so much and not be able to get it home! And she was young, she didn't want to die either. She thought of that lad, Matyukha. The wolves were getting quite close. What should she do? If she started to run, they'd go for her at once, tear her to pieces. If she climbed a tree, they'd wait underneath till she couldn't hold on any longer and fell.

The bog began to slope down to the Chusovaya. That was what the man had told her. If only I could get to the Chusovaya, she thought.

She walked along quietly, and the wolves kept following her. A whole pack of them. She'd got her axe, of course, but what could she do with that!

Suddenly two blue flames rose. Just like cat's ears, they looked—wider at the bottom, and a point on top. They were about fifty paces in front of her.

Dunyakha didn't stop to think where the flames came from, she ran straight to them. She knew wolves were afraid of fire.

She got close up, and sure enough, there were two fires, and between them a sort of little hump, just like a cat's head. And there Dunyakha stopped, between the two fires. She saw the wolves had fallen back, but the fires kept getting bigger and the mound higher. Dunyakha wondered to see those fires burning like that without any wood. She plucked up courage and stretched out her hand, but she couldn't feel any heat. She put her hand closer, and the fire flickered to one side, like a cat twitching its ear, and then burned evenly again.

Dunyakha feared a bit, but she couldn't run straight into the wolves' jaws. So she stood there in between the two fires, and they kept rising higher and higher. Got quite big. Dunyakha picked up a stone. It smelt of sulphur. Then she remembered the Earth Cat the Sysert man had talked about. She'd heard tell before of a cat with fiery ears that lived in the sands where copper's mixed with gold. Folks had seen the ears many a time, but they'd never seen the cat. It moved beneath the ground.

So Dunyakha stood there between the cat's ears and wondered what she should do now. The wolves had gone, but how far had they gone? If she left the fires, they'd be back at once. But it was cold standing there, she'd never hold out till morning.

Just as she thought that, the fires disappeared. There she was in the dark. She looked round—were the wolves coming back? No, no sign of them. But how could she go on in the dark? And then the fires jumped up again in front of her. Dunyakha ran straight to them. She ran and ran, but she couldn't catch them however she tried. And so she ran right to the river Chusovaya, and there were the ears burning away on the other side.

The ice was thin, of course, she couldn't trust it, but she didn't stop to pick a place. She cut two light staves and started to cross. She crawled over somehow without going through, though the ice kept cracking all the time. But the staves helped her.

She didn't stop when she got over but ran straight after the cat's ears. She looked round about, though, and found it was a place she knew— Pesochnaya. It had been a mine once, she'd worked there. She could have found the road home even at night, but all the same she followed the ears. If they've saved me like that once, she thought, they won't bring me to trouble now.

Just as she thought that, the ears flared up high and burned bright, as though to tell her: "Aye, that's right. Wise maid!"

The cat's ears led Dunyakha to the Povarenski mine, and that's close by Dumnaya Hill. Over there, it was. Right by the works, you might say.

It was night. Dunyakha went to her hut, but carefully, so as not to be seen. Wherever there were folks about, she'd hide behind a gate post and then slip through the vegetable plots. She got to the hut like that, and heard talking inside.

She listened a bit and found they were waiting for somebody. And it was her they were waiting for. The bailiff had ordered Granny to be kept at home with a guard over her. That's where Dunyakha'll come, he thought, if she manages to get back. And he kept coming himself to see the guard never went away for a minute, day or night.

Dunyakha didn't know all that, of course, but she could hear there were strangers in Granny's hut and feared to show herself. Still, she was cold, frozen to the bone. So she slipped through the back lanes to that young fellow, Matyukha, who'd gone with her to Kossoi Brod. She tapped softly at the window and then hid herself. And he came running out.

"Who's that?"

Then she showed herself. And Matyukha, he was real glad.

"Go into the bath-house quick," he said, "it's heated. I'll hide ye there, and tomorrow we'll find a safer place."

He put Dunyakha in the warm bath-house, locked the door and went off to tell folks he could trust.

"Our Dunyakha's here. The Fledgling's flown back."

They all came at once and started asking her about everything. And Dunyakha told them. At last she came to the cat's ears.

"If it hadn't been for them, the wolves 'ud have got me."

The men didn't take too much heed of that. She was tired, they thought, she was half asleep and dreamed it all.

"Eat and get some rest," they said. "We'll keep watch over ye till morning, and then we'll think where's the best place for ye to hide."

That was just what Dunyakha needed. The warmth had made her drowsy, she was nearly falling off her seat.

She ate a bit and went to sleep. Matyukha and five more young fellows stayed to guard her. But it was nighttime, everything quiet all round. And look what news Dunyakha had brought. Of course the lads started talking, and not so softly, either. Well, and other folks who'd come to hear it all, they didn't want to sit mum, they'd want to say this or that, or maybe give counsel what was best to do. The village was restless, like. The guards noticed it. So they started making the rounds. Found one man missing here, another there, and five young fellows all gathered at Matyukha's hut.

"What are you doing here?"

They all made the first excuse that came into their heads, but the guards didn't believe them and started to search. So there was naught to do but get hold of stakes. The guards were armed, of course, but stakes were handier in the dark. and the lads just smashed them down. Then other guards came running up, three or four times as many. They began to get the upper hand. One of the lads was shot down, but the others still went on fighting.

Dunyakha had wakened long ago. She ran out of the bath-house and saw two terrible blue fires rise behind Dumnaya Hill, as if the cat were hidden behind it with only the ears showing. Just ready to spring on the works.

Dunyakha cried out: "Those are our fires! The miners' fires! Go there to them, lads!"

She started running to them herself. The whole village was in an uproar. The alarm-bell began to ring. People all dashed out. They thought there was a fire the other side of the hill, and all went running there. But when they came closer, they stopped. There was something fearsome about those fires. Only Dunyakha ran straight to them. Then she stopped still, right between them, and called out: "Lay hold of those men o' the Master's! Time to make an end of them! Other works have settled wi' them long ago!"

Then the guards and watchmen of all kinds were in sore straits. Because folks had gathered in a great throng. The guards tried to run, this way and that. But you can't escape the people. Many were seized, but the bailiff they let slip. He managed to escape along the road to town. All the ones that were in chains were set free, of course. And then the ears disappeared.

The next day all the people gathered on Dumnaya Hill. Dunyakha told them what she'd heard in Sysert. Then some of the folks, mostly the older ones, began hanging back, sort of cautious.

"Who knows how it'll all end! Mebbe it's vain hopes you gave us yestereen?"

But others were all for Dunyakha.

"The maid's right! That's the way! What are we waiting for? We'll go and join the folks with that Omelyan Ivanych."

Then some more began shouting: "Kossoi Brod, that's where we'll go. They've got our lads shut up there. Have ye forgotten them?"

A whole crowd of men made for Kossoi Brod at once. They knocked down the guards, got their own men out and five from Sysert too. And they roused the Kossoi Brod folks. Told them all that was going on.

When they came back, folks were still arguing on Dumnaya Hill. With the young fellows away, the older ones had got the upper hand and folks were all mixed up. All they could say was: "Ought we to have killed those guards?"

"Served 'em right!" shouted the young ones.

Those who'd been shut up in Kossoi Brod were of the same mind, of course.

"Stop here if ye're afeard," they told the old ones. "We'll go and win what's rightly ours."

And so they parted. The older folks stopped there, to their own sorrow, and led others under the whips too. The bailiff came back with soldiers and guards from Sysert as well. He'd soon got his heel on the folks. He started off worse than he'd been before, but then he quieted down. Must have heard something that made him think. He tried every way to make up to the old men who'd put the folks wrong, to get them on his side. But they still had weals on their backs, they'd seen their mistake. The bailiff

The Frenchman saw flattery wouldn't help him any more than cunning; so he pulled two banknotes out of his pocket, a thousand rubles each they were, with Peter the Great's head on them, and put them on the bench.

"I'll pay a thousand if you'll tell me honestly all about it," he said, "and if you'll show me I'll give double."

Yevlakha looked at Peter's picture on the notes.

"A good ruler he was, none other like him, but one thing he didn't teach us—to sell our souls. Pick up your money, Master, and go your ways back where ye came from."

The Frenchman kept arguing and persisting, of course—what was the matter? Was he offended at something?

Well, then Zhelezko lost his temper and gave his visitor some straight words.

"You, with your white hat, calling yourself a craftsman! Tell you— why, ye'd sell it to the first that gives you a hat and gloves. Ye'd put snot in a gold setting and sell it as malachite for five rubles. D'ye understand that? Snot instead of our stone that holds the joy of the earth! But ye won't, never! We can use that stone ourselves. And we won't only make things like those covers for the Tsarina's album, we'll make things of such beauty, folks'll come from all ends of the world to set eye on them. And it'll be our work! Made wi' these hands!"

So the foreign craftsman got naught out of Zhelezko. But he did get the covers from Faberger. The great folks he was with talked the Tsar into making a gift of them.

Zhelezko died during the Civil War. There were still some who weren't sure how it would all end, but Zhelezko kept on saying: "Never you doubt it—workers' hands can do all! Some they'll grind to powder, some they'll gather up grain by grain and smooth them out carefully, and then ye'll have a whole stone of joy and beauty like none have ever seen. For the world to wonder at. And to learn from, too."

1940

it when his bullets go everywhere but where he wants. And he always tries to make up some reason. The sun blinding him, or a fly in his eye, or a sudden dizziness, or a mosquito that got into his nose and bit just as he fired. That sort of thing. And maybe that was the way one of them made up the tale about the cat's ears, to cover his bad shooting. Make it all look a bit better. And so the tale started.

Or maybe Dunyakha was one of those that bullets can't touch. After all, the old folks have a saying: A brave man stands on a hill and the bullets fly past, a coward hides in a bush and they find him.

So the men managing the works could never be sure of keeping their backs clear of Dunyakha's whip. The Master himself, they say, was scared some day she'd warm his hide. But she'd got her wits about her too.

What sense was there in her rushing in with only her whip, when the Master always had his guards, and every one of them armed?

1939

THE GREAT SERPENT

There was a man lived in our village once. Levonty, his name was. A mild man, and a hard worker. From the time he was young they kept him in the mines, in Gumeshky, that is. Getting copper. That's how he spent all the years of his youth. Crawled about underground like a worm, never saw the light till he was all pale and wan. Well, we know what it is underground. Damp, darkness and bad air. In the end he lost his strength. The bailiff saw there was no more to be got out of him there so he'd enough kindness to put him to other work—sent him to the Crown gold-fields at Poskakukha. Levonty started working there, but it didn't help him much. He was a real sick man. The bailiff turned it round in his mind, then he told Levonty: "You're a hard-working muzhik, I've spoken to the Master about ye, and he's going to reward ye. 'Let him work for himself,' the Master said. 'Let him work free, without quit-rent.'"

That's what they used to do in those days. When a man was worn out, no good any more, they'd let him work for himself.

So now Levonty was turned out, free. Well, he had to eat and feed his family too. And how was he to do it when he'd no farm, nothing at all? He thought and thought, and then decided to go prospecting, looking for gold. He was used to burrowing in the ground and it didn't take much in the way of tools either. So he looked round, got what he needed and called his boys.

"Well lads," he said, "come with me to look for gold. Mebbe luck will smile on little 'uns, and we won't have to beg our bread."

The boys were still only children, a bit over ten.

So off they went, our free prospectors. The father could hardly drag himself along, and the children, little as they were, tailed after.

Now in those days there was a good bit of gold along the upper part of the Ryabinovka. So that's the section Levonty asked for. It was easy enough to settle it with the office then. Just say where you wanted to go, and bring in the gold. Of course there was swindling too. What do you expect? Those in the office saw where the men went and what they brought in. If the takings were good, they'd grab the place. "We'll mine there ourselves, you go somewhere else." They used the prospectors to find the good spots. Well, and the men, of course, looked out for themselves too. Tried not to show all they got. Brought enough to the office to have something on the books, and sold most of it secretly to the merchants. There were plenty of them, those merchants, and clever—no watchman could ever catch them. So it was trickery all round. The office tried to trick the men, and they repaid in kind. It was the regular thing. Only by chance could you learn where gold was.

But they didn't keep anything back from Levonty, they told him all they knew. They could see he wouldn't last long, let him have a little comfort before his end.

Levonty came to the Ryabinovka, looked about him a bit and started working. But he'd little strength for it. He could only do a bit, then he'd have to sit down half dead to get his breath. And the children, what could they do? They tried their best, all the same. And so it went on for a week or maybe a bit more, and Levonty saw it was little enough they'd got, not enough for bread, even. What should they do? As for himself, he kept getting worse and worse, naught but bones he was, but all the same he didn't want to beg his bread, and sling a beggar's wallet on the children too.

When Saturday came, he went to the office to deliver the gold he'd washed.

"Stop ye here," he told the boys, "and watch the tools, for there's no sense carrying them back and forth."

So the boys stayed behind at the shanty. One ran down to the Chusovaya, it was quite close. He fished a bit, caught some gudgeon and perch, so they set about making fish soup. They lighted a fire, but soon it got towards evening. And the boys started to be a bit frightened.

That was when they saw an old man coming, one from the village. Semyonich, folks called him, but what his surname was I don't know. He'd been a soldier. Folks said that earlier on, when he was young, he'd been reckoned one of the best men round about at the iron furnace. But he gave the bailiff a pert answer one day, and the bailiff ordered them to take him to the fire station—to be flogged, that is. But Semyonich fought back and sent the men spinning—he was a real strong fellow. An iron worker, you know what they're like. Well, they got him down all the same. The firemen were all strapping fellows too, specially chosen. So Semyonich was flogged, and sent away to be a soldier because he'd fought. He came back to the village after twenty-five years, an old man. All his folks had died, and his hut was boarded up. There'd even been talk of pulling it down. It was in a real bad state. But then he turned up. He mended his hut and started living there, quiet as could be, all alone. But all the same, the neighbours got to whispering—something queer about him. He'd a lot of books there. And every evening he'd sit reading them. Folks thought maybe he knew ways of healing sickness, and they started coming to him. But he'd have naught to do with it. "I've no knowledge of that," he said, "and what healing can there be when you're doing this sort of work?" Then folks thought maybe he'd got some special religion. But that didn't seem right either. He went to church at Christmas and Easter like the other muzhiks, but it didn't look as if he made anything special of it all. And another thing to wonder at—he didn't work, so what did he live on? He'd a vegetable plot, of course, and an old gun, and fishing tackle. But that's not enough to feed a man. And he'd got money, sometimes he gave a bit to some man. With that he'd his own ways, too. One man might come and ask and beg and offer him something in pledge and promise everything, and still he'd refuse. And another he'd go to himself and say: "Here, Ivan," or maybe Mikhailo, "take this and get yourself a cow. Ye've a houseful of small children, can't get on your feet." A strange, crotchety old fellow. Folks said he dealt in black magic. That was mostly because of the books.

Well, up came this Semyonich to the boys and greeted them. They were real glad and called him to join them.

"Sit down, Grandad, have some of our fish soup."

He didn't refuse, he sat down and tried the soup, and praised it to the skies—fine soup, tasty, well made. He pulled soft fresh bread out of his wallet, broke it and piled up the hunks in front of the boys. They saw the old man liked the soup, so they set to work on the bread while Semyonich kept on praising the soup, saying he'd not had anything so good for a long time. This gave the boys heart, and they ate till they were filled, nearly finished all the bread. And the old man, he kept on with "it's long since I've eaten such soup."

Well, when the boys had finished, Semyonich began asking them how they were doing. They told him all about everything, how their father had been let off task work and was free to work for himself, and how they were washing gold there. Semyonich just kept shaking his head and sighing: "Eh dear, eh dear," and then he asked: "How much have ye washed?"

"About three drams, Father said."

The old man rose.

"Well, lads, I'll have to help ye. Only see ye keep still tongues. Not a word. Not to a single soul. . . ." And the way Semyonich looked at the lads, it was fearsome. Like it was some other man. Then he smiled again.

"Now then," he said, "sit ye here by the fire and wait till I come back. There's someone I must talk to a bit. Mebbe he'll help ye. Only mind, see ye aren't scared, or ye'll spoil all. Mind that well."

The old man went away into the woods and the boys were left alone. They looked at each other, but they didn't say a word. Then the elder took courage.

"Mind, Brother, don't forget—we mustn't be scared," he whispered, but his lips were white and his teeth chattered. And the younger one said: "I'm not scared a mite, brother," and he was white as a sheet.

So they sat there waiting. It was a dark night, and everything very quiet in the woods. They could hear the water rippling in the Ryabinovka. A good time passed, and nobody came, and their fear began to leave them. They put some more twigs on the fire and felt better. Then all of a sudden they heard talking in the woods. Somebody coming, they thought. Who can it be, this time of night? And it all got fearsome again.

Then two men came up to the fire. One was Semyonich, and the other was a stranger, and strangely dressed too. He was all yellow, his tunic and trousers were of gold, that brocade the priests wear, and his wide girdle with a pattern and tassels hanging from it was brocade too, only it shone greenish. His cap was yellow with red flaps on both sides, and his boots were red too. His face was yellow with a big wide beard that fell in tight curls, so tight you could see it would be hard to straighten them. And his eyes were green, like a cat's. But they had a kind look. He was the same height as Semyonich and not stout, but heavy. The earth sank under him where he stood. The boys were so interested they forgot to be afraid, they just sat staring at this man, while he asked Semyonich, joking like: "So these are your free prospectors? What they find they keep, eh? Don't have to give it up?"

Then he frowned a bit and said, as though he was taking counsel with Semyonich: "But what if we spoil these boys?"

Semyonich started saying the boys weren't pampered, they were good lads. But the strange man started again.

"All men are shoes from the same last. As long as they're poor and in need, they're decent folk, but let them come upon my golden trail, and evil grows up in them like toadstools, and whence come the spores none can say."

He stood awhile in thought, then he said: "Well, all right, we'll try it. It may work better with children. Though they're good lads, a pity if they're spoiled. The smaller one, he's got thin lips. Might turn out greedy. You must keep an eye on them yourself, Semyonich. Their father's not got long to live. I know him. He's on the edge of the grave, and still trying to earn a bit. Respects himself, stands on his own feet. But if ye give him riches, he'll be spoiled too."

He talked to Semyonich just as if the boys weren't there. Then he turned and looked at them.

"Now lads, watch carefully. Note where the trail goes. Along that trail dig on top; don't dig deep, for there you'll find naught."

And as the lads looked—the man wasn't a man any more. All of him down to the belt was a head, and from the belt down was a neck. The head was just exactly as it had been, only big, the eyes were large as goose's eggs, and the neck was a snake's. And the body of a great, huge serpent began to rise up from under the ground till the head was higher than the trees. Then the body bent down right over the fire and stretched out along the ground, and the wonder crawled towards the Ryabinovka while more and more rings of it still kept rising out of the ground. As though there would never be an end of them. And another marvel, the fire went out, yet it became quite light in the glade. But it was not a light like the sun, it was different, and sort of cold. The serpent went to the Ryabinovka and crawled into the water, and at once the water froze on both sides. Then he slid up the other bank, stretched out to an old birch tree standing there

148

and cried: "Mark it! Here you must dig. 'Twill suffice for orphans. But mind, beware of greed!"

As he finished speaking, he seemed to melt away. The water in Ryabinovka babbled again, the fire burned up, only the grass was still white, as though it had been touched by hoarfrost.

Then Semyonich explained it all to the boys.

"That was the Great Serpent. He is the master of all gold. Where he passes, there it lies. And he can pass over the earth or under the earth, and he can make a ring round as much space as he will. And that's how it sometimes happens; folks find a good vein, and then there's some fraud or fighting, and maybe a man's killed, and the vein's lost. That's because the Serpent came and took away the gold. Or it can be this way. Prospectors find a good place with loose gold and throw away their cares. But then the office suddenly tells them: 'Clear out, we're taking that for the Crown, we'll dig for gold there ourselves.' So they get machines there and drive all the folks to work, but there's no more gold. They dig deep down and out to all sides, but they get naught, just as if it had never been there. That's because the Serpent surrounded that place and lay there a night or two, and all the gold was drawn to him. And try as ye will, ye'll never find where he lay.

"He doesn't like trickery and swindling where there's gold, and worst of all he hates to have one man push another down. But those that work for what they need themselves, those he lets alone, and helps them at times, too, like he has you. Only mind, keep silent about it, or ye'll spoil it all. And mind, too, not to be greedy for gold. It wasn't for that he showed it ye. Ye heard what he said. Mind ye don't forget it, that's the main thing. Well, now, lie down and go to sleep, and I'll sit here a bit by the fire."

The children obeyed, they went into the shanty and fell fast asleep at once. When they wakened, it was broad day. The other prospectors had been at work a long time. The boys looked at each other.

"Brother, did you see aught last night?" asked one, and the other said: "So you saw it too?"

Then they made a pact. They vowed and swore every way they knew, they'd never tell a soul about it all, and they'd never be greedy. After that they started choosing a place to dig. They had a bit of an argument about it.

"We ought to start by that birch tree over the Ryabinovka. The place where the Serpent spoke last."

But the younger said: "Nay, that's no good, Brother. That'll be giving away the secret, because the other prospectors will come running to see the sand the Ryabinovka's bringing down. Then everyone'll know."

They argued a bit about it. They were sorry Semyonich had gone, there was nobody to ask. And then all of a sudden they saw a birch stuck in the middle of the ashes where the fire had been.

"That's the sign Semyonich left us, it must be," the boys said to themselves, and started digging.

And right away, they came on two small nuggets, and the sand was quite different, too, not what it had been before. So at the beginning it all went well for them, couldn't be better. Of course it took a bad turn later....

1936

THE SERPENT'S TRAIL

L evonty's two lads, the ones the Serpent showed the way to gold, soon began to prosper. Their father died, but just the same each year was better than the last. They built a hut—not over grand, just an ordinary well-built hut. Then they bought a cow and a horse, and in winter they'd three sheep under the roof. Right glad their mother was to see a little ease and comfort in her old age.

All this came from the good services of the old man, Semyonich. His was the head that guided them. He taught the boys how to dispose of the gold so the office wouldn't take note or the other prospectors look at them with envy. Guile was needed for handling gold, a man must have eyes all round. There were others seeking it, there were merchants like vultures, and the office watching you too. You had to be clever. How could children find their way about in it all? But Semyonich told them what to do. Taught them the ways of it.

And so it went on. The boys got big but they still washed gold in the same place. The other prospectors stayed round about too. They didn't get much, but still it was something. But the boys, they did real well. Even started to put a bit away.

But then the men on top noticed—two orphans, and not at all badly off. So one day—it was a holiday and their mother was just taking fish pies out of the oven—a messenger appeared.

"You've got to go to the bailiff. At once, he said."

They went, and the bailiff began bawling at them.

"How long d'ye think you're going to idle? Just look at ye—tall as flag-poles and never done a day's work for the Master yet! Who let ye off? Want to try the fit of a soldier's cap?"

Of course the boys explained.

"Our father, God rest his soul, the Master himself freed because he was past his work. And so we thought—"

"It's not for you to think! Show me the paper that says you're free!"

They boys hadn't any paper, of course, so they didn't know what to say. Then the bailiff told them: "Bring five hundred each and I'll give ye the papers."

He was probing, like, to see if the lads would say they'd got money. But they stood firm.

"If we sold all we've got, to the last thread," said the younger, "it wouldn't bring the half."

"If that's the way, then you go to work tomorrow morning. The supervisor'll tell ye where to go. And see you're not late for getting your task. If you are, ye'll get the whip on your first day."

Down in the mouth they were, those boys of ours. And when they told their mother she started weeping and lamenting.

"Oh misery! How shall we keep alive now?"

Their neighbours and relations all came. Some counselled writing to the Master, some said they ought to go to town, to the real big men over the mines, and some added up how much they could get if they sold everything they had. And others put fear in them, saying: "While you're talking and arguing here, the bailiff's men will take ye by the collar, flog ye and push ye into the mines. Put ye in chains there too. And then see how far ye'll get in seeking justice!"

Some said this and some said that, but none so much as thought that maybe the boys might have that five hundred the bailiff spoke of but fear to show it. Even their mother knew naught of it. When Semyonich was still among the living he'd warned them many a time: "Tell none of the gold put by, and especially tell no woman. Mother, wife, sweetheart—say no word to any. Ye never know what can happen. The guards from the mine can come, make a search, threaten this and that. A woman might have a close mouth in the ordinary way, but she'll be afraid for her son or her husband and show the place where it's hid. And that's just what the guards want. They'll take the gold and get rid of the man. And the woman, she'll just throw herself in the water or put a rope round her neck. I've known it happen. So be cautious! When ye grow up and wed, bear it well in mind. As for your mother, not a hint of it to her. She can never hold her tongue, she likes to boast of her children."

The boys took good heed of Semyonich's counsel and said no word to any of their hoard. The other prospectors guessed, of course, that the boys must have something put away, but how much and where, none knew.

So the neighbours talked the matter over this way and that, they felt for the two, but the end of it all was, they would have to go to work next morning.

"No way out of it."

As soon as all were gone, the younger lad said: "Come, Brother, let's go to the gold-fields. Take a last look at our place. . . ."

The other guessed what was in his mind.

"Why not, let's go," he said. "The fresh air'll mebbe make us feel easier."

Their mother put something together from the Sunday meal for them to eat on the way, and slipped in a pickle or two. They took a bottle as well, of course, and set off for the Ryabinovka.

They walked a good while with no word spoken. When the path turned into the woods, the elder brother said: "We'll hide here a bit."

They turned sharp off the path and lay down behind some briars. They drank a glassful each, then lay quiet and listened. Someone was coming. They peered out and saw Vanka Sochen plodding along the path with his pan and tools. Like as if he was off real early to the fields. Got a sudden craving for work, couldn't even wait to finish his bottle. Now that Sochen, he was an office cur, if they smelt a rat anywhere they sent him sniffing round. Folks had known that a long time. He'd been beaten more than once, but he still kept on. A real pest. The Mistress of the Copper Mountain herself gave him his quittance later on, and in such wise that he lay under the sod. Aye, but that's no matter here.... Well, along came that Sochen and the brothers winked at each other. Then the foreman passed on horseback. They waited a bit more, and Pimenov himself rolled past, driving his Yorshik. He'd got rods fastened to his light cart, as if he was going fishing.

Pimenov was the most daring of those that bought gold secretly those days in Polevaya. And everyone knew Yorshik. A racer from the steppes, he was. Not so very big, but he'd leave any three-span behind. Where could Pimenov have got hold of him? Folks used to say he'd got two hearts and two pair of lungs. He'd gallop fifty versts and be fresh at the end of it. Try to catch a horse like that! A real thief's horse. There's a lot of tales told about him. And his master was a stout, lusty fellow, not the kind you'd want to start a fight with. Not like those heirs of his that live in that big two-storey house over there.

When the two lads saw that fisherman they had to laugh. Then the younger one stood up behind the briars and called him—not too loud, though, a bit careful.

"Ivan Vasilyevich, have you your scales with ye?"

The merchant saw the lad was laughing and gave back jest for jest.

"Hard if I couldn't find any in the woods here! If there was something to weigh on 'em."

Then he reined Yorshik in. "If you've aught for me, get in, I'll set ye on your way."

That was how he always did it—bought gold with the horse ready. He knew what Yorshik could do. He'd only to say: "Yorshik—you'll get the whip!" and next minute there'd be naught but a spatter of mud or a cloud of dust.

"We haven't it with us," the lads said, and then asked: "Where'll we find ye tomorrow morning early, Ivan Vasilyevich?"

"What have ye got—something worth while, or just a pinch?" the merchant asked.

"As if you didn't know...."

"Oh, I know all right, but I don't know all. I don't know if you both want to buy yourselves free, or only one to start with."

He waited a minute, and then he went on—sort of warning them.

"Take care, lads, they're watching ye. Did you see Sochen?"

"Aye, we saw him."

"And the foreman?"

"We saw him too."

"They've maybe sent others. And there might be some smelling round on their own account. They all know you need to get money by the morn, so they're spying. I came specially to warn ye."

"And thank ye kindly, but we've got our own eyes open too."

"Aye, I can see you've got heads on your shoulders, but all the same— take care."

"Are you afraid it'll slip away from ye?"

"Nay, I've naught to fret about. There's none other would buy it, they'd be afraid."

"What'll you pay?"

Pimenov pushed the price down, of course. A hawk, after all. That sort don't let go their prey.

"That's all I'll give," he said, "there may be trouble."

155

So the bargain was struck. Pimenov whispered: "At dawn I'll drive by the dyke and pick ye up." He shook the reins. "Get on, Yorshik, catch the foreman!" Then he asked the lads: "D'ye want money for both or for one?"

"We don't know how much we'll be able to scrape up," said the younger. "Bring plenty, anyway."

The merchant drove away.

The lads were quiet a while, then the younger one said: "Pimenov spoke good sense, Brother. We'd better not show too much money all at once. It might end badly. They'd just take it and that's all."

"Aye, that's right. But what'll we do, then?"

"Mebbe this way. We'll go to the bailiff again, we'll beg him humbly to take a bit less. Then we'll say we can't get more than four hundred even if we sell all we've got. He'll let one of us go for four hundred, you'll see, and folks'll think we've given our last."

"That 'ud be all right," said the elder, "but who's to stay a serf? Looks like we'll have to draw lots."

Then the younger one started to cajole his brother.

"Aye, draw lots, that 'ud be the best way, of course. Then none can complain. No two words about it.... Though—there's one thing. You've got an injury. One eye's no good.... If you got in their ill books they'd never make a soldier of ye, but what 'ud save me? The first thing and they'd send me off. And goodbye to freedom then. But if you'd stand it a bit, I'd soon buy ye free. Before a year's past I'll go to the bailiff, and no matter what he asks, I'll pay it. Ye can rest easy about that. D'ye think I've no conscience? We've found it together. How could I grudge it?"

Now, the elder brother, Pantelei, was a simple, good-natured young fellow. He'd give the shirt off his back to one who needed it. And then that blemish, his injured eye, it seemed to have crushed him down. He was sort of quiet, and went about as if everyone was better and cleverer than he was. Not a word to say for himself.

The other lad, Kostka, was a bird of a different feather. Though he'd grown up poor, he was a proper figure of a man, tall and sturdy, good enough to put in a show. The only thing not so good was his carroty hair, real red it was. When he wasn't there folks always called him Red Kostka. And those who had dealings with him used to say: "Don't put your faith in every word ye hear from Kostka." And for making up to anyone—he knew just the way to go about it. Like a cat, rubbing and rubbing against you.

He soon got round his brother, of course. So it all went as he said. The bailiff knocked a hundred off the price, and the next day Kostka had a free man's paper, and claimed he'd made things easier for his brother too. The bailiff had Pantelei sent to the Krylatovskoye field.

"It's right what your brother says. It's the sort of work you're used to— mostly washing sand. And whether it's here or there, I've a need o' men. I don't mind doing ye a kindness. Go to Krylatovskoye."

So Kostka fixed it all up as he wanted. Got himself free and packed his brother off to a distant gold-field. Of course he'd no thought of selling the hut and holding. That was just talk.

Now he was rid of Pantelei, Kostka wanted to go back to the Ryabinov-ka. But how'd he manage alone? The only way was to hire a man, but that he feared to do. If things leaked out, others would be coming to the place. But he found one to suit. A bit lacking, he was. A tall, strong fellow, but couldn't count to ten. Just what Kostka needed.

He started off with this zany, but soon saw the place was getting worked out. He tried a bit higher, a bit lower, and on this side and that, but still there was no gold. Just a bit of colour here and there, not worth washing for. So Kostka decided to cross over to the other bank and try the place under the birch tree where the Serpent had stopped. It was a bit better there, but not what it had been when Pantelei was with him. Still, Kostka was glad to get that much, and he'd outwitted the Serpent too, he thought.

Other prospectors saw where Kostka had gone, and decided to try their own luck on the other bank. And they seemed to be getting something. So before a month had gone, there was a whole crowd on the spot. Folks even came from a long way off.

Some of the prospectors worked in parties, and there was a maid in one of them. She was red-headed too, a bit thin, but she drew the eye. When you've a maid like that, the sun shines even if it's raining. Now Kostka had loose ways, he might have been the bailiff or the Master himself. He'd given many a maid living at home with her parents cause to weep, and this was just a miner lass. So Kostka went right ahead, and burned his fingers.

The maid was young, simple in her ways, but he couldn't get near her all the same. Spirited, she was. Give her one word and you'd get back two, and both of them mockery. And as for touching her—better not try it. So there was Kostka like a fish on a hook. Went about moping, couldn't sleep at night. She'd got him twisted round her little finger.

There are maids who can do that real well. Where they learn it all I don't know. You see one—the milk's not yet dried on her lips, but she knows all the tricks. Kostka had always fooled them to the top of his bent, but now he changed his tune.

"Will you be my wife?" he said. "So it's not just anyway with us, but all honest and lawful.... I'll buy ye free."

But that maid, she just laughed at him.

"If you hadn't such red hair, now."

That stung Kostka, he didn't like it when they called him Red-Head, but he tried to joke it off.

"And what about yourself?"

"That's why I fear to wed you," she said, "I'm carroty, you're red, the children 'ud set the house afire."

Then she started praising Pantelei. She knew him a bit, she'd met him at the Krylatovskoye field.

"If it was Pantelei asking me, I'd wed at once. He caught my fancy. A proper lad. He may have only one eye, but it's a good one."

She said it just to torment Kostka, but he believed it. He ground his teeth, he could have torn Pantelei to pieces, and to make it worse, she went on with: "Why don't you buy your brother free? You panned the gold together, and now you're free and pushed him off to the back o' beyond."

"I've no money for him," said Kostka. "Let him find it himself."

"Ye shameless knave! Did Pantelei work less than you? Wasn't it mining he lost his eye?"

She got Kostka so wrought up he shouted: "I'll kill ye, ye jade!"

"Let that be as it may," she said, "but you'll never get me living. Red-haired and false—there's naught worse."

That was the way she flouted Kostka, but he kept after her all the more. He'd have given her anything in the world if she'd have stopped calling him Red-Head and looked at him a bit more kindly. But she'd have none of his gifts, not even the smallest thing. And she'd sting him with a tongue like a dagger.

"You'd do better to save that for buying Pantelei free!"

Then Kostka thought to give a big feast at the mine. He was clever, that fellow. When they all get drunk, he thought, there'll be none to mark who does what. I'll lure her away somewhere, and we'll see what tune she'll sing in the morning.

Of course, folks had their own ideas about it all.

"What come over our Red-Head? He must have made a strike. Better try that place where he is."

They might think this or that, but who'll refuse feasting with naught to pay? The maid, she came too. And in the dancing she stopped before Kostka in the ring, inviting him to step out with her. Folks say she was a real lightsome dancer. And Kostka, it just wrung his vitals.

But he didn't forget his plan. When all had drunk well, he seized hold of the maid, but she looked at him with such eyes that his hands fell and his legs shook, and fear took him.

Then she said: "Red-haired and shameless, will ye buy Pantelei free?"

That was like scalding water on Kostka. He flew into a rage.

"Nay, that I won't," he shouted. "I'd sooner drink it all, to the last kopek!"

"As you will," she said. "I've told ye. And as for drink, we'll help ye with that."

Off she went, dancing. She bent and twisted like a serpent and her eyes were fixed, unwinking. After that Kostka started to give feasts like that nearly every week. And it costs a bit to treat fifty or so till they're merry. Miner folks can hold plenty. No good trying to stint, or you'll be a laughing-stock, men will say: "Drained an empty mug at Kostka's feast and had a headache all week. Next time I'll take a couple o' bottles with me. Mebbe I'll feel better."

So Kostka saw to it there was wine and all the rest a-plenty. The gold he had soon flowed away and he was getting but a mite. Again there was no gleam in the sand, seek as he would. Even the zany who worked with him said: "Seems there's naught to be washed here, Master."

Well, that maid, she just tongue-lashed him on.

"Down i' the mouth, are ye, Red-Head? Danced the heels off your boots and no money left for the cobbler?"

Kostka knew he was riding to ruin, but he couldn't stop himself. You just wait, he thought, I'll show you whether I've enough for the cobbler or not. . . .

There'd been a deal of gold he and Pantelei had put by. They'd buried it the usual way, in their kitchen garden, deep under the ground. You dug down through the topsoil, and then came sand and clay. That's where they'd put it. They'd marked the place well, of course, measured it all to the inch. Even if it was found sometime, the mine watchmen couldn't do a thing to them. "A nugget?" they'd say. "Who'd ever ha' thought there was gold here? There we were seeking it in far places, and it lay right in our own garden!"

The place was as safe as it could be, but to get the gold out, that was bothersome, and they had to keep a sharp watch, too. But they'd thought all that out as well. They'd set bushes behind the bath-house, and a pile of stone, so it was all hard to see.

Now Kostka chose a dark night and went to his hiding place. He took off the topsoil, then filled a tub with sand, and carried it into the bath-house. He'd water there, all ready. He shut the window, lighted a lantern and started washing the sand. But not a thing could he find, not a grain of gold. What's this, he thought. Have I made a mistake? Out he went again, measured everything, and dug up another tubful. Not a 'speck. Then Kostka forgot all his care, he dashed out with the lantern. Checked everything again. All quite right. He'd dug at the exact spot. So he started getting out some more. Maybe I didn't go deep enough, he thought. This time there was a grain or two. He went still deeper and the same thing—just a gleam. Then Kostka fell into a frenzy, he started driving a shaft as they do in mines. But before he got very far he came up against solid rock. Real glad he was to see that, for not even the Serpent himself could carry the gold away through rock. It must be somewhere close. Then it suddenly flashed on him: "Pantelei's stolen it!"

As the thought came, that maid, the miner maid, suddenly appeared in front of him. It was dark, but he could see her plain as by day. She stood there, straight and tall, by the edge of the hole and looked hard at Kostka.

"It seems you've lost something, Red-Head! And blaming your brother? He'll come and take it in good time, and there'll be naught you can do about it."

"Who told you to come here, ye pop-eyed jade?"

He caught hold of her legs and tried to pull her down into the hole. Her feet were off the ground but she still stood straight up. Then she seemed to get longer and thinner, she stretched out and it was an adder he was holding. It curved over his shoulder and crawled down his back. And Kostka, seized with terror, let go the tail. The serpent struck with its head on the stone and sparks flew out, so bright they were blinding.

Then the serpent passed through the stone, and along its trail gold shone, in grains and whole nuggets. Gold, and much of it. When Kostka saw that he flung himself against the stone and his head struck it. The next day his mother found him at the bottom of the shaft. His head did not seem badly broken, but for some reason Kostka was dead.

Pantelei came from Krylatovskoye for the funeral. He was given leave. When he saw the shaft in the garden, he guessed there had been some mischance with the gold. That troubled him greatly, he had hoped that gold would give him freedom. He had heard bad reports of Kostka, but still he had trusted his brother to buy him off. He went to take a look, bent down over the shaft, and a light seemed to shine up at him from below. At the bottom was something like a round window of thick glass, and in that glass wound a trail of gold. And a maid stood below looking at Pantelei through the glass. She had red hair and black eyes, eyes that would make you fear to look at them. But the maid was smiling, and she pointed at that trail of gold as though to say: "There is your gold, take it. And have no fear." It was as if she spoke kindly, yet there was no word to be heard. And then the light vanished.

At first Pantelei was afraid, he thought it was a spook. But then he took courage and climbed down into the hole. There was no glass at all, only white stone, quartz. Pantelei had had to do with stone like that in the Master's mines. He was used to it, knew what to do. I'll have a try, he thought. Maybe there really is gold here.

He went and got all needful and started breaking away the stone at the place where he'd seen the golden trail. And there it was, gold, and not just grains, but nuggets and whole pockets. A real rich vein. By eventide Pantelei had got five or six pounds of pure gold. He went secretly to Pimenov, and then to the bailiff.

"What I've come about is, I want to buy myself free."

"Very good," said the bailiff, "only I've no time now. Come in the morn. We'll talk about it quietly then."

The way Kostka had been carrying on, the bailiff knew he must have had a good bit of money. So he made up his mind to squeeze Pantelei and get as much out of him as he could. But luckily for Pantelei, a man came running in.

"A messenger's come. The Master's in Sysert, he'll be here tomorrow. He's sent orders to have all the road to Poldnevnaya put in order."

The bailiff was likely afraid he'd lose all, for he said to Pantelei: "Give me five hundred, but I'll put four on the paper."

So he pocketed a hundred. Well, Pantelei didn't bargain. Gorge yourself, you dog, he thought, you'll choke some day.

So Pantelei was free. He dug a bit more in the hole in his garden. But then he stopped seeking gold altogether. A man lives quieter without it, he thought.

And that was how it was. He bought himself a farm, not so big, but he could get along. There was only one thing more that happened. And that was when he married.

He'd but one eye, of course. So he chose a plain, modest maid from a poor home. And he had his wedding quietly.

The next day his young wife took a look at her wedding ring. . . . How'll I wear that? she thought. It's so thick and fine, it must have cost a lot. What if I lose it?

So she said to her husband: "Why did you waste so much money, Pantelei? How much did my ring cost?"

"It's no waste when it's the custom," said Pantelei. "I paid a ruble and a half for the ring."

"Nay," said his wife, "never will I believe that."

Pantelei took a look, and saw it wasn't the ring he'd bought. He looked at his own hand and there was quite a different ring on his finger too, and it had two tiny black stones in the middle, like eyes sparkling at him.

When he saw those stones he thought at once of the maid who had shown him the trail of gold in the stone, but he said naught of that to his wife. Why trouble her for no good purpose?

She wouldn't wear that ring, all the same, she bought herself a cheap one. And what would a muzhik do with a ring? Pantelei wore his till the bridal days were over, and that was all.

After Kostka died, folks at the gold-fields asked each other: "Where's that maid, the one that danced so fine?" But she was gone. One would ask another—where did she come from? Some said from Kungurka, others from Mramor. Well, all sorts of things. Miner folk, they're always wandering. They've little time for thinking of who comes from what house. So they forgot her.

But gold was found on the Ryabinovka for a long time.

1939

ZHABREI'S PATH

At Kossoi Brod where the school is now, there used to be a stretch of wasteland. A big patch, anyone could see it, but no one wanted it. It was high up, you see. Planting vegetables there would mean plenty of sweat and little to see for it. So folks let it alone, and looked for easier places, more convenient.

Once, though, there was a hut there, folks say. A tumbledown sort of place with two windows, leaning forward as if it was just going to go somersaulting down the hill. There was a vegetable plot too, and a bath-house. Just a bit of a farm, you could call it. Naught to marvel at, but you could see it was there. And the folks all round about knew that hut well.

A gold miner used to live there, a prospector—Nikita Zhabrei, they called him. Getting on in years. A young fellow going grey, as the saying is. The lads could well have started calling him Grandad, but he still had all his strength. There were few could match him at work. He was a fine figure of a man, but naught to say for himself, as if he'd never learned the trick of speech. And surly—best leave him alone. He kept all away. 'Twas with good cause they called him Zhabrei the Nettle.

This Zhabrei generally prospected by himself, sought new places and sometimes found them. Then he'd come into the village and tell folks about it.

"Hark 'ee, muzhiks, in such-and-such a place there's gold turning up."

Those places were always worth working. Sometimes they were quite rich. But folks knew Zhabrei had a secret too. Now and then he'd have his pockets full of money. Nobody knew where he got it, but the talk went that he sold nuggets to merchants who bought on the quiet. And all the nuggets were the same shape, like bast shoes, small but heavy. And here was the marvel—each one was larger than the last, the first might have weighed about a pound, then they got bigger and bigger, but all of them were just like shoes.

The merchants and the other prospectors badly wanted to see where Zhabrei found those gold shoes, but naught came of all their trying. Nikita knew they were watching him, you see, and he was wily. He'd let them follow him hither and thither all day, and then when it got dark he'd plunge into the woods and be gone. Try to find the path he took through the forest in the dark of night!

They tried to get something out of his wife, but fared no better. She was the same sort as her husband. Prickly, best not touch her without gloves, and a sharp tongue in her head. Those that came for no particular reason she'd not let through the door. A man had hardly time to smooth his moustache and say: "Good day, Granny!" and she'd come back with: "And what else? What have ye come for?"

Well, the man would start to stutter and stammer, of course.

"How are you? How's your goodman? I hope ye're doing well."

"Aye, well enough," she'd say. "We go to none, we ask none to come to us, and them as come unasked get the broom in their faces."

Try to talk to that sort!

Sometimes the goodwives would come to borrow something. And them she might meet this way or that. Some she'd send packing straight away. "I've set naught aside for you, and don't ye come round again!" To another she'd give without a word--a bit of flour, or butter, or potatoes or whatever it might be, and never ask it back again; but she'd not say any more than she had to. As soon as the woman settled down to gossip, Zhabrei's wife would pick up bucket and floor-cloth.

"Off you go home, Stepanya. You've got little 'uns waiting. You've more to do than I have. And me, I was just starting to wash the floor, while you sit here as if ye'd naught to do."

So that was how Zhabrei and his wife lived, keeping to themselves.

Zhabrei did work in artels* sometimes, of course. That was when he showed the men a new place. And they were glad to get him. He did the work of two, or even three, and he had a real understanding of gold. Who'd refuse a man like that? But he never stopped long. Something would happen, and he'd leave them at once. All sorts can happen in an artel. There are quarrels about the work, or they find someone acting crooked, maybe someone gets a bit of a lesson; and Zhabrei couldn't stand all that. He'd listen a while to the bawling, then he'd just say, sort of scornful: "The mosquitoes in the bog singing again! If any want to harken, let 'em, I've had my fill."

He'd spit, take up his pick and spade, sling his pan and sack over his shoulder and be gone. Wouldn't even come to get his pay.

Once he went off like that and didn't come back for a long time. Folks reckoned him dead, when all of a sudden he appeared. It was just at

* Small co-operatives.—*Tr*

166

Trinity when all the rivers and streams overflow that he was washed up again.

It had been a bad year, they say. Little gold to be found. So the miners were down in the mouth. Here was a great holiday, and naught to make merry with. They talked and grumbled and wondered where they could get treated to a glass at least—and then they saw Zhabrei coming along the Polevaya road, all in new clothes. That was a plain token, he'd money in his pocket, now there'd be feasting and merrymaking all through the village.

And so it was. Nikita went straight to the tavern, poured a pile of rubles on the counter and called to the hostess: "Fill up, Ulyana, till they're all rolling! So not a mosquito of them all can whine that Nikita Zhabrei kept his gold in his pouch and showed it to none. Look ye—here it is!" And he kept pouring more and more rubles out on the counter.

If Nikita was giving a feast they knew he'd do it properly, till the last ruble was gone, so the whole village came running. Some, of course, had no other idea but—why not drink if you're treated? But most came with crafty thoughts, maybe Zhabrei'll get talkative, maybe he'll let slip the place where those bast sandals of gold are made. But Zhabrei knew how, much he could hold. He drank what he wanted, tipped some more money on the counter and told the hostess: "Pour out, Ulyana. Without stint. The men plain, the maids and wives red wine. All they can hold. If that's not enough I'll pay, and if it's more you can keep what's over. In the morn we'll start a new reckoning."

The hostess was so glad she didn't know what to do first, she poured out wine with one hand, gathered up the rubles with the other, bowed to Zhabrei—it'll all be done as you say, and whispered to her husband: "Go to the still, bring a couple of barrels, or we won't have enough."

From the tavern Zhabrei went straight to the shop, as he always did; and they'd been waiting long for him already. The shop-keeper was shrewd enough. The village was a small one, but there were always dear things on hand in case one of the miners had a stroke of luck—the sort of things no villager really needs.

From these Nikita chose gifts for his old woman. A shawl—a real fine one, buckled shoes, a length of silk and whatever else took his eye. He bought new clothes for himself too, and told the shop-keeper: "Take them to my old woman. Tell her Nikita Yevseyevich sends her a greeting and bids you say he's alive and well, and he'll soon be home. Let her make cabbage dumplings and kvass. Two cans at least."

The shop-keeper hurried away and Nikita sat on the bench till he came back.

"Well, what happened?" he asked.

"What could happen? I gave them to her."

"And what did she say?"

"She took the things, threw them in the corner, but said naught."

Nikita did not believe him.

"Nay, that can't be—that she just took her man's gifts without a word said."

Then the shop-keeper confessed: "Four words she did say."

"And what were they?" Nikita asked.

"When she took the things she sighed and said: 'Eh, the old fool!'"

Nikita laughed.

"Now that's the truth ye're telling. It's her way, my old woman. She's all right, in good health, no need to hasten home. We'll give the children a treat too. Bring a basket."

The shop-keeper knew what to do. He brought a basket measure and asked: "How much must I weigh out, and what kind?"

"Measure it wi' your eye, to the top! Every sort, but only the ones in paper wrappings, no naked ones."

The man couldn't do it without cheating, of course. The cheap sweets he poured in without stint, and the dear ones only a few, but he reckoned the cost the other way. Well, Nikita didn't argue. He handed over the money and went out on to the steps with the basket. And the children had come round from the whole village. But they didn't stand waiting by the door, they were just playing round about, some with knucklebones, some with a ball, and the maids with games of their own. They knew Zhabrei's ways: if he saw they were waiting for him, he'd take the basket back again. So the children always made as if they didn't know a thing, they'd just come there to play by chance.

Nikita would see they weren't waiting for him, and start scattering the sweets all round in handfuls. The children didn't often get sweets, of course, and they'd all make a rush for them, a real scramble it was. If one was knocked off his feet by chance, like, or two cracked their heads together, Zhabrei just laughed, but when they started quarrelling or fighting he'd grind his teeth, drop the basket and say: "Mosquitoes' brood are mosquitoes too!"

He'd scowl, and turn and go home. He'd climb his hill, sit down on the earthen bank and begin caterwauling. Best keep off him when he was like that, he'd knock any man off his feet. Only the old woman could deal with him.

All the village would be noisy with Zhabrei's feast, some singing, some dancing, and Zhabrei himself would sit there on the bank and all his song was: "Mosquitoes ye are, mosquitoes, a kingdom of mosquitoes."

When night came the old woman would lead him into the hut. He'd sleep it off and in the morning start all over again. First to the tavern, then new clothes for his goodwife and sweets for the children. Sometimes the old woman would have a whole corner piled up with things. Then when the money gave out she'd sell them back to the shop-keeper and get one kopek for ten paid What he'd sold for fifty he'd buy back for five, and what he'd sold for ten—for that he gave one.

When the children scrambled for sweets without fighting, Zhabrei would stop in the village till eventide. He'd sing with the other miners, and dance too; but when he went home he went alone, he needed no man's help. And if any tried to fasten on to him, Zhabrei'd make short work of the man.

"My friend ye are, but up my hill ye do not come. I have no love for it."

That was how these feastings always went on, until the money was gone. But this time it took a different turn on the first day.

Nikita brought out his basket of sweets and started to scatter them. Now, there was one among the children, Denisko the Orphan. He wasn't very old, but tall and lanky. The other lads of his age used to tease him. "Denisko, bend your back, double over so we'll be the same."

Because he was an orphan, he'd been washing sand a long time, and with that, and with his size, most reckoned him already grown. But still he was a boy at heart, and he was curious to see the merrymaking. So he came round the shop with the others and made as if he was playing. But when they all ran and scrambled for the sweets, Denisko just stood and watched. Nikita saw that and called out: "Hey you, Lanky, can't ye catch?" And he threw a whole handful right at Denisko. The other children made a rush for them, but Denisko himself just moved away a bit so he wouldn't be knocked off his feet.

Then Nikita asked him: "What's wrong wi' ye, Denisko? Hurt your back?"

"Nay, my back's all right," said the lad, "but all that's naught for me. I'm a man grown."

"If ye're a man," said Nikita, "off wi' ye to the tavern. Drink my health, even if it's only in red wine."

"When my mother was dying," said Denisko, "she told me: 'Till your beard's full grown, never touch a drop. After that, do as you see fit.'"

"So that's what ye're like," said Nikita, real amazed he was. "Here's this for ye, then!" And he threw down some silver coins. But Denisko didn't pick them up. "I need no charity now," he said. "I'm grown, I can earn my own bread."

That made Nikita angry, of course. He shouted at the other children: "Get away over there! We'll see how stiff his neck is!"

He pulled a bundle of banknotes, big ones, out of his inside pocket and tossed them down in front of Denisko. But this, seemingly, was a lad of character.

"I told ye I don't need charity," he said, "and least of all when it's thrown like a bone to a dog."

That put Nikita in a real rage, he just stood glaring at Denisko. Then he thrust his hand down the leg of his topboot, pulled out a bundle wrapped in a rag and took from it a nugget—five pounds' weight, maybe, and threw it down—bang!—at Denisko's feet.

"Don't brag!" he shouted. "That ye'll pick up!"

But Denisko, maybe he was just stubborn, or maybe he didn't know the real value of the nugget, anyway, he didn't pick it up. He just looked at it and said: "I'd like well to find a gold shoe like that myself, but other folks' I don't want.'

Then he turned to go. Nikita came to himself a bit, he ran and picked up the money and the nugget, and called out to Denisko: "What *do* ye want, then?"

"Naught," said Denisko. "I just came to look at you showing off before them all."

Nikita had little taste for being reproved by a boy, but he made no answer. Then after a bit he shouted: "Denisko, come back!"

The children caught it up with their own cry: "Denisko, bend your back! Denisko, bend your back!"

Denisko took no notice, he just came and stood there quietly. Then Nikita whispered, so no one could hear: "Come to me i' the morn, when I've sobered down a bit. Mebbe I'll show ye the ants' path, and after that it'll be your own affair. If the Lips of Stone let ye in, ye'll find it easy enough to get through the lard, either with heat or with water. And then ye'll find the shoes."

"Very well, Uncle Nikita," said the lad. "And thankful I'll be to ye for showing me the road."

"It's not for your thanks I'll do it," said Nikita, "but because I see no greed in ye. I've sought one like that a long time."

On those words they parted, and never saw each other again.

Zhabrei went straight to his hill. He walked slowly, as if he was thinking deep, and sang no song that day about mosquitoes. Folks saw him sitting with his old woman on the grass bank. A long time they sat there, just like folks new wed, talking and talking, confidential-like. The villagers were amazed to see them.

"Look at that, now, Zhabrei and his old woman can't get to the end o' their talk. As if they were going to die this night."

It was a jest, of course, but it was a true word. In the morning Denisko hastened to Zhabrei's hut and found all the doors unharmed, but a dire confusion within, this thrown down, that overturned, and the other thing smashed to splinters. In the middle of the room lay a heavy crowbar, but of people—not a soul.

Denisko was frightened, he ran back to the village and told folks what he'd seen—"something wrong there." They hadn't yet properly slept off their drink, but they went hurrying up the hill all the same. They took a good look at it all, then they sent to tell the magistrate. But no one could make head or tail of it. One thing was sure, though—there'd been a real hard fight, folks striking out in the darkness. Some hand had scraped everything out of the space under the stove, but the pile of clothes in the corner wasn't touched, they lay as the old woman had thrown them. There was no blood, and no tracks to be seen by the hut. The ground was hard and stony, it didn't show them. And besides, the whole village had been tramping round, anything there was had been scuffed away.

The magistrate had a guard set on the empty place, of course, and began questioning all the folks, asking who'd got something to tell.

But there seemed no one they could blame in the village. Some had been lying dead drunk, and the rest had all been together. Some thought maybe a gang from Kungurka had done it; folks had seen men in the village who served one of those merchants that bought gold on the sly. And many knew that merchant had often egged folks on to watch Zhabrei. But the magistrates weren't likely to accuse a man who paid them so well. So they turned it all round against Denisko the Orphan. He'd brought the robbers. Nikita had shown him money and a nugget. And hadn't he been the first there in the morning? That proved it.

A sin and a shame it was, of course. But they haled the poor lad away to jail, aye, and kept him shut up for many a year. Killed two birds with one stone—shielded the merchant and found a culprit. That's the way it was done, those times.

They soon forgot Denisko in the village. It's out of sight, out of mind with miner folk. Always plenty of coming and going. Denisko had no one of his own, none to grieve for him. So he stopped there in jail thinking to himself, maybe they'll find Zhabrei and his old woman, then it'll all be cleared up.

Well, in the end they let Denisko out and he came back, a man grown. The first thing, he wanted to know if aught had been heard of Nikita and his wife, and who was living in their hut. He asked round about, but none could tell him, and on the hill there wasn't a trace of the hut left. A hut won't stand long with none to own it, it's soon taken away bit by bit. And besides, folks didn't forget the robbers had hunted under the stove. So they started searching everywhere too. Pulled all to pieces, and where Zhabrei's hut had been they left naught but wasteland with a lot of holes dug in it.

It grieved Denisko sore. Here'd been a man who knew about gold. But he never piled up riches, he gave all away. Showed folks new places to find it. And his old woman, she harmed none. And now there was naught left to tell of them but this bit of bare ground and the holes dug in it.

He climbed the hill and sat there thinking. And then he called to mind Nikita's words, telling him to come the next morning.

What was that ants' path he spoke of? And what were the Lips of Stone?

He thought of it this way and that, and at last he decided—there are plenty of ants' paths, who can tell which is the right one, but Lips of Stone, those I can seek. Maybe by good chance I'll come across them.

As he thought that he happened to look down, and there he was, sitting right by an ants' trail. Just an ordinary one like any other, with ants crawling along it. But they were all going one way and none the other. Denisko found that queer.... I'll follow them, he thought, and see where their hill is.... So he went along that trail and it led him a long, long way. And here was a strange thing—the ants seemed to be getting bigger, and where the ground was bare, something seemed to sparkle on their feet. What could it be? He picked one or two up and looked at them, but naught could he see. It was all too tiny for his eye to take in. He went on and saw that the further the ants went, the bigger they got. Again he picked one up to look at it. And now he could see something like a tiny shining drop on each little foot. Denisko marvelled, and went on along the path. At last he came out on a glade with two stones thrusting out of the ground, shaped like flat cakes, one on top of the other. Lips, and naught else.

The path led straight up to those lips. And as soon as the ants came to the glade, they grew before his eyes. He was afraid to pick up any more, they were so big. And all of them with those shoes on their feet. They went to the Lips of Stone and vanished inside. So there must be a way in.

Denisko went up closer to take a look, and those lips opened wide, as though they wanted to swallow him. That scared him, of course. He jumped back but the lips didn't close, it was as if they were waiting, and the ants kept on going straight in, seemed to find nothing out of the way. Denisko took heart a bit, he came up closer to look in, and saw the path went down inside, steep like a slide. But it was all sticky clay, or rather, thick slime like lard. Even the ants had a hard job to get over it. Sometimes their shoes got stuck, but not all at the same place. The clay might hold them at once, then the ant would leave the shoes behind and run on all the easier. Another would go down unhindered, getting bigger all the time. An ant might go in the size of a beetle, and as it went on it got as big as a lamb, then a sheep, then a calf, a bull. And then it was like a great hill, and each shoe weighed a pood or more. As long as the clay didn't take those shoes it crept on slowly, but as soon as the last was off it slid down like a water-beetle, and got no bigger.

Well, now Denisko knew where the golden shoes had come from, though he marvelled that Nikita had not feared those great ants. But as he watched, they began coming one by one, and then no more entered.

So that's how it is, he thought. There's times they stop coming. But who knows how long that'll last?

The shoes, he thought, could be got out of the slime with his bare hands. He badly wanted to try his luck—to dig a bit, even if it was only on top. But it puzzled him how he would get up that steep, slippery slope again. He started looking round to see if he could find a knotted branch or a long pole, and stumbled across a bucket among the bushes. Not a very big one, but wide. And there was chopped wood beside it, and a hack and two spades, one iron and the other wooden.

Denisko had worked on the gold-fields since he was a boy, he knew what all that was for. He picked up the spades, hack and bucket, pushed a bundle of wood under his belt, went back to the lips—and they closed. Just two stones lying one on top of the other, and no path at all.

He was disappointed, of course, but what could he do? You can't lift stones like that with a crowbar. He turned to put everything back where he'd found it when the lips suddenly opened again. Opened quite wide and seemed to move a little—like getting ready to swallow him. Well, Denisko didn't fear, without stopping to think twice, in he went. He didn't find any gold shoes in the slime, of course, they'd sunk into the sand below. But for one that knew how, it was easy enough to get down to them. To lift up that slimy clay we call lard, folks take a hot iron spade or a wet wooden one, and it comes up in slabs like pancakes. Denisko set to work, soon got a place clear and started collecting gold shoes from the sand underneath. He got a lot of them, some big, others small. But then he saw it was getting darker, the lips were closing.... I'm being too greedy, he thought. What do I want with all these? I'll take one to buy masses for Nikita, and another for myself, that's enough.

As he thought that, the lips opened again, as much as to say: Go on out.

With a hack to help, it's easy to climb any slope. You push it in, pull yourself up, and so on. Denisko came out and put everything back where he'd found it. The smallest shoe he thrust down the leg of his topboot, the other—exactly like the one Nikita had had—he hid in an inner pocket. Then he went straight off to Kungurka.

He found the merchant there'd been talk about, waited till he could catch him in a quiet place, and then asked him: "Want the second shoe to make a pair?"

He took the shoe out of his pocket and showed it, keeping it in his hand. The merchant was pleased as could be.

"What d'ye want for it?"

"I'll give it ye for nothing," said Denisko, "if ye'll show me where ye hid Nikita and his old woman."

The merchant forgot caution in his greed, he said: "We threw them down the old pit at the marble quarries."

"Show me the place," said Denisko.

They went to the quarry and the merchant said: "This is it."

"Then take your payment!" And Denisko turned round and smash!—brought the shoe down on the man's forehead. It was about five pounds in weight. You can guess what happened when that came down on a man's head, and with an angry arm behind it.

Folks soon found the merchant and the gold shoe beside him—the seal that had left the mark.

After that, nearly all the judges got themselves in the dock because of that shoe. Each one wanted to grab it for himself, but the others didn't let him and complained to those higher up—he's a thief, he's a robber, he ought to be put in jail. And so it went on till it got right up to the top judge of them all. And he didn't think twice what to do.

"I'll take that shoe home," he said, "I'll test it with acids and find out if it's real gold or not."

So he took the gold shoe home and hid it away deep in a coffer; then he broke a piece off an old candlestick, cleaned it up a bit, and took it back.

"Not a bit of gold in it," he said.

Of course all could see the trick he'd played, it was plain enough, but none cared complain of the chief judge. And as for him, he was pleased as could be and very proud of himself. Tricked them cleverly, I did, he thought. No wonder I'm chief judge!

Back home he went, and straight to that coffer. But it seemed like worms had eaten a hole in it, and inside there was naught to be seen. He looked this way and that, but it was no good. There had been a gold shoe, now there was just a hole. And nothing he could do about it.

None ever found Denisko, however they sought. He'd seemingly gone to Siberia or some other place.

There was a good bit of talk and arguing about those Lips of Stone for a while, about where they could be. Some said they were near the Denisov mine, but that I don't know. And what I don't know, I won't say, for I make naught up. That's not my way.

1942

THE DANCING FIRE-MAID

A party of prospectors were once sitting round a fire in the woods. Four were men grown, the fifth was a boy. About eight he was, not more. Fedyunka, they called him.

It was long past the hour for sleep, but the talk was interesting. There was an old man in the artel, you see—Grandad Yefim. Ever since he was young he'd been getting grains of gold from the earth, and many's the strange thing he'd seen and heard. So he told them this and that, and they all listened.

Fedyunka's father kept saying: "You ought to go to bed." But the boy wanted to hear more.

"Just a bit longer, Father! I just want to stop a bit more!"

Well ... Grandad Yefim finished the tale he was telling. The fire was only embers now and they all sat looking into them.

Suddenly a tiny little maid jumped out of the very middle—just like a doll, she was, but alive. Her hair was red, her sarafan blue, and she held a blue kerchief in her hand.

She looked round at them merrily and her teeth shone white. Then she put one hand on her hip, raised the blue kerchief with the other and began to dance. And how light and pretty it was, is more than I can tell you. The miners held their breath. They looked at her and felt they could never tire of looking. But they said no word, just as though they were in deep thought.

First the maid circled on the embers, but that space was too small for her, she danced in a wider circle. The miners moved back to make room for her, and as she made another circle she grew a little bigger. The miners moved back again. She danced another circle and grew bigger yet. And when they were a long way back from the fire, she danced in between them and wove round them in loops. And then she went right outside and whirled round in a smooth circle again, and now she was as big as Fedyunka. She stopped by a tall fir tree, stamped her foot, her teeth shone, she flourished her kerchief and gave a shrill whistle: "Fi-i-it—iu-u-u!"

Then an owl hooted and seemed to laugh, and the maid was gone.

If it had been only grown men there, maybe that would have been the end of it. Each of them would have thought: That's what comes of looking at the fire too long. You get dazed with it. Queer, the things you can see when you're tired.

But Fedyunka didn't think that way, he asked his father: "Dad, who was that?"

"An owl," the man answered. "What d'ye think? Never heard an owl hoot before?"

"I don't mean the owl, I know owls and I don't fear them a mite. But who was that maid?"

"What maid?"

"Why, the one that danced on the embers. You moved back to give her room and so did all the others."

Then Fedyunka's father and the other men started asking him what he'd seen, and the boy told them. One man even asked: "How big was she?"

"At first she was only as big as my finger, but at the end she was nearly as big as I am."

Then the miner said: "I saw the same marvel as you, Fedyunka." And the father and the others said the same. Only Grandad Yefim sucked at his pipe and said no word. So the miners started asking him.

"And you, Grandad, what d'ye say about this?"

"What I say is, I saw the same, and I thought it was all fancy. But it looks like the Dancing Fire-Maid's paid us a visit."

"What Fire-Maid?"

Then Grandad Yefim told them all about it.

"I once heard tell from old folks that it's a sign of gold—a tiny maid that dances. If the Dancer shows herself there's gold in that place. It's not big nuggets, and it's not veins, it's in nests, like horse-radishes in the ground. They're wider at the top and as ye go down the gold gets less and less till there's no more of it. Dig out that radish of gold dust and then let the place alone for ye'll find no more there. The only thing is, I can't mind if ye have to look for it where the Dancer first appears or where she goes back into the ground."

"We'll soon settle that," said the men. "We'll drive a shaft down in the morn where the fire is, and after that we'll try under that pine. Then we'll see if it's just tales you're telling us, or if there's truth in it."

After that they settled down to sleep. Fedyunka curled up too, but he kept thinking: What did the owl laugh at? He wanted to ask Grandad Yefim, but the old man was already snoring.

Fedyunka woke up late the next morning and saw a big hole where the fire had been. The miners were standing under four big pines, all four saying the same thing—"She went down here!"

"Nay, you're all wrong!" Fedyunka shouted. "You've forgotten! It was by this pine the Dancer stopped. And here was where she stamped her foot."

Well, that put the miners in a real maze. "A fifth one's woken up and now there's a fifth place. And if there were ten of us, there'd be ten places. We're just wasting our time. Better let it alone."

All the same, they tried all five places but got naught from it. And Grandad Yefim said to Fedyunka: "Looks like we're out of luck."

The boy didn't like that at all.

"It's the owl spoiled everything," he said. "He hooted and laughed our fortune away."

"Nay," said Grandad Yefim, "the owl had naught to do with it."

"He had!"

"Nay, not he."

"He had!"

They went on that way till the others laughed at the two of them and at themselves to boot.

"Old 'un and young 'un, neither knows, and here we are standing like fools, losing the whole day harkening to 'em!"

From that time folks nicknamed the old man Yefim Gold Radish and the boy Fedyunka Fire-Dancer.

The village children got to know and gave the boy no peace.

"Fedyunka Fire-Dancer! Fedyunka Fire-Dancer! Tell us about the Fire-Maid!"

Little the old man cared what they called him. They could call him kettle so long as they didn't put him on the fire. But Fedyunka was a boy, he didn't like them making a mock of him. He quarrelled and he fought, and more than once he cried, but the children only jeered the more, he'd no peace or rest. And then something else happened. His father wed again. And the stepmother was as savage as a she-bear. So he'd no home you could call home at all.

Grandad Yefim didn't often come back from the gold-fields either. He'd be tired after the week's work, he'd no wish to make his old legs do more. And he'd no one awaiting him, he lived alone. So when Saturday came and the others went to the village, the old man and the boy used to stop there together.

What did they do with themselves? Well, they'd talk about this and that. Grandad Yefim told Fedyunka about all he'd seen and heard, and taught him the signs that show gold—things of that sort. They'd remember the Fire-Maid too. All as nice and friendly as you please. There was only one thing they couldn't agree on. Fedyunka said it was the owl's fault they'd found no gold, and Grandad Yefim said the owl had naught to do with it.

One time they got to arguing about it again. It was a still day, the sun was in the sky, but they'd made a fire by the hut—not so much a fire as a smudge to keep the mosquitoes off. Just a tiny bit of flame but plenty of smoke. Well, as they looked at it, a tiny little maid appeared in the smoke. Just like the one they'd seen that other time, only her sarafan was darker and her kerchief too. She looked at them with merry eyes, her teeth gleamed, she flourished her kerchief and began to dance.

First she made a small circle, then it got bigger and bigger and she began to grow too. The hut was in her way but it didn't hinder her. She danced right through it as though it wasn't there at all. Round and round she went, and when she got as big as Fedyunka she stopped under a big pine. She laughed, stamped her foot, flourished her kerchief and gave a whistle: "Fi-i-it—iu-u-u!"

And at once an owl hooted and laughed. Grandad Yefim was amazed.

"What's an owl doing here, with the sun still high?"

"You'll see! That owl's frightened our luck away again. Mebbe it's that owl the Dancer ran from."

"Why, did you see the Dancer?"

"Why, didn't you see her?"

They started asking each other what they'd seen and they found it was just the same, except for the place where the Fire-Maid had stamped, and there they'd seen her under different pines.

When they got to that, Grandad Yefim sighed.

"Eh-heh-heh! Seems like it was naught after all. Just our fancy."

Almost before he'd said it, smoke came curling out under the turf that roofed the hut. They dashed in and found the pole that supported it all smouldering. By good fortune they'd got water near. So they soon put it out.

There was nothing damaged save Grandad's mittens, they were burned a bit. And when Fedyunka picked them up he found the holes burned in them were just the shape of tiny feet. He showed this marvel to Grandad Yefim.

"Mebbe ye'll say that's just fancy too?"

Well, Yefim could find no word to say against that.

"Ye're right, Fedyunka. It's a true token—the Fire-Maid was here. We'll have to dig in the morn, try our luck."

They spent Sunday on that work. They dug three holes but not a sign of gold did they find. Grandad Yefim complained: "Our fortune's but a mockery."

Fedyunka blamed the owl again.

"That pop-eye hooted and laughed our luck away. I wish I could get at him with a stick!"

On Monday morning the miners came back from the village and saw fresh-dug holes right by the hut. They guessed the cause at once, and laughed at the old man.

"Our Radish has been digging radishes!"

Then they saw there'd been the beginning of a fire in the hut and changed over to storming at the two. Fedyunka's father rushed at the boy like a bear and was just going to beat him, but Grandad Yefim held his hand.

"Shame on ye, to beat a boy! As it is he's afeard to go home, for he's jeered at and hounded right and left. And is the fault his? I stopped here, blame me if ye've lost aught. I must ha' knocked out my pipe before it was dead, and that started the fire. The fault was mine, let the blame be mine too."

Aye, he chided Fedyunka's father. But later, when none were by, he said to the boy: "Eh, Fedyunka lad, she's laughing at us, that Dancer. If we see her again we'd best just spit in her face. Why must she lead folks astray and make them a laughing-stock!"

But Fedyunka still kept stubbornly to his way. "She doesn't do it a-purpose, Grandad. It's the owl hinders her."

The old man went on growling, but Fedyunka was sorry for the Fire-Maid.

"Don't be angry with her, Grandad. Look how jimp and pretty she is. She'd show us our fortune if the owl didn't stop her."

Grandad Yefim said naught about the owl, but he kept growling about the Dancer.

"A fine fortune she's given us! We're ashamed to go home, even."

However much Grandad growled, Fedyunka stuck to his own way.

"But how pretty she is when she dances, Grandad!"

"She dances pretty all right, but what good is that to us? I've no mind to look at her, even."

"Well, I'd watch her now if I could," sighed Fedyunka, and then he asked: "And you, Grandad—would ye turn your back? Doesn't she gladden your eyes?"

"Of course she does." It just slipped out of the old man, but then he stopped himself and began scolding Fedyunka. "A stubborn lad ye are, real stubborn. Get something in your head, and there's no getting it out! Ye'll be the same as me, go chasing after fortune your whole life long, and mebbe it's just a will-o'-the-wisp, naught else."

"How could there be naught when I've seen her myself?"

"Well, chase after it all ye want, but I stop quiet. I've chased enough. My legs ache wi' it."

They might argue all they would but they stayed good friends. At work Grandad Yefim taught Fedyunka, showed him all the ways of it, and when they were resting, told him stories of things he'd seen and done. Well, he just taught him how to live. And the best days were when they were alone at the gold-field.

Winter drove the miners home. The bailiff gave them other work to do till spring, all but Fedyunka, he was still too young so he was left at home. But life at home wasn't honey. And then came fresh trouble—his father was hurt at the iron works, so they took him to the sick-house. He lay there like dead. And then the stepmother got worse than ever, she gave the boy no peace day or night. He bore it as long as he could, then he said: "I'm going to live with Grandad Yefim."

What did she care? "Get out, then!" she screamed. "Go to your Dancer if ye want!"

So Fedyunka put on his felt boots and fastened his thin sheepskin tightly round him. He wanted to take his father's warm cap, but his stepmother wouldn't give it him, so he put on his own though it was much too small for him, and went.

As soon as he showed his nose outside the children came running after him, mocking him.

"Fedyunka Fire-Dancer! Fedyunka Fire-Dancer! Tell us about the Fire-Maid."

Fedyunka just went straight on. All he said was: "Eh, rattlepates!"

Then the children got a bit ashamed, and they asked him, quite friendly: "Where are you going?"

"To Grandad Yefim."

"Golden Radish?"

"Some call him Radish. I call him Grandad."

"It's a long way. You'll get lost."

"I know the path."

"Then you'll freeze. It's cold and you've no mittens."

"I've no mittens but I've got hands and I've got sleeves. Push my hands up my sleeves and they'll be warm. Didn't think o' that, did ye?"

The boys liked the way Fedyunka talked to them and they began asking him again, but without any mockery: "Fedyunka, did you really see that Dancer in the fire?"

"I saw her in the fire and I saw her in the smoke," said Fedyunka. "Mebbe I'll see her again somewhere, but I've no time to tell you about it all now." And he went his way.

Grandad Yefim used to live at Kossoi Brod, or maybe it was Severnaya. His hut was right at the edge of the hamlet, they say. And there was an old pine growing in front of the window. It was a long way, and bitter cold, the very middle of winter. Our Fedyunka was soon frozen to the bone. But he kept right on till he got there. He was just going to lift the latch when he suddenly heard: "Fi-i-it—iu-u-u!"

He looked round and saw a little flurry of snow on the road, and a sort of snowball in the middle of it; and that snowball looked like the Dancer.

Fedyunka ran closer to take a look, but before he got to the spot it was far away. He ran after it, but it went farther. So he kept running after the snowball till he got to a place he didn't know at all. It was a sort of glade, with the forest thick all round. In the middle of the glade stood a birch tree, very old, it seemed quite dead. The snow had drifted high all round it. The snowball rolled up to that tree and started circling round it.

Fedyunka was so eager he never noticed there was no path, he waded through the deep snow. I've gone so far, he thought, I'm not turning back now.

He got to the birch tree and the snowball fell apart, filling his eyes with snowdust.

Fedyunka could have cried with anger. But suddenly the snow melted round his feet and left a hollow. And at the bottom of that hollow he saw the Dancer. She gave him a merry look and a kind smile, then she flourished her kerchief and began to dance, and the snow melted in front of her. Wherever her foot fell there was green grass and flowers.

She danced round in a circle and Fedyunka felt quite warm; she kept making the circle wider and wider, and growing all the time, and the patch of grass and flowers grew too. Leaves were rustling in the birch tree. And the Fire-Maid danced all the faster and began to sing.

With me it's warm,
With me it's bright,
Golden summer-time!

She whirled round and round till her sarafan stood out like a bubble.

When she got to Fedyunka's size there was a big patch of grass and flowers all round, and birds were singing in the birch tree. It was as hot as the middle of summer. Drops of sweat rolled down Fedyunka's nose, he took off his cap and wanted to take off his sheepskin too. But the Fire-Maid cried: "Keep the heat you've got! Better be thinking of how you're going to get back, lad!"

Fedyunka had his answer pat.

"You led me here, you can lead me back again!"

The maid laughed at that. "Got a quick tongue, haven't ye? But what if I say I've no time?"

"You'll find time. I can wait."

"Take that spade, then," said the Fire-Maid. "It'll warm ye in the snow and lead ye home."

Fedyunka looked round and saw an old spade lying by the birch tree. It was all rusty and the handle was cracked.

He picked up the spade and the Fire-Maid warned him: "Mind, don't let it out of your hands! Hold it fast! And mark the path, for the spade won't lead ye back again. But ye'll be coming with the spring, won't ye?"

"That I will. I'll come with Grandad Yefim. Soon's spring comes we'll be here. And you come too, and dance again."

"I've no time. Do your own dancing, and let Grandad Yefim stamp the beat for ye!"

"But what work have you got?"

"Can't you see? I turn winter into summer and amuse lads like you. D'ye think that's naught?"

She laughed, whirled like a top and flourished her kerchief, and gave a whistle: "Fi-i-it—iu-u-u!"

Then the maid was gone, and the grass and flowers were gone, and the birch tree stood bare, as if it was dead. An owl sat high on the top of it. It didn't hoot, but it shook its head. And all round the birch tree the snow was drifted high. Fedyunka sank into it nearly to his head, and he threatened the owl with his spade. There was naught left of the Dancer's summer save that the spade Fedyunka held was warm, even hot. And his hands were warm, and he had a fine glow all through him.

Suddenly the spade gave a tug and pulled Fedyunka right out of the snow. He nearly dropped it at first, but then he learned to follow it, and got forward fast. Sometimes he would walk or run, sometimes it just dragged him through the snow. He liked that, but all the same he didn't forget to stop and blaze the trees. And that was easy, too—as soon as he thought to

187

make a mark, the spade jumped up with a "took-took" and there were a couple of even cuts all ready.

The spade led Fedyunka to Grandad Yefim's hut just as dusk was falling. The old man had cl mbed on the brick stove ledge to sleep. He was real glad to see the boy, of course, and started asking him all the hows and whys. Fedyunka told him all that had happened, but the old man couldn't believe it. Then Fedyunka said: "Take a look at the spade, then. It's standing in the entry."

Grandad Yefim brought the spade in and took a look at it. And there were golden beetles sticking to the rusty parts. Six of them. Then Grandad believed the boy.

"Can ye find the place again?" he asked.

"Of course I'll find it. I marked the way."

The next day Grandad Yefim borrowed skis from a hunter he knew.

They followed the marks with care and found the spot easily. Then Grandad Yefim was quite happy. He sold the golden beetles to a merchant who bought gold secretly, and lived in plenty to the end of the winter.

As soon as spring came they hurried away to the old birch tree. And what d'you think? With the first spadeful they came to such sand, no need to wash it even, they could pick the gold out with their fingers. Grandad Yefim even danced for joy.

But they couldn't keep their wealth secret. Fedyunka was just a child, and though Grandad Yefim was old, he'd little guile.

So folks came crowding in from all round. And then, of course, the Master had them all driven off, and took the place himself. That owl had known something when it shook its head.

Still, Grandad Yefim and Fedyunka did get something for themselves from the first findings. Enough to keep them in comfort for five years or so. Sometimes they'd talk of the Dancer.

"Eh, if she'd but show herself again!"

Well, she never did. But to this day the place is called Dancer's Gold-Field.

1940

THE BLUE SNAKE

There were two boys lived in our village, quite close together—folks called them Lanko the Rabbit and Leiko the Hat.

Who'd given them those nicknames and why, I can't say.

They were good friends, those two. And they matched each other well. One was as clever as the other, one was as strong as the other and they were the same height and the same age. There wasn't much difference in the way they lived either. Lanko's father worked in the ore mine, and Leiko's was at the gold-field washing sand; and both the mothers, of course, were busy with work about the house and yard. So neither could brag to the other.

There was only one thing different about them. Lanko didn't like his nickname, it was as though folks were jeering at him for a coward, while

Leiko didn't mind h's at all, he even liked it, it seemed sort of friendly. He'd often beg his mother: "Make me a new hat. They all call me Leiko the Hat, and I've naught but Father's fur cap and even that's an old one."

That didn't stop the boys being good friends, though. Leiko was the first to hit any boy he heard calling Lanko a rabbit.

"I'll give ye rabbit! Who's he ever been scared of?"

Well, so that's how they lived, always together. They'd quarrel, of course, but it never lasted long. Before you'd time to turn round they were together again.

There was another thing where they were the same—they were both the youngest in the family. And those always have more time to play. There's no little 'uns to look after. From winter's end to winter's beginning they only come home to eat and sleep. Plenty for lads to do—play knucklebones or skittles or ball, or go fishing and swimming, gather berries or mushrooms, climb all the hills, hop round every tree-stump on one foot. Early morning they'd be off, and try to find them after that! But nobody sought them over much. They'd come home at eve and their mothers would scold a bit: "So here ye are, ye vagabond! Roaming about all day, and now feed ye!"

But in winter-time it was different. Winter sends every beast's tail between its legs, and it doesn't spare menfolks either. It drove Lanko and Leiko into their huts. They'd little in the way of warm clothes and what they had on their feet—you couldn't go far in that. It was just enough to hold the warmth from one hut to the other.

They'd usually climb on to the ledge of the big brick stove so as to be out of the grown-ups' way, and sit there. It wasn't so dull when they were together. They might play at something, or they might talk about the summer, or they might just listen to the grown-ups talking.

They were sitting like that one day when some of the maids came to Leiko's sister Maryushka. It was getting near New Year, when it's the custom of our maids to tell fortunes. And that's what they were doing. The boys would have liked to look closer, but the maids wouldn't let them near. Drove them off at once, and Maryushka gave them a couple of clouts over the head too.

"Get back where ye belong!"

A bit of a shrew, she was, that Maryushka. She'd been a maid grown for many years but never a lad had courted her. She was a comely maid enough, but a bit wry-mouthed. Not much of a flaw, you'd say, but because of it the lads would have none of her. Well, it soured her.

The boys got up on the stove, snorted a bit and quietened down; but the maids were merry. They sprinkled ashes, they covered the table with flour, they tossed coal about and splashed each other with water. When they were all wet and dirty they just squealed with laughing at each other; only Maryushka was still downcast. She'd stopped believing in spells.

"It's all foolishness. Just a game."

Then one of the maids said: "There's a real way of knowing your fortune, but it's fearsome."

"What is it?" asked Maryushka. So that maid told her.

"My old Granny said the real way to cast a spell was this. Late at night when they're all asleep you have to hang your comb on a thread from the eaves and take it down in the morn, before they're awake. There'll be a sign that'll tell ye all."

Well, the other maids were all agog to be told the sign. So that one whose Granny had told her explained it.

"If there's a hair in the comb then ye'll be wed within the year. If there's none, then it's not your fate. And ye can tell by the hair what your man's hair'll be like."

Lanko and Leiko harkened to it all, and guessed Maryushka'd be sure to try her fortune that way. And they both had a grudge against her because of that clout over the head. "Just you wait!" they said. "We'll get even!"

Lanko didn't go home to sleep that night, he stopped with Leiko on the stove. They lay there, snored a bit, but all the time they kept punching each other—watch, keep awake!

When all the grown-ups had gone to sleep, the boys heard Maryushka go out into the entry. They crept after her and watched. She climbed up into the attic and fumbled about on the eaves. They marked the place and got back quick into the hut. Maryushka was right behind them; she was shivering and her teeth chattered. Maybe she was cold, or maybe it was fright. She lay down, shivered a bit more and then they could hear she was asleep. That was what the boys were waiting for. They climbed down, put on any clothes they found and crept quietly out. They'd thought before what they were going to do.

Leiko had a gelding, not quite a roan and not quite a bay, called Golubko. And the boys had got the idea of combing that gelding with Maryushka's comb. It was a bit fearsome in the attic at night, but each wanted to show a bold heart to the other. They found the comb under the eaves, combed some hair from Golubko's coat and put the comb back again. Then they went into the hut and fell fast asleep. They slept late, and when they woke up there was nobody in the hut but Leiko's mother, heating the stove.

Now, this is what had happened while the boys were asleep. Maryushka got up first in the morning and went to take her comb. And it was full of hair! Well, she was real happy, she was going to have a man with curly hair. So she ran to tell her friends all about it. They took a look at the comb, but there seemed something not quite right about that hair. Sort of queer, it looked. They'd never seen hair like that on any of the lads they knew. And then among it all they saw a hair from a horse's tail. So of course they all started laughing at Maryushka.

"It's Golubko that's to come courting you," they said.

Maryushka was put out and cross, she scolded and rated her friends but they just kept on laughing. And they gave her a nickname too—Golubko's Sweetheart.

Maryushka came running home to complain to her mother. But the boys hadn't forgotten those clouts on the head and they started jeering from up on the stove.

"Golubko's Sweetheart! Golubko's Sweetheart!"

Well, Maryushka burst out crying and sobbing, but her mother guessed whose doing it all was and scolded the boys.

"See what ye've done, ye shameless brats! The lads don't come to the maid as it is, and now ye must go and make her a laughing-stock!"

The boys saw the jest had turned out badly for Maryushka, and each blamed the other.

"You started it!"

"Nay, you did!"

Maryushka heard that and knew who'd played the trick on her.

"I hope ye both see the Blue Snake!" she screamed.

Then the mother turned on Maryushka. "Hold your tongue, ye ninny! Talking that way! Ye'll bring down trouble on the whole house!"

But Maryushka only said: "What do I care! I wish I'd never been born!"

She slammed the door behind her and ran out into the yard, and there she went chasing Golubko with a wooden spade as though it was his fault. Her mother went out, scolded the maid, brought her back in and tried to talk her round. The boys saw they'd be better out of the way so they went to Lanko's. They got up on the stove and sat there quiet as mice. They were sorry for Maryushka but what could they do now? And that about the Blue Snake, they couldn't get it out of their heads. They asked each other in whispers: "Leiko, have ye ever heard of that Blue Snake?"

"Never in my life, have you?"

"Nay, I haven't either."

They whispered about it a bit, then they decided to ask the grown-ups when the trouble blew over. And that's what they did. When folks had forgotten the trick they'd played on Maryushka, they tried to find out. But whoever they asked put them off with "I know naught of it," or even threatened them: "I'll take a stick and warm your hides! Let such things be!"

That made the boys even more curious. What sort of snake could it be that they mustn't even talk about?

But luck helped them. One day, a holiday it was, Lanko's father came home a bit tipsy and sat down on the earthen bank round the hut wall. Now, the boys knew he got talkative when he'd had a drop, so Lanko took his chance.

"Father, have ye ever seen the Blue Snake?"

That seemed to sober the man at once, he even got further away and muttered spells.

"Avaunt! Avaunt! Harken not, harken not, hearth and home! Not here that word was spoken!"

Then he warned the boys never to say anything like that again, but the wine was still in him and he himself wanted to talk. So after he'd sat a bit without a word spoken, he said to them: "Come to the river bank. It's a better place to talk freely of—of this and that."

They went to the bank. Lanko's father lighted his pipe, then he looked carefully all round about.

"All right, I'll tell ye," he said, "or ye may work mischief with your tongues. Harken, then.

"There's a little snake in our parts, bright blue. It's not more than seven inches long and so light it's no weight at all. When it goes over the grass it doesn't bend a single blade. And it doesn't crawl like other snakes do, it curls itself into a hoop with its head in front, and lifts itself up on its tail and jumps along—so quick ye'd never catch it. And when it jumps like that, it sends a shower of gold out on the right and a soot-black shadow on the left.

"If ye see it when you're alone it's real good fortune, for ye'll surely find surface gold where that shine went. And a lot of it. It'll be in big nuggets, right on top. But there's a catch in that too. If you pick up too much and drop any of it, even a little bit, then it all turns into plain stone. And ye can never come back for more because ye never find the place again, it goes right out o' your memory.

"But if the Snake comes to two or three together, or to an artel, then it's black sorrow. They all start quarrelling and such a hate comes on them, they can fight to the death. My father, he was sent away to jail because of that Blue Snake. They were sitting talking, the artel, when it came along. Well, and then there was a fight. Two were killed, and the other five went to jail. And there was no gold at all. That's why folks don't like to talk about the Blue Snake. They're afraid it may come when there are two or three of them together. And it can come anywhere—in the woods or the fields, in the hut or in the street. Aye, and they say there's times it takes the shape of a person, but you can always know it. Because it doesn't leave any tracks on the softest sand. Even the grass doesn't bend under it. That's the first sign, and the second is the gold falling from the right sleeve and the black dust coming from the left."

That's what Lanko's father told them, and then he warned them both: "Mind ye never tell anyone all this, and never even think of the Blue Snake when you're together. But if you're alone and no one round, then yell about it if ye like."

"And how d'ye call it up?" the boys asked.

"That," he said, "I don't know and I wouldn't tell ye if I did. For it's a dangerous business."

So their talk ended. Lanko's father warned them again to hold their tongues and never even to think of the snake when they were together.

At first the boys were careful, they'd keep reminding one another: "Mind out, see ye don't ever talk of—*that*, and don't think of it when we're together. Think of it when you're alone."

But what good was that when they were always together, and they couldn't get that Blue Snake out of their heads?

It was getting warmer. Water was running down in brooklets and streams everywhere. And where'll you find any better games than you can have with the water when it comes alive again—floating boats, making dams, or setting flutter-mills going? But the street where the boys lived went straight down to the pond and the streams ran away into it and stopped long before the boys were tired of playing with them. What should they do now? They each took a spade and away they went out of the village. There'd be streams coming down from the woods for a long time, they thought, they could play with any of them. And they were right. So they chose the best place and began making a dam. But then an argument started about which could do it best. They decided to settle it—each would make a dam alone. So they went different ways along the stream, Leiko went further down and Lanko maybe fifty paces up. They'd call to each other: "Oooh, look at mine!"

"And mine—you could build a water-mill by it!"

All the same, it was work. They both set about it seriously and soon kept their breath for the job, each one wanting to do it best. Now, Leiko had a way of singing when he was working, and he'd put any words to the tune, so long as they rhymed. He started that way now. And what came out was:

> *Are you awake,*
> *Little Blue Snake?*
> *Come along down the trail*
> *Hopping gaily on your tail!*

Then he saw something like a blue wheel rolling down the slope. It was so light the dry blades of grass didn't bend under it. It got quite close and Leiko saw it was a snake rolled up in a ring; then it pushed out its head and started hopping along on its tail. And golden sparks showered out from one side and a darkness from the other. Leiko stared at it, and the same moment Lanko shouted: "Look, Leiko, there it is—the Blue Snake!"

He found Lanko had seen the very same thing, but the snake had come up the hill to him. And as soon as Lanko shouted, the snake disappeared. Then the boys ran to each other to talk about it, each one boasting of what he'd seen.

"I saw its eyes plain as plain!"

"And I saw the tail. It stands up on it and hops."

"Didn't I see it too? It stuck out from the ring."

Leiko was a bit quicker on the uptake, and he ran back to his pool for the spade.

"Now we'll get the gold," he cried.

He came running with the spade and was just going to dig on the side where he saw the gold shine, when Lanko flew at him.

"Stop, what are you doing? You'll bring down sorrow! That's where black trouble was strewn!"

He pushed Leiko away, and Leiko yelled back and tried to stand his ground. Well, in the end it got to a fight. Lanko had it easier, he'd the hill behind him so he pushed Leiko down and kept on yelling: "You shan't dig there, you shan't! You'll bring sorrow on yourself! We must dig the other side!"

196

Then Leiko started on him. "I'll not let you! It'll bring misfortune! You saw yourself that was the side the black dust fell!"

So they went on fighting. Each was trying to keep the other from misfortune, and pummelling him to do it. They fought till they both got to crying. Then they stopped to think it all over and found out what had happened. They'd seen the snake from different sides, that was why left for one was right for the other. The boys marvelled.

"Look how it twisted us round. We each saw it coming to us. It just made a mock of us, got us fighting; and no chance to find the right spot now. Well, snake, we won't call you again, and don't take it ill. We know how, but we won't call you."

That's what they said, but all the same they couldn't get it out of their heads—they wanted another look at the snake. And each one was thinking—what if he tried it alone? But they were scared, and each one felt sort of awkward before the other. So a fortnight passed, or maybe more, and no word was said about the Blue Snake. Then Leiko spoke:

"What if we call the Blue Snake once more? Only we must both see it from the same side."

"And we must look to it we don't get fighting," Lanko added. "Think first, see if there's some trick."

They settled it that way, and then they each took a hunk of bread and a spade and went to the same place again. Spring had come early that year and young grass covered all the old brown turf. The streams of spring water had dried up and a lot of flowers were out. The boys went to their old ponds, stopped by Leiko's and started to sing.

> Are you awake,
> Little Blue Snake?
> Come along down the trail
> Hopping gaily on your tail!

They stood side by side as they'd settled. And because it was so warm, both were barefoot. Well, before they'd finished the rhyme, the Blue Snake

197

jumped out of Lanko's pond. It hopped quickly down over the young grass. And there was a thick cloud of gold sparks coming out on the right and a thick black cloud on the left. It made straight for the boys. They were just going to let it in between them when Leiko found his wits, took hold of Lanko's belt and pulled Lanko in front of him.

"Don't stop in the black side," he whispered.

But the snake was too clever for them, it shot down between their straddled legs. And each had one trouser leg all gilt while the other was black as if it had been smeared with pitch. But the boys didn't see that, they watched what would happen next. The snake hopped to a big tree-stump and then it vanished. They ran up to the stump and saw one side of it was all gold, and the other as black as could be, and hard as stone. And beside the stump there was a trail of stones, the ones on the right yellow and the ones on the left black.

Of course the boys didn't know the weight of gold nuggets. Lanko picked one up without stopping to think and felt at once it was too heavy for him, he'd never be able to carry it. But he feared to drop it, he minded what his father had told them—if you drop the tiniest bit it all turns into plain ordinary stone. So he called to Leiko: "Pick a smaller one! This is real heavy!"

Leiko heeded and took a smaller one, but that was heavy too, and he could tell Lanko would never be able to carry his home.

"Drop it," he called, "or you'll do yourself an injury." But Lanko answered: "If I drop it, it'll all turn into plain stone."

"Drop it, I tell you," Leiko shouted but Lanko still argued—no, I mustn't. Well, in the end they got to fighting again. They pummelled each other till they were both crying, then they went to take another look at the stump and the trail of stones, but none of it all could they find. Only an ordinary tree-stump and no stones at all, either gold or any other kind.

"It's all tricks with that snake," the boys told each other. "We'll never think of it again."

Off they went home, and found themselves in trouble because of their trousers. The two mothers warmed their hides, but marvelled.

"How did they manage to get themselves dirty both the same way! One leg all clay and the other pitch! Some trick, I'll be bound!"

Well, the boys were really angry with the Blue Snake.

"We won't talk of it any more!"

This time they kept their word. Not a thing did either of them say about the Blue Snake, they even kept away from the place where they'd seen it.

One day they went berrying. They each got a basketful, then they came to a meadow and sat down to rest. They sat there in the high grass, talking a bit—who'd got the most berries and whose were the biggest. Neither one nor the other had a thought of the Blue Snake. And then they saw a woman coming towards them across the meadow. They didn't pay any heed at first, plenty of women in the woods at that time, some berrying, some cutting hay. But then they noticed a strange thing. She came so lightly it was as if she was floating, not walking. And when she got closer they saw that not a flower or blade of grass bent under her. And they looked again and there was a golden cloud hanging on her right and a black cloud on her left.

The boys said to each other: "We'll turn our backs. We won't look. Or she'll make us fight again."

That's what they did. They turned their backs on the woman and shut their eyes tight as well. Suddenly they felt something lift them. They opened their eyes and saw they were sitting in the same place, but the grass that had been crushed was standing again, and round them were two wide rings, one gold and the other of black stone. The woman must have gone all round them and shaken the rings out of her sleeves. The boys jumped up to run away, but the ring of gold wouldn't let them out. As soon as they wanted to step over it, it rose up, and it wouldn't let them get underneath it either. The woman just laughed.

"There's none can get out of my rings till I take them away myself."

Then Leiko and Lanko started pleading. "We never called ye!"

"I came of myself," she said. "I wanted to take a look at lads who think to get gold without working for it."

"Let us go," the boys begged, "we'll never do it again. You've made us fight twice as it is!"

"Not every fight," she said, "is worthy of blame, some can even merit praise. You fought with good intent. Not for selfishness or greed, but to save one another. 'Tis not without cause the ring of gold protects you from the ring of black. But I want to try you once again."

She poured gold dust from her right sleeve and black dust from her left, mixed them on her palm and they became a slab of black-gold stone. Then she scratched it with her finger-nail and it fell into two halves. She gave one to each of the boys.

"If one of you wishes something really good for another, his will turn into pure gold, but if it's something trifling, it'll be a stone you can throw away."

Now, for a long time the boys had had Maryushka on their conscience for the unkind trick they'd played her. She'd not said another word to them about it, but they could see she was downcast. So they thought of that now, and each of them wished that folks should forget the nickname Golubko's Sweetheart, and that Maryushka should wed.

As soon as they'd thought the wish, the slabs in their hands turned to gold. And the woman smiled.

"Your wish was a good one. And here's your reward."

She gave each a small leather wallet tied at the top with a thong.

"This is gold dust," she said. "If the grown-ups ask where you got it, tell them: 'The Blue Snake gave it us, and said we shouldn't go for more.' They'll not venture to ask you further."

Then the woman stood the rings up on edge, rested her right arm on the ring of gold and her left arm on the ring of black—and rolled away over the meadow. The boys looked—and it wasn't a woman any more, but the Blue Snake, and the two rings had become dust, golden on the right and black on the left.

They stood where they were a bit, then put their gold slabs and the wallets in their pockets and started off for home. But Lanko said: "She didn't give us so much gold dust, all the same."

"Likely as much as we deserve," Leiko answered.

On the way Leiko felt his pocket getting heavy. He took out the wallet and found it grown bigger. So he asked Lanko: "Has your wallet grown?"

"Nay, it's just what it was."

Leiko felt awkward about it, that they'd not got the same, so he said: "Let me put some of my dust into yours."

"All right," said Lanko, "if ye don't grudge it."

The boys sat down by the path and opened their wallets; they wanted to make them equal but found they couldn't. Leiko took a handful of gold dust from his wallet and it turned into black dust. Then Lanko said: "Mebbe it's just another trick."

He took a pinch out of his own wallet but it stopped the way it was, gold dust. He put the pinch into Leiko's wallet and it didn't alter. Then Lanko guessed what it was—the Blue Snake had given him less because he'd been greedy, grumbled at the gift being small. He said that to Leiko—and his wallet began to fill up as he watched. So they both came home with wallets stuffed. They gave the gold dust and the slabs to their parents and said what the Blue Snake had told them.

Well, folks were real glad, of course, and at Leiko's hut there was more good news, matchmakers had come from another village to ask for Maryushka. She was running about all gay and merry, and her mouth had got quite straight. Maybe it was from happiness. The suiter had brown curly hair, with a bit of grey in it, that's true, but he had merry ways and was kind to the boys. They soon made friends with him.

The boys never called the Blue Snake again. They'd learned it would reward them itself if they deserved it, and fortune was always with them both. Seemed as if the snake remembered them and kept the ring of black away from them with the ring of gold.

1945

THE KEY TO THE EARTH

S eeking gems is a trade I've never had much liking for. I've found them, at times, but just by chance. You happen to be looking at pebbles washed down and you see something sparkling. Well, you pick it up and show it to someone with knowledge of those things—shall I keep it or throw it away?

With gold, now, it s simple. Of course there's different kinds with that too, some better, some worse; but it's not like those stones. With them neither size nor weight have any meaning. You can have a big one and a small one, they both shine the same, but when they're tested you find they're different. And for the big one folks won't give a copper, while they're all eager after the little one—amazing water, they say, it'll have the real fire.

There's times it's queerer still. They'll buy a stone from you and right there you watch them chip off half of it and throw it away. "That only spoils it," they'll say, "it dims the fire." And then they'll grind off half of what's left, and sing the praises of it too—"There's the pure water, now it'll sparkle so it'll shame the lamps!" And it's right, the stone'll end up tiny, but as if it was alive and laughing. But what it costs—that's no laughing matter, you hear it and gasp. Nay, I can make naught of those things.

But all that talk about stones that keep you from sickness, and stones that guard you when you're sleeping, or keep sorrow away and all the rest of it, that's just idle chatter to my mind, naught else. Though there is one tale about stones I heard from my old folks that took my fancy. It's a nut with a good kernel, for those with sound teeth to crack it.

They say there's a stone somewhere under the ground, and no other like it anywhere, it's the only one. None have ever found that stone. Not just in our land, but in other lands too, but the word of it's known all over. And the stone is under our soil. The old folks found that out. No one knows the spot where it is, but that's no matter, for the stone will come itself to the hand of the right one. That's another thing special about it. Folks learned it all from a young maid. This is the way they say it was.

Near Murzinka, or maybe it was some other place, there was a big ore mine. They found gold and all sorts of gems there. It was Crown land, those days. And the officials with their bright buttons—butchers in uniform, they were—used to drive folks to work with beat o' drum, and drum them through the lines running the gauntlet, with stripes raining down on them. A real place of torment, it was.

In the midst of it all was that little girl, Vasenka. She was born at the mine and she lived there, summer and winter. Her mother was a sort of cook at the barrack where the foremen lived; as for her father, Vasenka knew naught of him.

No need to tell you the sort of life children of that kind lived. Men had to hold their tongues under all the torment, but then it would get too much for them and then they'd curse her or clout her over the head because they had to let it out on someone. Aye, it was a bitter life she had. Worse than an orphan's. And there was none could save her from being put to work early, either. A child, with hands hardly strong enough to hold the reins, and she was put to carting. "Carry sand instead of getting under folks' feet!"

As soon as she grew a bit bigger she was given a board and sent off with the other maids and women to search the sand for gems. And then they found Vasenka had a real knack for it. She found more than any others, and all good ones, really valuable.

She was a simple-hearted maid, what she found she handed in at once to those over her. And glad they were, of course. Some they put in the bank, some in their pockets and some in their cheek. You know the old saying—what a big man puts in his pocket a little one has to hide. And one and all praised Vasenka as though they'd chosen the words together. They gave her a nickname too—Lucky Eye. As soon as one of them came along he'd make straight for Vasenka.

"Well, Lucky Eye, have you something worth looking at?"

Vasenka would give him what she had, and he'd gobble away like a goose. "Good, good, go-o-od! Seek well, my girl, seek well!"

Vasenka did seek, for she liked doing it.

Once she found a stone the size of her thumb and all the big folk came running to take a look. So that time no one could steal it, they had to send it to the bank. And after, folks say, it was taken from the Tsar's treasury to some foreign land. But that's not what I wanted to tell you.

Vasenka's luck made it worse for the other women and maids, the foremen never let them alone.

"Why can she find all those, and you bring us rubbish and little of that? You seek with only half a heart."

Instead of giving Vasenka good counsel the women banded together in spite against her. And her life wasn't worth living. And then a cur came slavering round, the chief foreman. He'd a nose for Vasenka's good fortune, so he said: "I'll wed that maid."

His teeth had all rotted away long before and on top of that you couldn't come within five paces of him for the stench, as if he'd rotted away inside too. And he kept snuffling: "I'll make a lady of ye, my maid. Mind that, and the stones you find give to me and to no one else. Don't let others even see them."

Vasenka was tall but she wasn't near the age to wed. She might have been thirteen, or fourteen maybe. But who'd pay heed to that if it was the foreman? The priest would write any age in the book. Well, Vasenka was real scared. Her hands shook and her legs too when she saw that rotting suiter. She'd make haste to give him all she'd found, and he'd keep rumbling: "Seek well, Vasenka, seek well! Come winter, you'll be sleeping in a feather bed."

As soon as he's gone the women would start jibing and jeering at Vasenka, and she was ready to tear herself to bits as it was, if she'd been able. After the evening drum she'd run to her mother in the barrack, but that only made it all worse. The mother was sorry for her, of course, tried to protect her all she could, but what could the barrack cook do when it was the chief foreman? He could hale her to the flogging post any day he wanted.

Vasenka managed to hold him off till winter, but she could do no more. He started coming to her mother every day.

"Give me the maid wi' good will, or it'll be the worse for ye."

No use saying the maid was too young to wed, he'd push that paper from the priest under her nose.

"Will you try to lie to me! The church book says she's sixteen. The lawful age. Better not cross me more, or I'll have ye to the whipping post tomorrow."

So the mother had to give way.

"Seems it's your fate, Daughter, and you can't escape it."

And the maid? Her arms and legs went weak, and not a word could she say. But by nightfall it passed over and she ran away from the mine. She didn't even take any special care, she just went straight off down the road, but where that road led she never even thought. All she wanted was to get as far away as she could.

The weather was warm with no wind, and at eve snow began to fall. Gentle flakes like little feathers. The road took her into the forest. There'd be wolves and other wild animals, but Vasenka didn't fear them. She'd made up her mind.

"Better be eaten by wolves than wed stinking offal."

So on and on she went. At first she stepped out bravely. She covered fifteen versts or maybe twenty. Her clothes weren't much to speak of but she wasn't cold, she even felt hot. The snow was deep, up to her knees, she could hardly plough through it, and that warmed her. And it kept on falling, thicker than ever, a real mass of it. Vasenka got tired at last, she felt she couldn't go another step, so she sat down by the roadside.

I'll rest a bit, she thought—she didn't know it's the worst thing you can do, to sit down in an open place in weather like that.

She sat there looking at the snow, and it kept on falling and clung to her. After she'd sat a bit she felt she just couldn't get up. But she wasn't afraid, she just thought: I'll have to sit a bit longer, rest myself properly.

Well, she rested. The snow covered her right up, she was like a shock of hay standing by the road. And there was a village near.

By good fortune one of the villagers came by in the morning—in summer time he used to seek gold, and stones too. Well, he came by with a horse and sledge, and the horse stopped and snorted and didn't want to go near that shock. Then the man took a look and saw it was some person buried in snow. He went up close and found the body wasn't frozen through, he could bend the arms. So he put Vasenka on the sledge, covered her with his sheepskin and off home with her. Then he and his wife set to work to thaw her and bring her to life again. And they managed it. She opened her eyes and her fingers loosened. And there in one hand lay a great shining stone, pure blue water. The man was really scared when he saw it, a thing like that could take you to jail, so he asked: "Where did you get that?"

"It flew into my hand by itself," said Vasenka.

"What? How—?"

So Vasenka told him all about it.

When the snow began to cover her right up, a passage into the earth suddenly opened in front of her. It wasn't very wide and it was dark too, but you could go along it. She could see steps, and it was warm. Vasenka was glad. None from the mines will ever find me here, she thought, and went down the steps. She went on for a long time till she came to a great field, so big there seemed no end to it. The grass grew in tufts and there were a few bushes scattered about, all of them yellow as they are in autumn. A river ran across the middle, and it was smooth and black with never a ripple as though it were black stone. On the other side, just opposite Vasenka, was a little mound and on top of it a big stone like a table and smaller ones round it like stools. But not the size folks use, much bigger. It was cold and sort of fearsome there.

Vasenka was just going to turn round and go back when a lot of sparks flew up behind the mound, and when she looked again she saw a pile of precious stones lying on the table. They sparkled all colours, and made the river seem less gloomy too. It was a joy to look at them.

Then somebody asked: "Who are these for?"

From down below came a shout: "For the simple."

The same instant the stones flew away to all sides like a shower of coloured sparks.

Another fiery flicker from behind the mound threw a fresh pile of stones on the table. A lot of them. Enough maybe to fill a hay waggon. And the stones were bigger. Again someone asked: "Who are these for?"

From below came the answer: "For the patient."

Just as before, the stones flew away to all sides. It was as if a swarm of May bugs were flying, only they shone all colours, some glowed red and some were green and there were blue and yellow—all sorts. And they hummed as they flew. While Vasenka was watching those May bugs, the fiery light came up behind the mound again and another pile of stones lay on the table. This time it was quite small, but all the stones were big ones and of great beauty. And the voice from below shouted:

"These are for the daring and for Lucky Eye."

The next moment the stones swooped and flew away to all sides like little birds. They were like tiny lamps swaying over the field. They flew quietly, without haste. And one stone flew to Vasenka and nestled in her hand like a kitten wanting its head stroked—here I am, take me!

When all the stones had flown away like birds, it got quiet and dark. Vasenka waited to see what would happen next. Then one stone appeared on the table. It looked just an ordinary one, with five facets, three lengthwise and two crosswise. And at once everything got light and warm, and the grass and trees turned green, the river sparkled and rippled. Where there had been bare sandy soil there was now thick, tall grain. People were there too, and they all looked happy. Some seemed like they were going home from work, and these were singing.

Then Vasenka herself called out: "Who's that for?"

The voice from below answered her: "For him who finds the true path for the people. This stone is the key which will open up the earth for him, and then what you have just seen will come to pass."

With that the light went out and everything vanished.

At first the prospector and his wife were chary of believing her, but then they thought—where could she have got such a stone as that one in her hand! They asked where she came from and who she was, and she told them all about herself, keeping naught back. And she begged them: "Don't let them know back there where I am!"

They thought it over a bit, the man and his wife, and then they said: "All right, stop here and live with us. We'll hide ye somehow, but we'll call ye Fenya. Remember, that's the name you answer to."

Their own daughter had died not long before, you see—Fenya had been her name. And she'd been just the same age as Vasenka. And another thing that would help, the village wasn't on Crown land, it was on the Demidov estate.

So that's how it ended. The Master's Elder marked at once that the maid was new to the place, but what did he care? It wasn't him she'd run away from. An extra pair of working hands was no bad thing. So he just gave her her task with the other folks.

Of course life wasn't all honey on the Demidov estate either, but it wasn't like the Crown mines all the same. And the stone Vasenka had had in her hand helped too. The miner managed to sell it secretly. He didn't get its real price, of course, but all the same he got a good sum. So they were able to live easier for a bit.

When Vasenka was a maid grown she wedded a lad in the village. And with him she lived till she was old, and reared children and grandchildren.

Granny Fedosya, as she was called, maybe came to forget her old name and her nickname of Lucky Eye, and she never spoke of the mine. But when folks talked of lucky finds, then she always had her word to say.

"Little skill it needs," she'd say, "to find good stones, but it's little fortune they bring our folks, too. 'Twould be better to seek out the key to the earth." And then she'd tell them: "There is a stone, it's the key that opens the earth. But none will find it before the proper time—not the simple, nor the patient, nor the daring, nor the lucky. But when the people take the path which is the right one for all, then he who goes in front and shows the way, into his hand that key to the earth will fly of itself.

"And then all the riches of the earth will be opened and life will be quite different. That's what ye must seek for!"

1940

THE BLUE CRONE'S SPRING

There was once a lad called Ilya in our village. Alone in the world he was, for he'd buried all belonging to him. And each of them had left him something.

From his father he'd shoulders and hands, from his mother sharp teeth and a tongue, from his Grandad Ignat a hack and a spade, and from Granny Lukerya a special remembrance. Let that be told first.

Now—she was real canny, that old woman, she used to pick up feathers in the street and put them by to make a pillow for her grandson, but she didn't have time to finish it. When she felt her end was near, she called Ilya to her.

"Look ye here, Ilya lad, how many feathers your Granny's got together! Nearly a whole sieveful. And what feathers they are—all of a size, little and bright-coloured, a joy to your eye. Take them as a remembrance. They'll come in useful.

"When ye come to wed, if the maid brings a pillow ye'll not be put to shame. Aye, ye can tell her, I've got my own feathers too, my Granny left them me.

"But don't ye seek after it, a feather pillow. If she brings one, take it, but if not—don't fret. If ye live with a gay heart and work hard, ye'll sleep sound on straw and your dreams'll be sweet. Keep bad thoughts from your head and all will go well wi' ye. The bright day will cheer ye, the dark night will caress ye and the golden sun will bring ye joy. But if ye let bad thoughts in, then ye might as well smash your head on a tree-stump, for ye'll have no stomach for aught."

"But what are those bad thoughts, Granny?" asked Ilya.

"Thoughts o' money," she said, "thoughts o' wealth. There's none worse. They bring a man only unease and torment. Honest ways'll not even get ye feathers enough for a pillow, so how'll ye ever get wealth?"

"But then," said Ilya, "what about the wealth underground? Will you say that's bad too? Sometimes it happens—"

"Aye, it happens, but it's not to be reckoned on. Comes in grains and goes in dust, and only brings trouble with it. Don't ye think o' that, don't fret yourself. Of the wealth underground, they say there's only one kind that's clean and sure. That's when the Blue Crone turns into a fair maid and gives it ye wi' her own hands. And she gives it to them as have quick wits and daring and a simple heart. None else. So keep in mind, Ilya lad, my last charge to ye."

Then Ilya bowed low to his grandmother.

"Thank you, Granny Lukerya, for the feathers, but thank you most for your teaching. I'll mind it all my days."

His grandmother died soon after. Ilya was all alone, with none elder and none younger. Of course old women came hurrying along to wash the body and lay it out and perform all the rites. It was bitter want sent those old women to corpses. And some would ask for this or that, and others would spy out what they could take. They soon got hold of all Granny had left. When Ilya came back from the graveyard he found the hut swept bare. He'd naught but what he hung on the nail—his coat and cap. Somebody had even made off with Granny's feathers, emptied the sieve to the bottom. Only three little feathers were left—one white, one black and the third red.

Ilya was grieved that he hadn't been able to take care of his grandmother's gift. I'd better save these last three feathers, at least, he thought. It would be a shame for me to leave them. Granny worked hard to collect them, it's as if I cared nothing for it.

He found a bit of blue thread on the floor, tied the feathers together with it and fastened them in his cap. Just the right place for them, he thought. When I put it on or take it off I'll think of Granny's words. They'll be good guidance for me. I'll always keep them in mind.

Then he put on his cap and coat again and went back to the gold-field. He didn't fasten his hut because there was naught in it. Only the empty sieve, and that wouldn't be worth picking up if it was lying by the roadside.

Ilya was a grown lad, he'd long been of an age to wed. He'd been working at the gold-fields six or seven years. It was serfdom in those times, and lads and maids had to go to work when they were still children. Many a one worked ten years for the Master before wedding. And as for Ilya, you could say he'd grown up at the gold-fields.

He knew all those parts up and down. The road to the gold-fields was a long one. At Gremikha, I've heard tell, they were getting gold nearly by White Stone. So Ilya thought to himself: I'll take a short cut through Zuzelka Bog. It's hot weather, it'll be dried up a bit, I'll be able to get across. I'll save three versts, maybe four.

So that's what he did. He cut straight through the woods, the way folks did in autumn. At first it was easy going, but then he got tired and found himself off the right way. You can't keep a straight path when you're jumping from tussock to tussock. You have to go where they are, and it may not be the way you want. He jumped and jumped, till he jumped himself into a sweat. At last he came to a glade with a hollow in the middle. There was grass growing there—feathergrass and such like, and pines grew up the sides. This was where the dry ground began. The only trouble was, Ilya didn't know which way to go next. With all the times he'd been round about there, he'd never seen that little gully before.

Ilya walked up the middle with the banks rising on both sides. He went on till he came to a little round pool like a spring, only he couldn't see the bottom. The water was clear, but a blue web covered the top; in the middle sat a spider, and that was blue too.

Ilya was glad to see water, he pushed the web away from one side to take a drink. But as he did so his head began to swim and he nearly fell in. He felt real sleepy.

Look how tired I've got on the bog, he thought. I'd better rest an hour or two.

He wanted to get to his feet but couldn't. Still, he did manage to crawl away a couple of yards to the slope. There he put his cap under his head and stretched himself out. He looked back—and there was a little old crone rising up out of the water. She wasn't more than twenty inches tall. Her dress was blue and so was the kerchief on her head, and she was sort of blue herself too, and so thin you'd have thought the first puff of wind would blow her away. But her eyes were young, and so big they didn't seem to belong to her face.

She fixed those eyes on the young fellow and stretched out her arms towards him. They kept growing longer, those arms, until the hands were close to his head. They seemed to have no substance, like wisps of blue mist, there was no strength in them that you could see, there were no claws, and yet they were fearsome. Ilya wished to crawl further away, but weakness overcame him.

I'll turn my head away, he thought, it won't be so awful.

He did so, and his nose came up against the feathers. And at once he had a fit of sneezing. He sneezed and sneezed, blood gushed from his nose, and still he could not stop. But he felt his head get lighter. Then Ilya seized

213

his cap and got on his feet. And there was the crone, standing in the same place, shaking with fury. Her hands stretched to Ilya's feet, but she could lift them no higher from the ground. Ilya saw the crone's scheme had failed, she had not the strength to clutch him. He sneezed a couple of times more and blew his nose.

"So you didn't manage it, eh! The nut's too hard for your teeth!"

He laughed, spat on the hands and turned to go. But the crone called after him, and her voice was as clear and loud as a maid's.

"Wait a bit, don't crow too soon! Ye'll not take your head away safe next time ye come!"

"I just won't come," Ilya answered.

"Aha! Ye're scared! Scared!" the old woman cried gleefully.

That stung Ilya, he stopped and said: "If that's the way, then I'll come just to spite you—and get some water from your spring."

Then the crone laughed and began to jeer at the lad.

"A braggart ye are, a braggart! Ye ought to thank your Granny Luker-ya that ye've got away safe, and here ye are bragging! The man's not born that can drink from this spring!"

"We'll see about that, whether he's born or not," said Ilya.

But the crone kept on. "A windbag, that's all ye are! How'll ye get the water when ye're afeard to come close? Big words and naught else—unless ye bring others wi' ye. More stout-hearted than you are."

"You'll have to wait a long time for that," shouted Ilya, "for me to bring others to you! I've heard tell of ye before, about your ill deeds and how you beguile folks "

But the crone kept on with the same song.

"Ye won't come! Ye won't come! Too big a bite for you to chew! It's not for the likes o' you!"

Then Ilya cried: "All right, then. If there's a good wind Sunday, you can expect me."

"And what d'ye want a wind for?" asked the crone.

"Wait and see," said Ilya. "Wipe the spittle off your hands. And don't you forget."

"And what's it to you," said the crone, "what the hands are like that pull ye down to the bottom? I see ye're a bold lad, but all the same I'll get ye. Ye needn't put your faith in the wind, or your Granny's feathers either. They won't help ye!"

Well, so they parted with hard words and Ilya went his way, marking the path carefully. So that's what she's like, the Blue Crone, he thought. Looks as if she's just clinging to life, but got eyes like a maid's, they'd put a spell on you, and a voice that rings young too. I'd like to see her when she turns into a maid.

Ilya had heard a lot about that Blue Crone. There'd often been talk about her at the gold-fields. Folks might see her in empty bogs or in old mines. And wherever she sat, there would be wealth. If you could get her away, there'd be a whole pile of gold and precious stones. Scoop up as much as you could hold. Many sought her, but they either came back empty-handed or didn't come back at all.

It was evening when Ilya came to the gold-fields. The supervisor sent for him at once.

"Where've you been all this time?"

Ilya explained—he'd buried his Grandmother Lukerya. The supervisor was shamed a bit by that and sought something else to find fault with.

"What are those feathers on your cap? Adorned yourself for a feast?"

"They were left me by my grandmother," said Ilya. "I fastened them there to remember her by."

The supervisor and those who were by laughed at such an inheritance, but Ilya went on: "Aye, and mebbe I'd not change these feathers for all the Master's gold-fields. Because they're not plain feathers, they've got power in them. The white one's for the bright day, the black one's for peaceful nights and the red one's for the golden sunshine."

He spoke in jest, of course. But there was a fellow standing by—Kuzka Double-Snout. He was the same age as Ilya and their name-days were in the same month but that was the end of the likeness. That Double-Snout came from a well-to-do family. By rights he needn't have come to the gold-fields at all, he could have got easier work at home. But Kuzka had been hanging round the fields for a long time with thoughts of his own—mebbe I'll lay hands on something good, I'll be able to get it away all right. And sure it was, he'd guile and long practice in getting other folks' property into his own pocket. Take your eyes off something and before you knew, Double-Snout would have got hold of it, and you'd never see it again. In a word—a thief. He bore a mark for it, too. One miner had left his signature with a spade. It hit him slanting but left a scar for a reminder—his nose was slit to the lips. That's how he got the name Double-Snout.

Now, Kuzka had a bitter envy for Ilya. You see, Ilya was a strong lusty fellow, robust and gay, and his work seemed to get done of itself. When it was finished he'd eat, and then begin singing or maybe set a dance going. In an artel that can happen too. How could Double-Snout compare with a lad like that when he'd neither the strength nor the will, and he'd different things on his mind as well. But Kuzka accounted for it in his own way. . . . Ilya must know some spell, that's why fortune was with him, and he could work without wearying.

When Ilya spoke of the feathers, Kuzka said to himself: That's it, that's where his magic power lies.

So of course that night he stole the feathers.

The next morning Ilya found them all gone. He thought he must have dropped them, and started searching about. Folks laughed at him.

"Where's your wits, lad! All these feet tramping about, and you think to find tiny feathers! They've been crushed long ago. And what's the good of them anyway?"

"What good, when they're my remembrance of Granny!"

"Remembrances you should keep in a safe place," they told him, "or else in your head, not carry them on your cap."

It's true what they say, Ilya thought, and he stopped searching for the feathers. It never even entered his thoughts that ill hands might have taken them.

Kuzka had his own care, to watch how Ilya managed now, without his grandmother's feathers. And he saw Ilya take his mining pan and go into the woods. Double-Snout made after him—he thought Ilya had found gold-bearing sand somewhere. But there was no sign of sand, and Ilya simply set about fixing a long pole to the pan. Over eight yards long, it must have been. That was no good for washing sand. But what could it be for? Kuzka watched closer than ever.

It was near autumn, with strong winds blowing. When Saturday came and the workers at the gold-fields went home, Ilya asked leave to go too. The supervisor made difficulties at first—"Not long since you went, and what d'ye want to go for, at that? You've no family and all the property you'd got, those feathers, you lost.".... But in the end he let him off. And Kuzka would never miss a chance like that, he slipped off in good time to the spot where the pan on the long pole was hidden. He'd a good while to wait, but that's part of a thief's trade. You know the saying—a thief can out-wait a dog, let alone its master.

Early in the morning Ilya came, got out his pan and said aloud: "A pity the feathers are gone. But there's a good wind. It's whistling now, by midday it'll be blowing hard."

The wind was strong enough to make the trees groan with it. Ilya followed his marks, while Double-Snout slunk after him full of glee. "Here they are, the feathers! The ones that show the way to wealth!"

It took Ilya a long time to find his way back by the marks, and all the time the wind was getting less. When he came to the gully it had dropped entirely, not a twig was moving. Ilya looked at the spring and there was the crone standing by it, waiting.

"Ha, the cock-sparrow's back again!" she cried and her voice rang fresh and clear. "You've lost your Granny's feathers and guessed wrong with the wind too. What'll you do now? Run back and wait for a breeze? Mebbe it'll come to help ye!"

She stood a bit to the side, she didn't reach out for Ilya, but there was a mist over the spring like a blue fog, so thick it looked solid. Ilya took a run and thrust the pole with the pan on the end right into the middle of that blue fog; and not only that, he shouted: "Hi, look out, old crone, or I may happen to hit you!"

He scooped a panful from the spring but found the pan so heavy he could hardly get it out. The old woman laughed and her teeth shone white and young.

"Aye, let's see how you'll get your pan back again, whether you'll drink deep of my water!"

Mocked the lad, she did. Ilya felt it really was too heavy for him and lost his temper.

"Drink it yourself," he shouted.

He gathered all his strength, managed to lift the pan a little and tried to pour the water over the crone. She moved. He went after her. She got further off again. Then the pole broke and all the water was spilt. And the old woman laughed again.

"You'd do better to fasten your pan to a tree-trunk. More chance then!"

"You wait, you miserable crone," Ilya threatened. "I'll souse ye yet!"

Then the old woman said: "Well, enough. We've fooled a bit, now let be. I can see you're a daring lad and bold. Come here on a moonlight night, whenever ye will. I'll show ye wealth of all kinds. Take all you can carry. And if I'm not here on top, say only: 'I have brought no pan,' and you'll get all."

"And I'd like well to have you turn into a pretty maid too," said Ilya.

"About that we'll see," laughed the old woman and showed those young teeth again.

Double-Snout saw it all and heard every word.

"I'd better go back to the gold-fields," he thought, "and get some wallets ready. If only Ilya doesn't get it before me!"

So Double-Snout hastened back. But Ilya climbed the slope and made his way home. He crossed the swamp from tussock to tussock, got home and found a surprise—his grandmother's sieve was gone.

Ilya marvelled—who would want a thing like that? He went to see his friends, talked a bit with this one and that, and walked back to the gold-fields with the others, not across the swamp but by the road.

Five days passed and Ilya couldn't get it all out of his head. He thought of it at work and he dreamed of it at night. He'd keep seeing those blue eyes and hearing the ringing voice: "Come here on a moonlight night, whenever ye will."

At last Ilya made up his mind. I'll go. At least I'll see what wealth looks like. And maybe she'll show herself as a fair maid.

There had been a new moon not long before and the nights were getting lighter. And all of a sudden Double-Snout had vanished, everyone was talking about it. They sent to the village but he wasn't there. The supervisor had men search the woods—no sign of him there either. Though truth to tell, they didn't wear themselves out searching. Good riddance to bad rubbish, they thought. And that was the end of it.

Ilya went when the moon was full. He got to the place and found nobody. Still, he did not go down the slope, he only said quietly: "I've come without a pan."

As soon as he had spoken the words the old woman appeared and said kindly: "You're welcome, dear guest! I've waited long. Come and take all ye can carry."

She passed her hands over the spring as if she was opening a lid, and there it was, filled with treasures of every kind. Right up to the top. Ilya would have liked well to take a closer look, but he didn't go down the slope. The crone began to urge him.

"What are ye standing there for? Come and take all ye can put in your wallet."

"I've no wallet with me," he said, "and Granny Lukerya told me different. Only those riches are clean and secure that ye give a man yourself."

"So that's what you're like, no pleasing ye! Want it brought to ye! Well, be it as ye will!"

As the old woman spoke, a column of blue mist rose from the spring. And from this column came a maid, very fair to see, dressed like a tsarina, and half as tall as a good pine tree. In her hands she bore a golden tray heaped up with treasures of all kinds. There was gold dust, and precious stones, and gold nuggets nearly as big as a loaf. And that maid went up to Ilya and with a bow offered him the tray.

"Take it, fair lad!"

Now, Ilya had grown up at the gold-fields, he'd seen gold weighed and could guess the burden. So he looked at that tray and said to the old woman: "You're making a mock of me. There's no man on earth with the strength to lift that."

"Ye won't take it?" asked the old woman.

"No thought of it," Ilya answered.

"Be it as ye will. I'll offer ye another gift," she said.

In an instant the maid with the golden tray had vanished. Again a column of blue mist rose from the spring. And another maid came out. She was smaller. But she was fair too, and her dress was that of a merchant's daughter. In her hands she bore a tray of silver heaped with treasures. But Ilya would not take that tray either.

"It's beyond human strength to lift it," he said. "And besides, you're not giving it me with your own hands."

Then the old woman laughed, and her laugh was like a maid's.

"Very well, be it as ye will! I'll please you and myself too. But see ye don't regret it, after. Wait."

With her last word the maid with the silver tray was gone, and so was the old woman herself. Ilya waited and waited, but no one came. He was getting wearied of it, when he heard the grass rustling away to the side. He turned and saw a maid coming. An ordinary maid of ordinary human height. About eighteen, maybe. Her dress was blue and so was the kerchief on her head, and she had blue slippers on her feet. And fair she was, that maid—no words can tell. Eyes like stars, brows like bows, lips like raspberries and a thick russet braid thrown forward over her shoulder with a blue ribbon on the end of it.

She came up to him and said: "Take this gift, dear Ilya, it is given without guile."

With her own white hands she gave him Granny Lukerya's sieve filled full of berries. There were wild strawberries, and raspberries, and golden cloudberries and black-currants and bilberries. Every kind of berry. The sieve was full to the brim. And on top lay three feathers. One was white, one black and the third red, and they were tied together with blue thread.

Ilya took the sieve and stood there like one who'd lost his wits, he couldn't think where that maid could have come from and where she'd found all those berries in autumn. So he asked her: "Who are you, fair maid, and what's your name?"

Then she laughed and told him: "Men call me the Blue Crone, but to those who have quick wits and daring and a simple heart I show myself as you see me now. Only that comes but rarely."

Then Ilya knew who he was talking to, and asked: "Where did you get the feathers?"

"It was this way," she said. "Double-Snout came looking for wealth. But he fell into the spring and went down, and all his wallets with him. Only these feathers of yours came to the top. It's plain you've a simple heart."

Ilya did not know what more to talk of, and she stood there too and said naught, only played with the ribbon on her braid. At last she spoke.

"So, there it is, dear friend Ilya. I am the Blue Crone. Always old, always young. And placed here to guard the wealth for all time."

She was silent again for a moment, then she asked: "Well, have you looked your fill? Let it suffice, or you'll be seeing me in your dreams." With those words she sighed so it was like a knife in the lad's heart. He would have given all could she but have been a real maid. But she was gone.

For a long time Ilya stood there. The blue mist from the spring spread through the whole gully, and only then he turned to make his way home. It was light when he arrived. And just as he entered the hut, the sieve suddenly got heavy, the bottom tore out and nuggets and precious stones scattered all over the floor.

With wealth like that, Ilya bought his freedom from the Master at once, built himself a new house and bought a horse, but somehow he could not bring himself to wed. For he could not forget that maid. Peace of mind and sleep had left him. And Granny Lukerya's feathers were of no help either. Many a time he said: "Eh, Granny Lukerya, Granny Lukerya! You taught me how to get the Blue Crone's wealth, but how to rid myself of longing—of that you said naught. Likely you didn't know yourself."

So he pined and fretted, and at last he thought: Better go and throw myself in the spring than bear this torment.

He went to Zuzelka Bog, but still he took his grandmother's feathers with him. It was berrying time and folks were going out for wild strawberries.

Just as Ilya came to the woods he met a party of maids. Ten of them, maybe, with full baskets. One of the maids was walking a bit off to the side. About eighteen, she'd be. She'd a blue dress, and a blue kerchief on her head. And fair she was—no words can tell. Eyes like stars, brows like bows, lips like raspberries and a thick russet braid thrown forward over her shoulder with a blue ribbon on the end of it. The very picture of that other one. Only one thing was different—that maid had had blue slippers, while this one's feet were bare.

Ilya stood dumbstruck, staring. And she flashed him a look and another with those blue eyes, and laughed sort of teasing, showing her white teeth. Then Ilya came to himself a bit.

"How's it I've never seen you before?"

"Well, take a look now if it pleases ye," she said. "Ye can have it free, I'll not charge a kopek."

"Where d'ye live?" he asked.

"Go ahead and turn to the right," she said, "ye'll see a big tree-stump. Take a good run and smash your head against it till the sparks fly—then ye'll see me."

She was just teasing him with pert talk, the way maids do. But then she told him who she was and where she lived.

Aye, she told him honest and truthful, and all the time those blue eyes of hers enticed and drew him.

With this maid Ilya found his happiness. But not for long. She came from the marble quarries, you see, that's why he hadn't seen her before. Well, we know what that marble cutting meant. There were no maids fairer in our parts than the ones from there, but he who wed one was soon a widower. They worked with that stone from the time they were children, and they were consumptive one and all.

Ilya didn't live long either. He may have got the sickness from this maid or the other one. But however that may be, a big gold-field was found under Zuzelka Bog. You see, he didn't keep it secret, where he'd got his wealth. So folks started digging there, and came on rich gold.

I can mind the times they used to get a lot there. Only the spring none ever found. But there's a blue mist you can see there today, it always shows where there's gold.

It's little we've done yet, though. Just scraped the top a bit. We've got to go deeper. Far down, they say, is the Blue Crone's well. Real deep. Waiting for those who seek its riches.

1939

SILVER HOOF

There was an old man used to live in our village called Kokovanya. He'd none of his own family left, so he thought he'd take some orphan into his hut to be a child to him.

He asked the neighbours if they knew of anyone, and they told him: "Grigory Potapov's children were left orphans on Glinka not long ago. The bailiff sent the older girls to the manor sewing-room, but there's a little girl of six nobody wanted. That would be the child for ye."

But Kokovanya said: "I'd be unhandy-like wi' a maid. A lad 'ud be better. I'd teach him my trade and he'd help me, too, when he got bigger. But what can I do wi' a maid? What can I teach her?"

But then he thought about it all again. "I knew Grigory and his good-wife too," he said. "They were lusty workers and right merry folk. If the maid takes after them it won't be dull in the hut. I'll have her. But mebbe she won't come?"

"Eh, her life's none so sweet," the neighbours told him. "The bailiff gave Grigory's cottage to some poor devil, and told him to look after the orphan till she grows up. But he's got a dozen of his own. They haven't enough for their own mouths. And the wife nags at the orphan child and grudges her every crust. She's little, but she's big enough to understand. She feels it. Wouldn't ye say she'd want to get away from it all? And then ye'll talk to her a bit, and she'll take to ye."

"Aye, that's true," said Kokovanya. "I'll talk to her kindly-like."

When the next holiday came round he went to the place where the orphan lived. He found the hut crowded with folks, young and old. A little girl sat by the stove nursing a brown cat. The child was small and the cat was small too, so thin and bedraggled it was a wonder anyone would let it in. The child was stroking the cat and it purred so you could hear it all over the hut.

Kokovanya looked a the girl and asked: "Is that Grigory's giftie?"

"The same," said the goodwife. "And as if it's not enough feeding her, she's got to drag in that mangy beast too. We can't get rid of it. And it scratches the children. And then on top of all I've got to feed it!"

"They must tease it, your children," said Kokovanya gravely. "When she has it, it purrs." Then he turned to the child. "Well, Podaryonka,* how'd ye like to come and live wi' me?"

The child stared.

"How d'ye know I'm called Daryonka?"

"It just came," he said. "I didn't think, I didn't know, I just happened on it."

"But who are you?" the child asked.

* Podaryonka—a gift.—Tr.

"I'm a sort of hunter," said Kokovanya. "Summer-time I wash sand and look for gold, and winters I go to the woods and look for the goat, but I never get a sight of it."

"Will ye shoot it if you do?"

"Nay," said Kokovanya, "I shoot ordinary goats, but that one I won't. I want to see where he stamps his right forefoot."

"What for?"

"Come and live wi' me, and I'll tell ye all about it," said Kokovanya.

The little girl wanted very much to hear about the goat, and she could see he was a merry, kind old man. So she said: "I'll come. But take my Pussy too. Look how good she is."

"That's as sure as I stand here," said Kokovanya. "Only a fool would leave a cat that sings like that. She'll be as good as a balalaika in the hut."

The goodwife heard their talk, and she was as glad as could be to get the orphan off her hands. She started putting Daryonka's things together all in a hurry. She was afeard Kokovanya might think better of it.

The cat seemed to understand all about it too. She kept rubbing up against their legs and purring: "R-r-right! You'r-r-re r-r-right!"

So Kokovanya took the orphan home. He was tall and bearded, and she was a bit of a thing with a button nose. Down the street they went with the draggled cat trotting along behind.

That was how they came to live together—Grandad Kokovanya, the orphan Daryonka and Pussy. The days passed, they didn't get rich but they had enough and there was plenty for everyone to do.

In the morning Kokovanya went to work, Daryonka tidied the hut and made soup and porridge, while Pussy hunted mice. In the evening they were all at home, very comfortable and merry.

The old man was a wonderful teller of tales. Daryonka loved to listen, and Pussy would lie purring: "R-r-right! You'r-r-r-re r-r-right!"

But after every story Daryonka would remind the old man: "Now, tell me about the goat, Grandad. What is he like?"

At first Kokovanya tried to put her off, but then he told her.

"That's a very special goat. On his right forefoot he's got a silver hoof. And when he stamps with that silver hoof he leaves a gem there. If he stamps once there's one gem, if he stamps twice there are two, and if he begins to paw the ground there'll be a whole pile."

He told her, and then he was sorry, because after that Daryonka could talk of nothing but the goat.

"Grandad, is he a big goat?"

Kokovanya told her he was no taller than the table, with thin legs and a pretty head. But Daryonka kept on: "And has he got horns, Grandad?"

"Aye, that he has, and fine ones too. Ordinary goats have two horns, but this one's got antlers, with five tines."

"And does he eat people, Grandad?"

"No, he doesn't eat people, he eats grass and leaves. Well, and he may nibble a bit of hay from the stacks in winter."

"And what colour is he?"

"In summer he's brown like Pussy here, and in winter he's silver-grey."

Autumn came and Kokovanya got ready to go to the woods. He wanted to see where the goats were feeding. But then Daryonka started begging and pleading.

"Take me with ye, Grandad! I might get a look at the goat, even if he's a long way off!"

"A long way off ye wouldn't know him," said Kokovanya. "All goats have horns in autumn. And ye wouldn't see how many tines there are. In the winter, now—that's different. Ordinary goats haven't got horns then, but Silver Hoof has them all the time. So then ye can know him even when he's far away."

With that talk he managed to quiet her. Daryonka stopped at home, while Kokovanya went to the woods. On the fifth day he came back.

"A lot of goats are feeding Poldnevsk way this year," he said. "That's where I'll go when winter comes."

"But how'll ye sleep in the woods in winter?" asked Daryonka.

"I've got a bit of a hut there, by the glade where we go mowing," he said. "It's a stout one with a window and a stove. I'm all right there."

Then Daryonka started off again: "Will Silver Hoof feed there too?"

"Who knows? He may."

Then the child started off with her begging and pleading: "Take me with ye, Grandad! I'll stop in the hut. Maybe Silver Hoof'll come up close and then I'll see him."

At first the old man wouldn't hear of it. "What! Take a little girl into the woods in winter! Ye'd have to go on skis and ye don't know how. Ye'd sink in the snow. What would I do with ye? Ye'd freeze too!"

But Daryonka wouldn't let him alone. She kept begging: "Take me, take me, Grandad! I can ski a little bit!"

Kokovanya talked this way and that, but at last he thought to himself: "What if I do take her after all? If she tries it once she won't ask again."

"All right," he said, "I'll take ye. Only see ye don't start crying when we get to the woods or asking to go home."

When winter was really come, Kokovanya loaded a hand sled with two sacks of rusks, some hunting supplies and other odd things he'd need of. Daryonka made herself a little bundle too. She took some scraps of cloth to make a frock for her doll, a hank of thread and a needle, and then she put in a rope too.

I may be able to catch Silver Hoof with it, she thought.

She was sorry to leave the cat, but there was naught else to be done with it. She stroked it and talked to it, and explained all about everything.

"Grandad and I are going to the woods, Pussy, and you must stop here and catch all the mice. When we see Silver Hoof we'll come back home again and I'll tell you all about it."

Pussy looked up with cunning eyes and purred: "R-r-right! You'r-r-re r-r-right!"

So Kokovanya and Daryonka set off. And all the neighbours stared in amaze. "The old man must be doting! Taking a little maid like that to the woods in winter!'

Just as Kokovanya and Daryonka were leaving the last houses behind, they heard all the dogs making a big fuss and commotion, barking and howling as though some wild beast had got in. They looked round, and there was Pussy running down the middle of the street, spitting and swearing at the dogs. Pussy was a fine big cat now, and able to look after herself. There wasn't a dog anywhere that would try a fight with her.

Daryonka wanted to catch her and take her back home, but just try to catch Pussy! She ran into the woods and up a tree in a flash. Get her out of there if you can! Daryonka called and called, but Pussy wasn't to be lured down. So what could they do? They had to go on. And when they looked round, there was Pussy running along near them, off to one side. That was how they came at last to the hut.

So all three of them lived there. And Daryonka liked it. "It's nice here," she said. Kokovanya agreed, "Aye, it's more cheerful-like." And Pussy curled up in a ball by the stove and purred loudly: "R-r-right! You'r-r-re r-r-right!"

There were a lot of goats that winter. Ordinary goats. Kokovanya brought one or two home every day. The hides piled up and the meat was salted—far too much to be taken back on the hand sled. Kokovanya saw he would have to go home for a horse, but how could he leave Daryonka alone in the woods with only the cat? But Daryonka had got used to the woods and she spoke of it herself.

"Grandad, why don't ye go to the village for a horse? We ought to take the salt meat home."

Kokovanya was astonished.

"What a wise head on little shoulders! As sensible as a woman grown. Thought of it all by yourself. But won't ye be frightened, all alone?"

"Why'd I be frightened?" she answered. "Ye say yourself the hut's a good strong one, the wolves can't get in, and besides they don't come here. And I've got Pussy with me. I won't be frightened. But come back quickly all the same!"

Kokovanya left. And Daryonka stopped behind alone with Pussy. She was quite used to being alone in the daytime when Kokovanya was tracking goats. But when it began to get dark she felt a bit queer-like. So she looked at Pussy and saw she was lying comfortable and contented. That made Daryonka feel better. She sat down by the window and looked out towards the glade and—there!—something like a little ball bounced out of the woods. It came closer and she saw it was a goat. He had thin legs and a slender head, and five tines on his horns. Daryonka ran out at once, but she found nothing there. She waited and waited, and at last went back to the hut. "I must have dreamed it," she said, "it was just my fancy."

Pussy purred: "R-r-right! You'r-r-re r-r-right!"

Daryonka went to bed taking the cat with her, and slept soundly till morning. Another day passed. No Kokovanya. Daryonka felt dull and lonely but she did not cry. Instead she stroked the cat.

"Don't fret, Pussy," she said. "Grandad'll come tomorrow, you'll see."

Pussy only sang her usual song: "R-r-right! You'r-r-re r-r-right!"

Again Daryonka sat by the window looking at the stars. She was thinking of going to bed when she suddenly heard a pitter-pitter-pat behind the wall of the hut. She jumped up, frightened, and there was the pitter-pitter-pat by the other wall, then back by the first one again, then by the door, and at last up on the roof. It was not loud, it sounded like very quick, light footsteps.

Suddenly Daryonka thought to herself: What if that's the goat that came yesterday? She wanted so badly to see it that even fright couldn't hold her back. She opened the door and peeped out, and there was the goat, quite close, standing as quiet as could be. It raised its front foot to stamp and a silver hoof gleamed on it, and the horns had five tines. Daryonka did not know what to do, so she called it as she would an ordinary nannie or billie.

How that goat laughed! Then he turned and ran across the glade. Daryonka went back into the hut and told Pussy all about it.

"I've seen Silver Hoof. I saw his horns and I saw his hoof. Only I didn't see him stamp and leave precious stones. He'll show me that next time."

Pussy sang her usual song: "R-r-right! You'r-r-re r-r-right!"

The third day passed and still no Kokovanya. Daryonka's face was quite clouded. She even cried a bit. She wanted to talk to Pussy, but Pussy was gone. Then Daryonka got really frightened and ran out to look for the cat.

It was a light night with a full moon. Daryonka looked round and there was the cat, quite close, sitting in the glade with the goat in front of her. Pussy was nodding her head and so was the goat, as if they were having a talk. Then they began running about on the snow.

The goat ran here and ran there, then he stopped and stamped.

They ran about the glade for a long time, and disappeared in the distance. Then they came right up to the hut again. The goat jumped up on the roof and began stamping with his silver hoof. And precious stones flashed out like sparks—red, green, light blue, dark blue—every kind and colour.

It was then that Kokovanya returned. But he did not know his hut. It was covered with precious stones, sparkling and winking in all colours. And there stood the goat on top, stamping and stamping with his silver hoof, and the stones kept rolling and rolling down.

Suddenly Pussy jumped up there too and stood beside the goat purring loudly—and then there was nothing, no Pussy and no Silver Hoof.

Kokovanya scooped up half a hatful of stones, but Daryonka begged him: "Don't touch them, Grandad! I want to look at it just as it is in the morning."

Kokovanya did as she asked. But before morning heavy snow fell and covered everything up.

They cleared the snow away afterwards, but they couldn't find anything. Well, they didn't do so badly after all, with what Kokovanya had collected in his hat.

So it all ended well, though it was a shame about Pussy. She was never seen again, and Silver Hoof didn't come back either. He'd come once, that was enough.

But after that people often found stones in the glade where the goat had run about. Most of them were green ones, chrysolites, folks call them. Have you ever seen them?

1938

THAT DEAR NAME

It was in the days when the Old People still lived here. They lived on that sand where folks get gold, only it's grown over with turf now.

There was a lot of it then, and chrysolite and copper too. Pick it up, all you want. But the Old People had no use for it, what did they need it for? The children could play with the chrysolite, but none could find any use for gold. Yellow grains and sand—what could you do with that? Nuggets of several pounds or even half-a-pood would lie right in the path and nobody bothered to pick them up. If one was in the way, someone would kick it to the side, and that was all. Though there was one thing they used them for. When they set off to hunt, they'd take some of those nuggets with them. They weren't so big, you see, but they were heavy. Easy to hold and throw straight. A lucky throw and you could kill a good-sized beast with one of them. Easily. That's why you sometimes find nuggets in places where there oughtn't to be any gold at all. It's the Old People threw them, that's how they came there.

Copper nuggets, those they did seek a bit. They made axes from them, and other things they used. Spoons for cooking and all sorts of pots and such like.

Gumeshky was left us by the Old People. Only of course they didn't dig any mines, they just took what was on top, not like it is now.

They hunted, they caught fish and birds and that's how they lived. There were a lot of wild bees then, and all the honey you wanted. But as for bread—they didn't even know the name of it. And livestock—horses, or cows, or sheep—they'd none. They'd no understanding of such things.

They weren't Russians and they weren't Tartars, but how they were named and what was their faith and belief no one knows. They lived there in the forest. They were the Old People.

They hadn't any houses or outbuildings like bath-house or shed, none of that at all, and they didn't live in a village. They lived in the hills. There's a big cave in Dumnaya Hill. A path went up there from the river. You can't find it now, it's covered with slag. Maybe twenty-five yards thick. But the biggest cave was in Azov Hill. It was a really vast one, went under all the hill. You can still see the opening, though inside it's fallen in a bit. But secret things are there. And that's what I'll tell you about now.

Well, so they lived, the Old People, they went their own ways, troubling none. But other folks started coming to these parts. First the Tartars rode past, and tramped a whole road from the foot of Dumnaya Hill to Azov Hill. From south to north it went, straight as an arrow from a bow. You can't find it now, but our grandparents heard of it from theirs, it used to be quite plain. A real broad track like a road, only without ditches at the sides.

They'd ride back and forth, the Tartars, they'd carry one sort of lead from the north, another from the south, but they gave no heed to the gold.

233

Maybe they didn't know what it was, or else they'd no use for it. At first the Old People were wary of them, but then they saw no one touched them, so they went on with their old way of living. Caught birds and fish, stunned beasts with nuggets of gold and finished them off with copper axes.

But then all of a sudden a lot more Tartars started coming from the south. Whole swarms of them, and all with spears and sabres—as if they were going to war. Then a bit later they came back, running. They just fled without stopping to look behind them. And that was because Yermak and his Cossacks had gone to Siberia and beaten all the Tartars there. And those who came to help them, into them he put the fear of death. He'd got firearms, you see, and that was all new then, they turned the Tartars' bones to water.

Those Cossacks had once been free, but they came to Siberia bought men. They'd sold themselves to the merchants, and the Tsar had made them rich gifts too. The biggest of them, that Yermak, he'd a silver shirt, armour, that is, that the Tsar had sent him. He never took it off. Proud of it, you see. And he was drowned in it, too—in that gift of the Tsar.

When Yermak died, all sorts of trouble started. There were plenty of rascals had gone along with the Cossacks. So now they just did as they liked. Anyone they met, they'd take by the throat, give up what you've got. They'd lay hold of the women and maids, even those that weren't full grown. It was just as bad as it could be.

A band of them came to these parts—not a big one, and on foot. But their leader must have been a real robber. And they marked the gold at once. They started grabbing at it all together so they near killed each other for it. But then they came to their senses and saw there was a lot of it, more than they could carry off. So what was to be done now? They started nosing about here and there, maybe there were folks living near, they could get horses. And so they came to the Old People. Well, of course, they started asking them: "What folk are you? What faith and tribe? What Tsar d'ye pay tribute to?"

They harassed the Old People, but these had only one answer—we want aught o' yours, we don't hinder ye, go your ways. So the Cossacks sought to scare them and fired their flint-locks. Then panic seized the Old People and they fled to the hill. The Cossacks went after them, thought they'd put fear into them, but they were wrong. The Old People were brave. It was only at first the firing had frightened them. They thought it was fire from the sky. But then they threw off their fear. And they were big, strong men. They ran to their cave, and then they started hurling gold nuggets, so the Cossacks didn't know where to hide. Killed nearly all of them. But two or maybe three managed to get away. And the Old People let them go. Got rid of them, and that's enough. Let them go their ways, so long as they leave us alone. The Old People looked at those who were dead and marvelled to see every man had such a lot of yellow stones, why did he want to carry all that heavy stuff? They never guessed, the Old People, what the stones were for. Thought it out their own way and decided the Cossacks had gathered them to fight with. They looked at the flint-locks, and one of them was loaded. Well, somebody got hold of it, he twisted it and turned it and pulled this and pushed that till suddenly it went off. It gave them a fright and bruised the man a bit, but no one was killed. Then the Old People saw the fire didn't come from the sky at all. And they wanted to make a gun fire again. They took everything off the dead men, they looked at everything, felt everything, smelt everything. They found powder and they found lead, but what it was all for they couldn't make out.

But those three who'd run away, they managed to get back to their company again. And they told their leader all about it—a strange tribe attacked us and killed near all, only us three got away.

That leader, maybe he was a bit drunk, he just said "All right." It was war, they were winning Siberia. All sorts of things could come about. They'd been killed, well, so they'd been killed. And that was the end of it. But about the gold those three said naught. We've got it, they thought, we'll take our ease and our pleasure a bit. But gold is gold. It may be heavy but it always comes up to the top. The first thing, it must be changed into money. And that set them scratching their heads. They'd got hold of real big nuggets, but if they let folks see them, what would happen? They'd be asked where they'd got them. . . . But soon they found a way. They broke the nuggets into small pieces and sold them to a merchant. But they kept it secret from each other. Gold's gold. So one went to a merchant, then the second and then the third. They went round all of them the same way. And the merchants were glad enough. They paid money, but they kept their thoughts to themselves. And that money the Cossacks got, what could they do with it? First they got rich clothes, each to fit his fancy, and then started feasting and drinking. Spent their whole time in the tavern and treated all who came. Well, of course the other Cossacks marked them—where'd they got all that money? So they set to work to discover it, and when a man's drunk that doesn't take long. They soon had it all out of them, and then they got a band together to go after that gold.

But those Cossacks, they weren't all the same. There was one, I don't know what they called him, but he'd come from Solikamsk. He'd been looking for a good life, but he found there was only robbery and drink, and he began to shun the others.

When he heard them planning another robber raid, he tried to bring them to better ways of thinking. "Have ye no shame? Before, ye stripped the merchants and the boyars, but what are ye doing now? Robbing the folks here of their last and giving it to the merchants. Isn't that how it is?"

This talk wasn't to their liking, and they were all armed, so a fight started with sabres and other weapons. Well, that fellow from Solikamsk was bold and agile He beat them all off, but he was sore wounded. He got away and then he hid in the woods so they wouldn't find him. And those woods were thick and fearsome—where'd you seek a man there? So the Cossacks hunted a bit and made a lot of noise, and then they went back. And the Solikamsk man, wounded he was, started thinking what he'd do now. If he went back, they'd kill him, or maybe give him to the headsman for his talk. So he thought: I'll go to the folks they wanted to rob. I'll warn them.

He knew the way they'd meant to take. But that way was long and he'd got naught to eat with him. He got weary after a while and his wounds pulled him down too. He could hardly drag himself along. He'd lie down a bit and then go on again. And right by Azov Hill, just over there, he couldn't get up any more.

The Old People, they saw a stranger lying there, all blood, and a gun with him. The women went to him the first. Whatever tribe or people, it's always the women are pitiful and delight in tending those as are hurt. And there was one maid among them, the daughter of their elder. Daring she was, and resolute, she could well have worn men's clothing. And fair to look at—none to compare. Eyes like coals, cheeks like roses in bloom, a braid that reached to her heels and all else right and proper. You could wish no better. At dancing there was none to equal her, and when she sang with trills like a bird, well. . . . In a word, a joy to behold. Only one thing there was—she was tall, a giant, you could say. She was of an age to wed. Eighteen, just ripe for it. And the stranger seemed to take her eye. He was a tall man too, as we count it. Good to look on, with curly hair and big eyes. She was curious about him. So while the other women were oh'ing and ah'ing, that maid just picked up the wounded man, carried him to the cave and started to tend him, gave him water and bound up his wounds. Her father and mother had naught against it, took it as quite natural. And the neighbours, they held their tongues and helped a bit, gave her what she wanted. The women were sorry for him, and the men had their own thoughts—maybe he'd teach them how to fire those guns.

After a bit the wounded man began to come to. And he saw strange folk busy about him. They were taller than ours, and they didn't know the Tartar tongue. He knew just a little bit of Tartar, he'd hoped a lot from that when he went to seek them. Well, naught to be done, he started making signs, pointing to this thing and that to find out what it was called. Learning their talk, that is. And the maid never left him, like as though she was bound to him. And he, well, he was young too, and he liked her well. But he was slow in getting his strength. That was because they'd no bread. She gave him all the best they had, that maid did. Fish, meat, bowls of honey filled to the brim, but his stomach turned against it. He'd have been glad to see even a crust of barley bread. He asked her for it, and she didn't know what bread was. Even cried, she did. And of course a Russian man can't get along without bread. So how could he really pick up strength? Still, he did get on his feet and learned something of their tongue too. And the maid learned his Russian speech, and so quick it was a marvel. Wise she was, and no simple maid, seemingly, but possessed of secret powers.

So that man from Solikamsk began walking about a bit. He got to know the place, and he showed them how to use the flint-lock guns, and explained about it all.

"Those yellow stones, and the yellow grains and sand and shining green stones—they'll bring ye misfortune. Now the merchants have smelt them, they'll never let them be. And when it gets to the Tsar, you'll have no life worth living. Now," he said, "this you must do. Take these stones, those nuggets, and put them out o' sight. Take them into Azov Hill if you will. And the chrysolites too. And cover the grains and sand with earth. Dig up the black soil from beneath so grass'll grow. Till that is done, let no stranger come near. And so that none should come by chance," he said, "put those ye can trust to keep guard on Dumnaya Hill. Let them watch the road and if they mark a stranger, let them light a fire as a sign."

The maid told her people all he had said. They saw his care was for them and they harkened. They set guards as he counselled, and all began gathering the nuggets and chrysolites and carrying them into Azov Hill. They stacked it all up—great piles, dreadful to look on, and chrysolites like heaps of coal. Then they covered the rest of the grains and sand, and all the time they let no stranger come near. If the guard on Dumnaya Hill or Azov Hill saw one coming on horseback or on foot, he lighted a beacon fire. Then they would all go running, and overpower the man and kill him. Kill him and bury him in the ground. For now they'd no fear of firearms.

But men are drawn to gold like flies to honey. No matter how many perish, more follow after. And it was like that here too. Many perished but still more kept coming. That was because the talk of gold went further and further. And someone must have brought it to the Tsar. Then it was really bad, for men came with cannon. Came from all sides. The forest was thick and fearsome but they found a road.

The Old People saw they could do no more, here their strength counted for naught. So they went to that wounded man to ask counsel. Now, he was on Dumnaya Hill. The maid used to carry him there when he felt weak. Azov Hill was covered with woods, but on Dumnaya Hill there were great rocks with the free wind blowing on them. So she used to take him there. All her thought was to make him well and sound again.

There they took counsel for three days. And that is why it is called Dumnaya.* Before that it had another name. They thought this way and that, but could find no way but to seek some new place to live where there would be no gold, but beasts and birds and fish a-plenty. And he, that man from Solikamsk, he explained and showed them which way they should go. And so they started to make ready for the road. The Old People wanted their good counsellor to go with them, but he would not.

"Death," he said, "is close to me, and moreover I may not go."

Why he must not go he didn't say. And the maid said: "I shall not go either."

Her mother and sisters wept and wailed, her father stormed and threatened, her brothers tried to change her: "What are you saying, Sister! Your whole life's before you!"

But she would not be moved.

"Such is my fate. I will never leave my dear one."

She said it, and she'd hear naught against it. Like a stone, she was. In every way right and perfect. They saw there was naught to be done with her, so they took leave with all love and tenderness, for they thought to themselves—there'd be naught more in life for her anyway. Maids whose sweethearts die, they're worse than widowed. For the sorrow is with them to the end of their lives.

So all were gone and those two were alone on Azov Hill. Strange folk were round them on all sides. Digging with spades, aye, and fighting each other with them too.

* From *dumat*, to think —*Tr.*

The wounded man's strength was nigh gone, and he said to his betrothed: "Farewell, my bride! It's not our fate to live and love and rear our children."

She broke out in tears as women do and would have none of it, but tried to make him believe different.

"Let be and don't fret yourself, my love. I'll tend you and make you well, and then we shall live our lives together."

But he only said again: "Nay, my dear one, I'm not long for this life. Now even bread would not help me. I feel my hour is come. And I'm no mate for you, either. See how tall you are, I'm like a child beside you. With us it's not seemly that a wife should carry her husband like a child. You'll have to wait and wait long before a man lives on earth fit to be your mate."

But of that she would hear naught.

"What talk is that! Don't even think such thoughts. For me there's none other."

But he would not heed her.

"I'm not saying it to wound you, beloved," he said, "but because it must be so. It came upon me clear when I saw how you lived amid gold with no merchants. A time will come in our land when there will be no more merchants or Tsar, and even their names will be forgotten. Folks hereabouts will grow tall and strong, and one of these will come to Azov Hill and loudly call your dear name. When that day comes, bury me in the ground and go to him with a brave gay heart. For he will be your mate. And when that day comes, let them take all the gold, if indeed those folks have use for it. But for this time farewell, beloved." He sighed once more and died as if he fell asleep. And in that moment Azov Hill closed.

For seemingly those were not idle words he spoke. He had wisdom, the wisdom of hidden powers. In Solikamsk they know much of these things.

From that time none could ever come within Azov Hill. Now folks know the entrance to the cave, but it's fallen a bit. A man starts in, then it falls some more and he fears to go further. So the hill stands empty. Trees have grown over it, and those who don't know would never guess what's there, inside.

But in the hill there is a great cave. And all of it a wonder to look on. The floor is smooth, of the best marble, with a spring in the middle, and the water like tears. And all round gold is stacked like we stack wood, and chrysolites in heaps like coal.

It is arranged some way, so it's always light in the cave. And there lies a dead man, and a maid so fair there are no words to tell of it sits by him and weeps always, and becomes no older. As she was at eighteen, so she is now.

Many have wished to get into that cave. They've tried every way. They drove shafts but naught came of it. Even dynamite was no good. Then others thought to get that wealth by trickery. They'd come to the hill and shout out words of all kinds, one queerer than the other. They hoped, you see, to chance on that dear name which will open the cave of itself. Fools they were, of course. They'd lose their wits with it. Mumble all sorts of gibberish that none could understand. Always seeking new names.

Nay, the spell is a strong one. Until that hour comes, Azov Hill won't open.

Once there was a sign. That was when Omelyan Ivanych* came and the workers used to gather on Dumnaya Hill. Our grandfathers told us at that time a song came from inside the hill, like a mother playing with her little one and singing him a merry tune.

But there's been naught of that since. Only groaning and weeping. When folks stopped being serfs, many went to Azov Hill to listen. But still there was naught but groaning. Seemingly more pitiful than before.

A true sign, it was. Money drives folks worse than the Master's whips. And as the years go on, it seems to get more power. Our fathers and grandfathers, when they came to my years, could sit in quietness on the stove, but I must keep watch on Dumnaya Hill. For all must eat and drink to the day when death takes them.

* Emelyan Ivanovich Pugachev—leader of a peasant uprising.—*Tr.*

Aye, I'll not live to see the day, seemingly, when Azov Hill opens. I'll not see it. . . . But if I could but hear a gay song coming from within. . . .

For you it's different. You're young. Maybe you'll have the fortune to live to that time.

Then folks will make gold of no power. Mark my words, it will be so. That Solikamsk man spoke with wisdom.

Those of you who live to that day will then see the treasures of Azov Hill. And they will know the dear name that opens up that wealth.

Aye, that's how it is. This is not a simple tale. It's one to think on, and draw the wisdom from it.

1936

THE EAGLE'S FEATHER

It was in the village of Sarapulka. Not so many years ago. Just a bit after the Civil War. Village folks still hadn't much learning yet in those days. But all the same, all those that were for Soviet power started thinking what they could do to help it.

Now, we all know in Sarapulka that from ancient times our fathers and grandfathers used to seek stone. Between sowing and harvesting, or any other time they'd got to spare, they'd go off looking for it. Well, folks minded that and they set up an artel. Started seeking graphite. Seemed to go all right, too. They reckoned to get a thousand poods, but then soon after they stopped. Why they stopped—whether the graphite was bad or the price too low—I can't say. They gave it up, that's all I know, and turned their eyes to Adui.

Now, that's a place everyone hereabouts knows something of. The main thing there was aquamarines and amethysts. And there'd be other stones too. One of the artel boasted: "I know a crack in the old digging that's promising." And the others snapped at it. And at first they did well. Came on two or three pockets. Basket stones, we call them, because they're counted by the basketful. And when folks saw what they'd got, a lot more came to Adui—d'ye mind if we try our luck too? Well, the working was a big one, you couldn't forbid them. But then it started going wrong—they made a mistake, or else they overlooked something. And the artel that had gone there first lost the vein. That often happens with stones. They hunted and searched, but they couldn't find it. What now? Well, in Berezovka there was an old prospector living. He was far on in years, but he was famed all round. So folks from the artel went to him. They told him the place where they were working and asked him: "Do us a kindness, Kondrat Markelych, find us the vein."

Of course they'd brought good food and wine to set before the old man, and they spoke him fair, and promised much. And the Berezovka prospectors came round too and bragged of their aged prospector.

"Our Markelych is masterly wi' them things. You'll not find another like him in miles around."

The ones that had come, they knew that for themselves, of course, but they said naught. Talk like that would help them, it might spur on the old man to show his skill. But with it all he'd only a nay for them.

"I know those veins that lose themselves at Adui. My eyes 'ud never find them now."

But the artel folks kept on. They'd put more meat and drink before the old man and tell him—you're our only hope. If you can't find it, who'll we go to? Now, the old man liked well to hear all that, and he'd had a few glasses too. He straightened up his shoulders and started boasting—he'd found this and he'd found that and he'd opened a place here and shown one there. Well, to cut it short they got their way. The old man was real hot after a while, he thumped on the table. "I may be old but I can still show ye how to find a vein!"

That was just what the folks from the artel wanted.

"Show us, Kondrat Markelych, show us, and we'll thank ye well. Half the first pocket'll be yours."

But Kondrat would have none of it.

"That's not what I'll go for. I want to let ye see what a real miner can do if he'd got the wits and understanding."

Well—you know the saying, what a man in wine promised, a man sober must fulfil. Markelych had to go to Adui. He asked how the vein had been going, he tapped and tapped, and thought hard where it should be sought, but no vein could he find. The men who'd got him to come saw he was puzzled, so they soon dropped the whole thing. If Kondrat can't find it, they thought, it's no good wasting more time on it.

The other prospectors who'd been working round about, they gave it up too, one after another. After all, haying time was near. Every man wanted to get in enough. So folks all disappeared from the Adui workings as if the wind had swept it clear, not a one would be seen. Only Kondrat still kept working and working away. He was stubborn, that old man. At first he'd tried because folks asked him, but when he saw the stones mocked him and wouldn't show themselves, then his anger rose. "I'll find it all the same! I will!"

Week after week the old man toiled alone. He got weary and weak, and still naught to show for it. Ought to have given it up long ago, but he felt shame. What—the best miner in the whole district and couldn't find a vein?! Not to be dreamed of! Folks would laugh at him. So at last Kondrat thought to himself—what if I try it the old way?

In other days, folks say, they used to seek ore with a divining rod and stones with an arrow they'd woven spells on. Kondrat had known of all that since he was a boy, but he'd never had any use for it, held it to be foolishness. He d mocked at it all, but now he made up his mind to try it.

"If naught comes of it, I'll waste no more time here."

Now, the way of it was this. You had to rub an arrow-head with load-stone, and then with the kind of stone you wanted to find. And there were spells to be said. Then this magic arrow must be shot from an ordinary bow, but you must shut your eyes and turn round three times before shooting it.

Kondrat knew all the spells and the rules, but he felt ashamed to do it himself, so he thought to have his grandson do it, or maybe it was his great-grandson. He didn't grudge the trouble, but went back home. Of course, he wouldn't let folks there see it had been too much for him. When any of the Berezovka prospectors came to ask, he put a good face on it, and told them he'd have to be away another week.

He went to the bath-house and steamed himself well, rested a day at home, then when he was making ready to go again he asked his grandson: "Would ye like to come wi' me, Mishunka, to look for stones?"

The boy was flattered at his Grandad asking him.

"That I would," he said.

So Kondrat took his grandson to Adui. He made the boy a bow, prepared the arrows after all the old rules, told Mishunka to shut his eyes, turn round three times and shoot at random. The boy was eager to help, of course. Did it all just like Kondrat told him. He shot three times. But Kondrat saw naught would come of it. The first arrow struck in a tree-stump, the second fell in the grass and the third hit a stone and went sliding down. The old man scratched a bit in all those places—but it was mostly so as to follow the old custom to the end. Of course, the boy started playing with the bow and arrow, ran about with it till he was tired. The grandfather gave him supper and put him to bed in the shanty he'd built, but he'd no wish for sleep himself. He felt low in spirit. Shamed in his old age. He went out of the shanty and sat thinking, maybe he ought to try again? And then the thought came to him—what if the arrow didn't go right because it wasn't the right hand that shot it?

"The lad knows naught yet. Ye'd think he'd be the best for it, but he's never sought stones himself, and that's why the arrow gives no guidance. Seems like I'll have to try myself."

He spoke the magic words over the arrow, made everything ready the way it ought to be, shut his eyes, turned round three times and shot it. But it didn't go the way the workings were at all, and there was some stranger coming along the path. He was travelling light. He'd only a plaited basket in his hand, the kind our women use when they go berrying. He picked up the arrow, for it fell quite close to him, and said with a laugh in his voice: "It doesn't suit your years, Grandad, to play with child's toys. It's not fitting."

Kondrat felt awkward, being caught out doing a thing like that, and he said with anger: "It's no concern o' yours! Go your ways!"

The stranger laughed.

"How's it none of my concern when I nearly got your arrow in my foot!"

He went up to the old man, handed him the arrow and said chidingly yet with a bit of a laugh: "Eh, Grandad, Grandad! Many years ye've lived, yet you don't know the saying: It's no arrow if it isn't tipped with an eagle feather."

Markelych had no taste for that sort of talk.

"There's none o' those birds in our parts," he said angrily. "There's no feather to be got."

"You're wrong," said the stranger. "There's eagle feathers everywhere, but they must be sought under the high light."

Kondrat could make naught of it all.

"Ye talk in riddles. Ye're making a mock of an old man, I see; but in my work I'm no worse than others."

"And what is your work?" the stranger asked.

And suddenly talk flowed from the old man. He told this stranger his whole life. He marvelled at himself, yet he went on talking. The stranger sat down on a stone, listened and put in a word to help him on.

"Aye, like that, was it, Grandad? And then?"

The old man finished his tale and the stranger spoke good words.

"Ye've worked well and honestly, Grandad. Ye've done much that is of good use. But why did ye shoot that arrow?"

Kondrat didn't keep that back either. And the stranger, he sort of peered at him, with his eyes a bit narrow, and he said: "Aye, that's how it is. Your arrow lacks an eagle's feather."

Then Kondrat lost his temper. Here he'd opened up his whole life, and this man started off with his feathers again; making a fool of him, that's what it was.

"I'm telling ye, there aren't any o' them birds in our parts," he cried, real angry he was. "Ye'll never find a feather. Are ye deaf, or what?"

The stranger laughed a bit, and asked: "Would you like me to show ye?"

Kondrat didn't believe him, of course, but all the same he said: "Show me if ye can, if ye're not trying to make a fool o' me."

Then the stranger took a big stone out of his basket. About double the size of your fist. It was cut flat at the top and bottom, and the sides were five facets. It was dark, he couldn't see the colour, but it looked like red quartz, what we call eagle-stone in our parts. On the top there were white spots, you could hardly see them, one over each of the facets.

The stranger put the stone down beside him, pressed one of the spots with his finger, and all of a sudden there was a light all over and round them, like as if they were in a great bell. It was very bright, and sort of blue, but where it came from he couldn't see. It wasn't very high, that bell of light, three or maybe four times man's height. Swarms of midges danced in it, and bats fluttered about, and at the top a flock of little birds flew over, and each of them dropped a feather. They went round and round in the air as if they didn't want to seek the ground.

"D'you see the feathers?" the stranger asked.

"Aye, I see them," said Kondrat, "but those aren't eagle feathers."

"You're right, they're more like sparrows' than eagles'," said the stranger, and then he explained: "That's your life, Grandad. You've seen much, you've toiled much, but your wings were small and weak, they couldn't raise you high. Midges got into your eyes, and all kinds o' vermin hindered you. But now see how it's going to be."

He pressed his finger again on one of the spots, and the bell of light got much bigger. And there was green mixed with the blue of it. Under their feet it was as if the top of the ground had been taken away, and birds flew past overhead. Lower down there were ducks and geese, then cranes higher up, and still higher—swans. And each of the birds dropped a feather, and these fell straighter down to the ground, because they were heavier.

Then the stranger pressed his finger on another spot, and the bell of light spread out and rose up to a great height, and the light was so bright it nearly blinded him. And it glowed blue and green and red. Under the earth all could be seen for five yards deep, and birds flew past overhead. Each of them dropped a feather and they fell straight down to the ground like arrows, close to the spot where the stone stood. The stranger looked at Kondrat, his smile was like the light.

"There are other birds that fly higher than the eagle," he said, "but I fear to show ye, your eyes would not bear the sight. Try now with your arrow."

He picked up some feathers from the ground and fixed them on quickly, as if he'd done it all his life, and told the old man: "Shoot in the place where you think the vein should be; but there's no need to turn round three times or shut your eyes."

Kondrat did as the stranger bade him. As the arrow flew, the hollow opened to meet it. And he could see all—not just the veins, but all the pockets. One of them was very big. Aquamarines, nearly enough to fill a cart, and just like they were laughing. The old man forgot all, of course, and ran to take a closer look, and the light went out.

Then Markelych cried: "Stranger, where are ye?"

The answer came back: "I have gone on."

"But where'll ye go in the dark? Robbers may do ye a hurt! They might even take that thing from ye!" cried Markelych.

But the stranger answered: "Don't you be feared for me, Grandad! This thing works only in my hands, and in those to which I give it."

"But who are ye?" asked Markelych.

The stranger was already far away, and his answer carried back faintly: "Ask your grandson. He knows."

Mishunka had not been asleep, the light had wakened him, and he'd been looking out of the shanty. And as soon as the old man came back there, Mishunka said: "Grandad, that was Lenin wi' ye."

But the old man felt no surprise.

"Aye, Mishunka, that's who it was. It's right, then, what folks say, that he wanders through our parts. He does. And teaches folks wisdom. So they shouldn't take pride in their little wings, but reach up to the high light. To the eagle's wings, that is."

1945

CPSIA information can be obtained at www.ICGtesting.com
Printed in the USA
BVOW05s0654281114

376806BV00002B/541/P